Praise for

Vulnerable

Here's what some readers have to say about the first book in the McIntyre Security Bodyguard Series...

"I can't even begin to explain how much I loved this book! The plot, your writing style, the dialogue and OMG those vivid descriptions of the characters and the setting were so AMAZING!"
– Dominique

"I just couldn't put it down. The first few pages took my breath away. I realized I had stumbled upon someone truly gifted at writing. " – Amanda

"*Vulnerable* is an entertaining, readable erotic romance with a touch of thriller adding to the tension. Fans of the *Fifty Shades* series will enjoy the story of wildly rich and amazingly sexy Shane and his newfound love, the young, innocent Beth, who needs his protection." – Sheila

"I freaking love it! I NEED book 2 now!!!" – Laura

"Shane is my kind of hero. I loved this book. I am anxiously waiting for the next books in this series." – Tracy

Praise for

Fearless

Books by April Wilson

McIntyre Security, Inc. Bodyguard Series:

A Tyler Jamison Novel:

Somebody to Love

A TYLER JAMISON Novel

by

APRIL WILSON

Cover Artist: Steamy Designs
Photographer: Golden Czermak/ FuriousFotog
Model: Daniel Rengering
Editor/Proofreader: Christina Hart
(Savage Hart Book Services)

Published by
April E. Barnswell
Wilson Publishing LLC
P.O. Box 292913
Dayton, OH 45429

ISBN: 9781653883653
First Printing: December 2019

Dedication

For Tyler, who waited so patiently for his story to be told

1

Homicide Detective Tyler Jamison

Another Friday night alone, sipping whiskey in a downtown Chicago bar. Another fucked-up night in my fucked-up life. At least today I put a murderer behind bars. I guess that makes it a good day after all.

"Another round, detective?"

I nod to Glenn, the balding, middle-aged owner of Tank's, a middle-class watering hole located just north of downtown. "One more."

I tap the rim of my tumbler, and Glenn pours a splash of liquor into my glass. This is my last one for the night. Then I'm heading home. *Alone.*

Always alone.

A shift in the air around me, accompanied by a whiff of expensive perfume, heralds the arrival of a woman who sits on the empty barstool to my left. I don't bother looking up. The last thing I want to do is encourage her.

Glenn gives me a pitying glance before he turns to the woman. "And what can I get you, beautiful?"

"I'd love a glass of white wine," she says, her voice silky smooth.

"Coming right up," the bartender says just before he walks away.

I focus on the half-inch of amber liquor in my glass, mesmerized by the translucent color that resembles a mix of honey and fire, swirling it gently before taking a biting, neat sip. The burn makes me grimace. I've never really gotten used to the taste of whiskey, but I like how it warms my belly. It centers me.

"What's that you're drinking?" the woman asks. "Whiskey?"

Still avoiding eye contact, I nod.

She sighs. "I'm more of a wine lover myself, although I can certainly appreciate fine liquor when the occasion calls for it. I'm... flexible."

I resist the urge to laugh. *There's no sexual innuendo in that statement. No, not at all.*

"Did I say something funny?" she says.

I guess I'm not as subtle as I think I am. Or maybe it's the whiskey affecting me. "No. Sorry."

I still haven't made eye contact. There's no point. She's the third woman to hit on me tonight, and I'm not interested.

Yeah, she smells good and she sounds good, but my body and mind just aren't on board. Every time I hook up with someone, the result is always the same. I come away from the experience feeling empty. And frankly, I'd rather be lonely than feel nothing at all.

I'm defective.

I was born defective. The only thing I've ever successfully cuddled up to is a tumbler of whiskey, and that's only on Friday nights. I don't allow myself to drink hard liquor any other time during the week. I have... rules. And rules are meant to be followed. Otherwise, chaos ensues.

"Do you live around here, detective?" she says.

For an instant, I think she might know me from work. But then I realize I left my badge lying on the counter. I pick it up and slip it into my pocket.

Her voice is sultry and sophisticated. I should be thinking about taking her up on the offer I know is coming. Sometimes I do, when the loneliness gets to be too much. But afterward, I end up feeling worse. It's just not worth it anymore.

I toss back the contents of my glass, savoring the burn and the subsequent fire in my gut. It's time for me to go. I don't want to sit here and field come-ons all night from women looking for sex.

I finally get around to answering her question. I may not be interested, but I'm not a complete ass. "Yeah. I live around here."

I toss two twenties on the bar and step off my barstool.

"Don't go," she says with a pout.

Finally, I meet her gaze. Ice blue eyes, platinum blonde hair swept up in a fancy twisted arrangement, a cream-colored business suit and matching heels. There's a thin gold chain around her slender neck. She's got *attorney* written all over her, but I don't recognize her. As a homicide detective, I've come across a lot of attorneys in Chicago, but not this one.

"It's late," I say, grabbing my jacket off the empty stool to my right. "Been a long week."

With a parting nod, I leave her and head for the men's room so I can take a piss before heading home. The men's room door opens as I approach, and a young guy walks out—in his late twenties, lean, fit, but not overly muscular. We make eye contact briefly as we approach each other. He's easily fifteen years younger than me, about my height, six-foot. His brown hair is cut close on the sides and back, longer and wavy on the top. His jaw is covered by a trim beard.

I notice a flash of interest in his green eyes. When he nods at me, heat blooms in my chest, unbidden and unwelcome, and my belly tightens.

I'm stunned by my physical reaction.

Oh, hell no.

I break eye contact and continue into the men's room. Fortunately, I'm the only one in here. I quickly empty my bladder, trying to ignore what just happened, and wash up, my motions quick and efficient. I'm careful not to look at my own reflection in the mirror, afraid of what I'll see. My face still burns from that brief encounter in the hall.

When I exit the bathroom, he's there, leaning casually against the wall, his arms crossed over his chest. I finally notice what he's wearing—ripped jeans, a tight-fitting gray t-shirt with faded text on it. That t-shirt hugs his lean torso and biceps. He's clearly no stranger to physical activity.

For a moment, I stare, unable to look away as my heart starts pounding.

His gaze sweeps over me from head to toe. "I'm just trying to figure you out."

The sound of his voice sends a shiver down my spine, and my thoughts race as I try to keep up. "Excuse me?"

He pushes away from the wall and steps in front of me, meeting me eye-to-eye, a cocky grin on his face.

His gaze searches mine, as if he's looking for answers. "I watched three hot-as-hell women hit on you tonight, and you brushed off every single one of them. My friends say you turn down offers from both women *and* men." He looks at my hands. "I don't see a ring. Is there someone special?"

This close, I can see flecks of gold in his eyes. His lashes are long, the color of fine chocolate. My ears start ringing and my chest tightens as it heats up. He's so...brazen. I don't know how to respond.

When I stand there like a tongue-tied idiot, he shakes his head and chuckles. And then he walks away, leaving me dumbfounded.

My God, he's... I don't even know how to describe him. He's so... fearless.

I head for the exit, skirting around the crowded dance floor and tables filled with loud, half-drunken people. I just want to get out of here. As I step out onto Superior Avenue on a crisp, cool June night, I dodge the steady stream of pedestrian traffic. It's only ten p.m., and there are plenty of people still out, many of them tourists.

I have no trouble flagging a ride from the line of cabs idling out front. Since I knew I'd be drinking tonight, I didn't bother driving. I give my driver the address to my condo in Lincoln Park, and a moment later he darts into traffic, heading north. As I settle into my seat, I'm painfully aware that my heart is pounding, and I'm breathing like I just jogged up two flights of stairs.

Closing my eyes, I try to force the picture of that guy out of my head. I focus on other things... about the cases I'm working on, about my sister who's pregnant with her second child, about her son—my nephew—who's just about to turn one. I think about anything other than a pair of green eyes and the way his chest and arms filled out that damn t-shirt.

Shit. I should have taken the woman up on her offer. At least she would have given me something else to think about tonight. Something else to focus on.

As soon as I get home, I strip off my suit and tie and hit the shower. My body is a live wire, charged, crackling with electricity. I need a release. I need something, anything to redirect my thoughts.

I lean into the cold tile wall and attempt to shut off my brain as I jerk myself off. My fist is relentless, as brutal as it is unforgiving. *Punishing.*

I stroke myself roughly, my grip firm, and try desperately to empty my mind. Before long, my balls draw up tight, and I feel the fire of an impending climax searing my spine. My mouth falls open as air billows in and out of my lungs.

Just as I'm about to come, I picture a stranger with green eyes and a lean, muscular body. *Fuck!* With a hoarse cry, I shoot my load into the spray of water, gritting my teeth as my body bucks hard into my orgasm.

Damn it! I sure as hell didn't want to envision him.

No fucking way. It just can't happen.

* * *

My phone rings at three in the morning. That's nothing unusual for me. Chicago never sleeps, and if you're going to kill someone, the middle of the night is a good time to do it. Murderers never take holidays, which means neither do I.

Blinking away sleep, I reach for my phone on the top of my nightstand and check the caller ID. "Jamison," I say, my voice little more than a hoarse rasp. I maybe got three hours of sleep. I clear my throat. "Sorry, Captain. Go ahead."

Captain Walker's voice is clipped, matter-of-fact. "You're needed down at the St. James Yacht Club, slip forty-three. Someone called in a dead body on a yacht. Uniforms are already on scene, and I've dispatched a forensics team."

I sit up and swing my bare feet to the floor, already reaching for my trousers.

"And Tyler?"

"Yeah?"

"Heads up. The victim was strangled with a garrotte."

"Shit." That's not what I want to hear. It'll be the third such case in two weeks. Already I'm reaching for my trousers. "I'm on my way."

2

Ian Alexander, voluntarily unemployed

The cops are nice enough to give me a moment while I puke my guts into Lake Michigan. I've seen some pretty bad shit in my life, but never anything remotely like what I just saw.

A dead man, his throat sliced nearly clean through.

All that blood and such a horrific, gaping wound. I shudder. *Poor Eric.* Who could do something like that to a fellow human being? Who could hate another human being so much? Who could hate *Eric?* He and I both are used to dealing with haters, it comes with the territory, but this?

The officers talk quietly as I collect myself, wiping my mouth on the hem of my t-shirt. They're waiting for a homicide detective to show up and take charge of the crime scene. I hear one of them mention a garrotte. *Jesus!* The killer must have used a wire for it to cut that deeply into Eric's throat. If it was a wire, it means someone brought it onto the boat with him. And that means it was premeditated.

Who in the hell would want to kill Eric? He's a harmless flamer. Promiscuous, yes, but harmless. And he's my friend. Or, he was.

I'm shaking, but I don't think it's from the chilly late-night air. I think I'm in shock. *Fuck.* I sit down hard on a wooden crate, before I keel over, and lower my head between my knees, hoping it will help with the nausea.

One of the officers takes pity on me. "Slow down your breathing, buddy. Take deep breaths or you'll hyperventilate."

At least I'm still breathing. I can't say the same for poor Eric.

I can't get the image of his dark, lifeless eyes out of my head. The shocked grimace on his face. Whoever did this overpowered him. And since Eric was bound and gagged, he probably didn't get a chance to fight back.

It's a quarter 'til four in the morning, and the night sky is pitch black. The only ambient light comes from the lamp posts spaced strategically along the pier. It's eerily quiet this time of night— or rather this early in the morning. The boats rock gently as the water slaps their hulls. The air is tainted with the faint stench of rotting vegetation and dead fish.

Off in the distance, a siren shatters the quiet.

My yacht, *Carpe Diem*, is moored right next to Eric's on a dock that juts out perpendicular from the pier, at least fifty yards from shore. My boat rocks gently beside Eric's, undulating in the dark, murky water.

My friend is dead.

Hanging my head, I fight against the nausea that just won't let up. *Shit, I feel numb.*

"Here he comes," says one of the officers.

"Thank God," I mutter. The sooner we get this over with, the sooner I can escape to my boat and get drunk.

I hear his footsteps long before I see him. His heels strike the wooden boards, sharp and precise, as he approaches.

"Is this the guy who found the body?" says a male voice, deep and authoritative.

"Yes, sir," an officer says. "His name's Ian Alexander. His boat is moored next to the victim's. He found the body about an hour ago."

I find myself staring down at a pair of perfectly polished black loafers. I look up, and... *damn!* My heart slams into my chest. It's *him*. It's the guy from the bar earlier this evening. He's looking a little worse for wear at the moment, his black hair tousled, as if they got him out of bed for this. He must have finger-combed it on his way over here.

He's wearing the same black suit he had on earlier tonight, with a wrinkled white shirt and a black tie. There are faint shadows beneath his startling blue-green eyes. Even as rough as he looks, he still takes my breath away.

I see a momentary flash of awareness when we finally make eye contact. He looks away for a second, scrubbing his hand roughly across his trim, black beard. But just as quickly as it came, the moment passes, and he's all business as he pulls a black leather wallet out of his jacket pocket and shows me a very shiny, very official looking badge.

This is surreal. I can't believe it's the same guy. "You're a homicide detective," I say. It's not a question.

He nods. "Homicide Detective Tyler Jamison, Chicago PD."

I laugh. "So, you drew the short straw."

He ignores me as he pockets his badge. "Don't go anywhere, Mr. Alexander," he says. "After I see the body, I'll need to ask you some questions."

My pulse flutters as I nod. *Hell, he can ask me all the questions he wants.*

And then he walks away, his stride purposeful and strong, and all I can do is stare after him.

Once the detective disappears inside Eric's boat, where the forensics team is already at work, I turn to the officers keeping me company. Honestly, I'm not sure if they're guarding me or containing me.

"Can I go sit on my boat?" I point to mine just a few yards away. "I'm about to fall over."

Taking pity on me, one officer nods. "I'll have to go with you, but sure."

"Thanks."

Officer Swanson, according to his name tag, follows me onto my boat. He steps onto the swim platform right behind me, and we climb the few steps to the main deck.

"Have a seat," I tell him, motioning to the cushioned benches along the stern.

The seats are arranged like a squared-off horseshoe. I sit on one side, leaning forward with my arms resting on my thighs. The cop sits opposite me.

My upbringing kicks in. "Can I get you something to drink, officer? Water? A soft drink?" I figure beer is out of the question under the circumstances, even though I could sure as hell use one. Now's not the time to be playing host, but my mother has drilled proper etiquette into my head if nothing else.

Officer Swanson grins at my obvious discomfort. "No, thank you. I'm fine."

Lying back on the long, padded bench, I prop my feet up on the chrome railing and close my eyes. I breathe deeply, in through the nose and out through the mouth, and let the rocking motion of the boat lull me. I find it comforting.

Once my stomach has somewhat settled, I sit up. I puked not half an hour ago, and my mouth tastes like shit. "I need some water."

When I stand, the officer stands, too, as if he's going to follow me. But the wet bar is right here on the main deck, beneath the overhang of the cockpit, so I don't have far to go. When I grab a bottle of sparkling water from the mini fridge, he relaxes and sits back down.

Too restless to sit, I stand, leaning against the bar and sip my fizzy water.

Not long after, there he is. Detective Jamison stands at my railing. When our gazes meet, my belly tightens. Tall, dark, and handsome. I know it's a cliché, but he sure as hell meets all the requirements.

He grips the railing. "Permission to come aboard?" he says with a straight face.

Did he just crack a fucking joke? "Permission granted," I say, grinning.

The detective steps onto the swim deck and climbs up to join us on the main deck. "My condolences. I understand from my colleagues on the forensics team that the victim was your friend."

A knot forms in my throat as I nod toward Eric's boat. "We've been neighbors for several years."

"I'm really sorry." He sounds genuine.

"Eric was a sweetheart. I don't know why anyone would want to hurt him, let alone kill him." Still feeling a bit dizzy, I return to my seat, leaning forward with my arms propped on my legs.

Jamison points at the section of seating catty-corner to mine. "Mind if I sit?"

"Go right ahead." It's then that I notice Officer Swanson is gone, leaving the two of us alone. I'm alone with one of the sexiest men I've ever met. No, *the* sexiest.

"I need to ask you some questions," he says as he pulls out a small black notebook and a pen.

"I didn't kill him, if that's what you want to know. We were friends." My gaze snaps to his. If he was inside Eric's boat, then he knows Eric was gay.

Eric was flamboyantly loud and proud. He wore his sexuality draped over him like a gay pride flag. There are framed photographs on his boat, posters... prominently displayed... that leave no doubt as to his sexual orientation. Or as to some of his more unusual proclivities.

"Just how close were you to the victim?" Jamison says, eyeing me directly.

"Are you asking me if I've had sex with Eric?" I shrug, outing myself in the process. If the detective was wondering about *my* sexual orientation, he now knows. I'm tired, though, and I just want to get this interview over with. "No, I haven't. He was into some pretty extreme stuff, like pain. That's not my thing."

Jamison makes a notation in his notebook. Then he makes eye contact once more, his expression taut. "Are you aware that two homosexual men have been killed in the city in the past two weeks?"

I'm aware. I read the news. "Gay."

"I'm sorry?"

"We prefer to be called *gay.*"

"All right, then. Two *gay* men."

I lean back on the cushioned railing. "Yes. It's all anyone's talking about at the clubs."

"You're referring to gay clubs, I take it?"

"Yes."

Jamison nods. "The first two victims were both strangled with a garrotte."

"Like Eric was?"

Grimly, he nods. "I thought you should know, since you saw the crime scene. In effect, you're the closest thing we have to a witness."

"And you think their deaths are related to Eric's?"

"It's not conclusive at this point, but based on what I've seen here tonight, I have little doubt."

"Shit. You're talking about a serial killer."

"Can I ask what you were doing on the victim's boat at—" he pauses to check his notes and then says, "—approximately two-thirty a.m.?"

"I'd just gotten home from clubbing, and I saw his lights were on. That's not unusual for Eric. He's a night owl, up most of the night and asleep all day. I popped in to say 'hi' and found him lying in a pool of blood."

"Did you see anyone on or near his boat? Did you hear anything unusual?"

"No. Nothing."

"Did you notice anyone on the pier or in the parking lot?"

"No."

Jamison makes another notation in his notebook before meeting my gaze once more. "Mr. Alexander—"

"Ian."

"Ian. Three gay men have been murdered within a five-mile radius of this location in the past fourteen days. One of them apparently lived right next door to your boat, and you discovered the body."

"What are you saying? That I'm in danger, too?"

"If the killer thinks you're a possible witness, yes. You should be vigilant until the killer is apprehended. Is there somewhere else you can stay tonight, other than on this boat? Somewhere more secure?"

I nod, my mind reeling. "I have a townhouse not far from here, in the Gold Coast."

"Then I suggest you go there tonight. I'll have officers escort you home."

"Thanks, but is that really necessary?"

"Under the circumstances, I'm afraid it is." He stands. "Be vigilant, Mr. Alexander. The killer appears to be targeting gay men. I'd advise you to keep a low profile until we catch the perpetrator."

"I will."

"One more thing." He holds his hand out to me. "Give me your phone."

"Why?"

"I need your contact information. It's just a precaution."

I hand him my phone, and he keys in his number and sends a brief text from my phone to his. "Now you have my number, too. If you think of anything else pertinent to this case, please let me know."

I watch him climb off my boat and stride purposefully back toward Eric's boat. *Damn.* He is one fine specimen of a man.

3

Tyler Jamison

It's Saturday morning, just after six a.m., when I finish up at the marina. I head straight to the office to file my initial report. It doesn't matter that it's the weekend; my job doesn't have regular hours.

The moment I saw the murder victim, I knew why the captain assigned the case to me. It's the same apparent MO as two other cases I'm working. Unless we discover otherwise, I have to assume it's the same killer. Three gay men, all dead within a two-week period. A knot forms in my gut. I hate serial killers.

Someone who kills in a fit of passion is usually easy to catch.

In the heat of the moment, they make mistakes. They're often careless, and they don't think things through. But a serial killer? That's a different story. They plan ahead, think it through.

Right now, I'm not aware of any link among the three dead men, other than the fact they were all gay and they all frequented gay nightclubs in the local area. I'm still working on making the connections. But the fact that Ian Alexander's boat is moored right next to Eric Townsend's boat doesn't sit well with me, especially if Ian was a friend of Eric's. The killer might already know this, and that only puts Ian more directly in harm's way.

Ian Alexander. What are the odds that I would run into the guy I encountered at Tank's last night through the course of my job? I've read the reports written by the responding officers over and over, gleaning every detail. Ian Alexander, twenty-eight years old. He splits his time between his small luxury yacht at the St. James Yacht Club and an expensive, two-story townhouse in the heart of the Gold Coast. He's apparently unemployed, so I have to wonder where the money comes from.

I look up from my keyboard just as Captain Walker steps into my office. The sixty-five-year-old African American man is probably the closest thing I have to a father figure. When my dad died, in the line of duty as one of Chicago's finest, he and Jud Walker were partners. At my father's grave site, Jud stood beside me and held me up when I would have collapsed. I was eighteen years old at the time, and I'd just lost my hero. Saying that I was devastated is an understatement. Besides my mom and sister, Jud is the only connection I have left to my dad.

"I just assigned a twenty-four-seven protection detail to Ian Alexander's townhouse," Jud says.

"That was fast."

Walker shrugs. "Not when you realize who his father is."

"His father? Who's that?"

"Martin Alexander."

My eyes widen. "The federal judge? Well, that explains a lot." It certainly explains the money. The Alexanders are loaded, thanks to old family money on the father's side. Ian Alexander was born with a silver spoon in his mouth.

Walker nods. "The protection is warranted, though. As a possible witness to a murder—"

"He says he didn't actually see anything or anyone. He said he only *found* the body."

The captain shrugs. "I don't think it matters. If there's any chance the killer thinks Ian knows something, he's in danger."

I nod. "I'm going to talk to him again later this morning. If he was friends with the victim, he may know more than he realizes."

Walker nods. "If he does, it could put him at serious risk. I talked to Judge Alexander this morning. He's worried about his son's safety."

This is my case and, as much as I'd like to avoid seeing Ian Alexander again, I can't pass it off to another investigator. I'm going to have to deal with Ian myself, no matter how much he unsettles me.

* * *

I arrive at Ian's Gold Coast townhouse at eleven that morning. There's a police cruiser parked in the driveway, and I hope the visible police presence is enough to dissuade anyone with bad intentions from trying to get to Ian.

I park behind the cruiser and, as I pass by, I wave at the uniformed officer sitting behind the wheel. After climbing the steps to the front door, I ring the bell. When there's no answer, I ring again. Ian's expecting me. I called ahead to let him know I was on my way over. I try again.

The door opens with a flourish, and there is Ian Alexander, obviously just out of the shower. He's wearing nothing but a gray towel that hangs low on his lean, cut waist.

For fuck's sake. He knew I was coming. He could have at least put some clothes on before answering the door.

I look away, but not before I get a good look at the man's smooth, bare chest. He's lean, muscled, and sports a few scattered tattoos. But what really catches my eye are his pierced nipples. *Jesus.* My belly clenches hotly at the sight of two silver barbells threaded through his dusky pink nipples.

I tear my gaze away from the piercings only to notice the thin line of hair that disappears beneath the towel, drawing my eyes to a very healthy erection straining against the material.

"Detective!" He sounds winded, as if he raced down the stairs to answer the door. "Come in, please."

Ignoring my heated face, I do my best to maintain a neutral expression. *Who the hell answers the door in nothing but a towel?* "This isn't a social call, Mr. Alexander."

He steps back to invite me in. "Ian, please."

I frown, not wanting to make this personal. If I call him by his first name, it becomes personal. When my gaze catches once more on the barbell running through his right nipple, my heart stutters. *What does that feel like? Is the metal warm to the touch, or cold?* I force myself to ignore the heat surging through me. "I have more questions."

As I walk past him, I detect a faint whiff of soap and damp male skin. My body reacts, my chest tightening. My pulse is hammering.

I stop just inside the foyer. "I'll wait while you get dressed," I say, not giving him any alternative. There's no way I'm interviewing him while he's half-naked. I can't even think straight.

"Fine." He sounds disappointed. "Have a seat in the parlor, and I'll rejoin you shortly."

Parlor?

Ian leaves me to wait for him in a small, fussy room that is as pretentious as it sounds. This townhouse dates back to the mid-nineteenth century, as does the furniture in this room. It surprises me that such a hip young guy would furnish his home with antiques. As I take it all in—the polished dark wood floors and dark paneling, the fine furniture and ornate light fixtures, the thick rugs on the floor—I find myself reluctant to admit he has good taste.

Seeing him again has set me on edge, and I'm too wired to sit. Instead I pace, staring out the front bay window at the quiet, residential street.

When he rejoins me, he's dressed in worn jeans and a faded blue t-shirt advertising a local seafood restaurant. His long feet are bare, and his hair is still damp from his shower, the honey-brown waves on top thick and unruly.

The guy could easily make a killing as a fashion model if he wanted to. He's young, handsome, edgy. But then I remember who he is—the son of a prominent, wealthy Chicago family. He doesn't need to work a day in his life.

He's watching me intently.

I mentally shake myself. "Mr. Alexander—"

"Ian, please."

I sigh, because calling him by his first name feels too intimate. "I don't think—"

"Say it," he says, breaking into my thoughts.

There's a wicked gleam in his eyes, and I realize he's toying with me. "Say what?"

"My name. *Ian.* It won't kill you to say it."

I blow out an exasperated breath. "Ian," I say forcefully, as if I have something to prove.

He grins as if he's just cornered me in a brilliant Chess move. "So, what can I do for you, Tyler?"

I fight to keep from grinning. *Well played.* He's enjoying this way too much. "Detective Jamison, please."

He laughs. "Oh, come on! Are you always such an uptight stick-in-the-mud?"

I've clearly lost control of this conversation. "Yes, I am. Can we please get back on track here? I have questions about Eric

Townsend."

Ian's expression sobers at the mention of his deceased friend's name, and he sinks down onto an upholstered armchair. "All right. Ask your questions."

All of his bravado evaporated almost immediately, and I realize his cockiness is just a show.

Feeling like an ass, I take a seat on the chair across from him and pull out my notebook and pen. I ask him to go through his movements during the previous night. Where did he go? And at what time? When did he arrive at the marina? How often is he on his boat? Does he sleep there often? Does he know if Eric was seeing someone in particular?

"There were lights on below deck, and I heard music. I figured Eric was still up so I boarded and knocked on the galley door. When he didn't answer, I knocked again, louder, and called his name. He should have heard me. The music wasn't that loud. When there was still no answer, I let myself in."

"The door wasn't locked?"

"No."

"Go on."

"There's not much else to say. I spotted him immediately, lying on the floor in a pool of blood. It was obvious someone had slit his throat." Ian motions toward his own throat and shudders. "It was gaping." He makes a hand gesture. "Open."

"Did you happen to notice if he was still bleeding at the time?" I'm still waiting on a preliminary autopsy report for an estimated time of death, but knowing if he was still bleeding would help narrow down the timeframe.

Ian nods. "It was sluggish, but the blood was still coming out."

Sluggish. Townsend must have nearly bled out by that time. "And you saw no one?"

"Not a soul. I went up on deck, called nine-one-one, and then I threw up over the side."

"Tell me about your friend. What was his routine? Where did he typically hang out, and with whom?"

"Eric was all over the place, flitting from club to club late into the night. He was very outgoing... and very promiscuous. We used to go clubbing together a lot, and it wasn't unusual for him to hook up with one or two guys in one night."

"Used to?"

Ian shrugs. "Not so much lately. Eric had started doing some pretty hard partying, drugs included. That's not my thing."

"These are gay clubs you're talking about, I presume?"

Ian smiles. "Yes, *gay* clubs, where *gay* men congregate and sometimes engage in *gay* sexual activity in the bathroom or back alley."

Again, my face heats. I really wish he wouldn't push me this way. I don't know what he's trying to accomplish, but it's counterproductive. "Let's just stick to the facts, okay? I'm not here to do any gay bashing."

"Sorry." He gives me a contrite half-smile.

"How do you feel about the police presence outside?" I ask him, redirecting my thoughts.

He shrugs. "Dad told me he was going to arrange it."

"Your father has a lot of pull with Chicago PD." That's not a question.

Ian sighs. "Dad usually gets his way. I've learned not to fight him on the small things."

"And you consider your protection from a possible serial killer a small thing?"

"I'm not afraid, if that's what you're asking," he says. "Life's too short to live in fear. *Carpe diem.*"

He meets my gaze defiantly, and I find myself holding onto my breath. I've never known anyone like him. He's a free spirit. He's electrifying. "Seize the day. That's the name of your boat."

He nods.

I force myself back on track. "I need you to make a list of all the clubs Eric frequented. Can you do that?"

"Sure. You think his murder is connected to one of the clubs?"

"It's possible. All of the victims frequented a number of gay clubs in the area. I'm investigating these murders as possible hate crimes, and sexual orientation is the obvious common denominator."

Ian laughs harshly. "Three gay men strangled to death, nearly decapitated? Yes, I'd say these are hate crimes. People don't go around strangling people they like. This killer *hated* his victims."

"That's why you need to be vigilant. Let the police do their jobs. Let them protect you. Stay here in your townhouse for the foreseeable future and avoid the marina. In fact, I think it's advisable for you to remain here, safely indoors, until the killer is apprehended."

Ian's expression darkens. "I won't be locked up, Tyler."

"It's just for a little while." My God, the thought of this vibrant young man becoming another statistic shakes me to the core. "Ian, please. It's for your own safety."

He relaxes, his posture losing its defensiveness. "I'll think about it."

I rise from my seat to hand him my notebook and pen. "How about that list of clubs, then?"

As he starts writing, he shakes his head. "Pen and paper? You do have a smartphone, don't you? And a note app? You're so old school. How old are you, anyway?"

There's a hint of curiosity in his voice, but since my age is irrelevant, I ignore his question. When he hands me the notebook, I study the list. Four clubs, all located in Boystown. I meet his gaze. "Stay away from these clubs."

For a moment, he looks like he's going to refuse. But then he relaxes into another half-smile. "Whatever you say, Tyler."

I know it's pointless, but I correct him anyway. "Detective Jamison, please."

He rolls his eyes, reminding me just how young he is. "Whatever you say, *Detective*."

I leave Ian's townhouse with an uneasy feeling, and I'm tempted to tell the officers on guard duty to watch him closely. I have zero confidence that he'll heed my warning.

I suspect Ian Alexander does whatever the hell he wants. As a straight-laced stick-in-the-mud, I kind of admire that about him.

4

Ian Alexander

It's midnight, and I can't sleep. I'm usually out at this time of night, hitting the clubs with friends. My phone is lit up with text messages from Chris and Trey asking me where the hell I am. I keep tossing and turning in bed, the covers a twisted wreck.

I've got a raging hard-on, thanks to a certain someone I can't stop fantasizing about. I've already rubbed one out tonight, with his face front and center in my mental spank bank. And now I'm ready for another go.

The man is hot. In spite of his old school, uptight, repressed manner, he makes me tingle. I can't figure him out, though.

I think that's because he hasn't figured himself out. My heart pounds every time I'm near him and he sears me with those mesmerizing blue-green eyes.

When I saw him the other night at Tank's, my pulse kicked into overdrive. I was there with some straight friends that night, and when I pointed him out to the guys, they told me he was a regular. They said he'd show up every Friday night at eight p.m. and sit at the bar drinking alone until around ten, when he'd leave, almost always alone. They told me he was hit on frequently by both women and men and, occasionally, he'd leave with a woman.

But the way he looked at me outside the men's room that night—*damn!* I can still remember the blatant hunger in his eyes as we made eye contact. He made my body light up like fireworks. And I would have sworn he was feeling it too. *He has to be at least bi.*

That man is so tightly wired. I can't imagine what it would be like to be on the receiving end of all that intensity. *God, what I wouldn't give to find out.*

When I saw him that night at the bar, the ground shifted beneath my feet. I know it sounds sappy as hell, but I felt it. My entire body vibrated with arousal.

I couldn't figure him out that night, and I still can't. The way he watched me tonight, his eyes roaming over my chest when I met him at the door in nothing but a towel. Of course, I did it on purpose. I wanted to see his reaction. And, wow, did I get a reaction! The way his eyes locked onto my body... he looked like he wanted to eat me alive. But I want more than just his gaze on me.

I want those hands on me as well. And that sexy-as-sin mouth.

My thoughts turn to Eric, and I'm immediately flooded with guilt. He and I had grown apart the past few months as we saw less and less of each other. He'd gotten involved with someone who was into bondage and pain. I don't mind a little rough sex, but no one is hog-tying me or sticking a ball gag in my mouth. No fucking way.

Tonight, I gave Tyler what he asked for: a list of the clubs Eric frequented, and when I think of a certain uptight homicide detective visiting those clubs, I can't help smiling. I'd give anything to see the look on Detective Jamison's face when he visits the more flamboyant clubs.

I scroll through my Instagram feed and watch some You-Tube. Then, still feeling desperately horny, I jerk off one more time, with Tyler's face plastered across my mind. I imagine him here with me, in my bed. I imagine his hands on me, strong and fierce. Controlling. His mouth on me, his tongue teasing my nipple piercings. His cock sliding in deep. Pushing, pounding into me, grazing my prostate, making my nerves sing. More pounding, deep inside, hard, harder! I grip my cock mercilessly, stroking myself with frantic need. I come hard, my back arching off the mattress. I let out a strangled cry as my climax rushes through me.

Finally, after I've milked the last little bit of pleasure, I'm left shaking.

* * *

After showering and dressing the next morning, I make coffee and slather a toasted bagel with strawberry cream cheese. I've been under house arrest essentially for twenty-four hours now, and I'm ready to climb the walls. I cannot handle being cooped up.

I used to drive my parents crazy sneaking out of my bedroom at night. They'd find me sleeping on a sofa or crashed out on the floor of my baby sister's room.

The best I can do right now is take my breakfast up to the roof of my townhouse and sit in the greenhouse so I can watch the boats skimming across Lake Michigan. I bought this townhouse because of its proximity to the lake. The lake is one of my escapes—my happy place. And the view from my rooftop is priceless.

I've always loved the water. My parents would take me out on their yacht, and I felt like Peter Pan and Tinker Bell rolled into one. I'd climb up to the highest point on the boat—up above the cockpit—and pretend I was one of the lost boys. It was mind-blowing adventure on the open water. The perfect antidote for a kid with severe claustrophobia.

When I turned twenty-two, I bought my own yacht—the biggest one I could manage to operate on my own. When I'm on my boat, with the wind in my face and the sun on my skin, I'm free. I'm able to leave the shadows and the darkness of my past behind. No one's ever locking me up again.

Up in my greenhouse, reclining on an old futon sofa and surrounded by lush ferns and potted trees, I make my daily phone call to my sister, Layla. My sister and I are tight. Maybe it's because we're both adopted, or maybe it's because we both have issues and got rough starts in life.

I remember the day my parents brought her home. I remember staring at a baby with jet-black hair and dark eyes. Her birth parents, both teenagers in high school, relinquished their parental rights when she was diagnosed with juvenile diabetes. Layla was labeled "medically fragile," and her teenaged parents were ill-equipped to meet her needs.

It wasn't until she hit twenty that Layla's mental health issues began to surface. She can be a challenge, but God I love her.

Now my sister is twenty-one and currently enrolled at University of Chicago, majoring in psychology. She has a full-time bodyguard, who is an asshole as far as I'm concerned. My parents have been reluctant to replace him as Layla doesn't handle change well. If it was up to me, I'd have already fired him.

Layla and I are as close as any two siblings can be, probably because we have so much in common. We both came from bad situations, both of us abandoned by birth parents who were unable to care for us. I give the Alexanders a lot of credit for loving us no matter what. They helped make us into the people we are today.

"How's it going, sis?" I ask her when she answers my call.

She turns down the music in the background. "Hey, Ian! I'm good. How're you?"

"Peachy." I'm not about to tell her about Eric's murder or the police guarding my townhouse. She has enough to worry about without me adding to it. I know my parents won't tell her. "How's school?"

She sighs. "Final exams are coming up and then, thank God, it's summer break."

She tells me about her classes and the guy in her English lit class she likes. Then she tells me she has to get ready to leave for class. Before hanging up, I promise I'll come by for a visit. I'd offer to take her out for lunch, but I can't make any promises until this murder investigation is over. I won't do anything to put my sister in danger.

We hang up, and I go back to staring longingly at the boats on the lake, wishing I was out there instead of in here. I head back downstairs to my workout room on the lower level to run a few miles.

By now, my measly breakfast has worn off, and I'm sweaty and hungry. After a quick shower and some lunch, I watch a movie on the big screen TV in the living room, and then I surf the Internet for a while, just killing time until the sun sets.

Just knowing I'm house-bound sets me on edge. It brings back bad memories that I've worked hard to bury. My dad calls me, just to say hi, but I wonder if there's more to his call than that. I suspect he's checking up on me, just making sure I'm doing okay.

Finally, when the sun has set, I head down to the basement and slip out of the house through an old access tunnel that leads underground to the carriage house in back, which serves as my garage. From there, it's a piece of cake to slip through the back gate and down the alley, leaving my police protection detail none the wiser.

I hoof it over to Rush Street, where I hail a cab and head for Boystown. It's here that Eric most often frequented gay clubs. Maybe I can ask around, find out who he was spending time with. I'm not about to sit home and do nothing when I can do something to help.

I'll have a much better chance of finding out who might have wanted to hurt Eric than Tyler. He'd probably get hives just from stepping foot inside one of these clubs.

* * *

The taxi drops me off right in front of Diablo's, one of the most popular gay clubs in the village. I go to the end of the line and wait my turn like a good little boy. If Bruno—the bouncer—saw me, he'd let me go right in. But I'm not looking for special treatment, and I don't mind waiting.

Half an hour later, I'm at the front of the line, and Bruno waves me forward.

"Hey, man, I'm sorry about your friend," he says in his deep bass voice. "Eric was a great guy."

"He was. Thanks, Bruno."

Bruno ushers me inside. The club's interior is pumping, as usual, the darkness lit up by multi-colored disco balls suspended from the ceiling. The music is pounding, and the place is packed.

Heading to the bar, I work my way through the diverse crowd. Guys of every type, color, and creed are here, from young to old. Other than the paid dancers on raised pedestals, dressed in

G-strings stuffed with cash, almost everyone else is either standing around in small groups talking and drinking, or they're on the
dance floor, which is jam packed.

I stop at the bar to grab a beer and shoot the breeze with the
staff. Three guys work behind the bar. Two of them are dressed
in jeans and t-shirts. The third—Roy, the owner—is bare-chested
and wearing a black leather harness and tight black jeans. Flashing strobe lights glint off the rings piercing his nipples.

Roy sees me and waves me over. "Ian!" When I take a seat at
the bar, he reaches over to clasp my hand, giving it a comforting
squeeze. "I'm so sorry about Eric!" He has to yell to be heard over
the music.

"Thanks!"

"What can I get you?" he says.

"Beer."

Roy grabs a bottle out of the case, pops the top, and hands it to
me. "It's on the house."

I take a swig. "Was Eric in here much lately?"

"Yeah." He steps away to fill another customer's drink order.
When he returns, his expression is pensive. "I saw him in here a
lot the past few weeks. Why?"

"Do you remember if he was here Friday night?"

Roy thinks for a moment, and then he nods. "Yeah, I think so."
He motions me closer, leaning over the bar so he can be heard
over the pounding music. "Is it true what I heard on the news? He
was strangled with a garrotte?"

The reminder makes my stomach twist into a knot. I nod. "Did you see him talking to anyone? Was he seeing anyone?"

Roy shrugs. "I didn't notice anyone in particular. I saw him with a lot of guys, you know?" And then he's pulled away again when more customers arrive at the bar.

I turn to face the crowd and sip my beer, watching the mix of familiar faces and new ones. A couple of friends come up to say hi and invite me to join them on the dance floor, but I decline. A guy seated beside me at the bar offers to buy me a drink, but I pass. I'm not looking to hook up. I'm here to see if I can find out anything about Eric. I owe it to him.

One hour and two beers later, after having talked to at least a dozen people, I have nothing to show for my efforts. I think my best bet will be to let folks know I'm asking around. Maybe that will lead to something.

While I'm waiting to get Roy's attention, so I can settle up my bar bill, a strong hand grips the back of my neck. I glance back, expecting to see one of my friends, but no. I'm staring into a pair of angry blue-green eyes. He's clearly pissed, his jaw clenched tightly. His nostrils are flaring.

I'm so happy to see him, I can't hide my smile. "Hello, detective! Fancy meeting you—"

"What in the hell are you doing here?" he growls through gritted teeth. "You're supposed to be at home! Did you sneak out?"

My smile widens because, God, he's hot when he's pissed. I'd do it again in a heartbeat just to feel all this intensity. "I'm here for the same reason you are! I thought I'd ask around, see what I could find out."

He shakes his head and points toward the exit. "You're leaving—now!"

I reach into my pocket and pull out some cash, which I toss onto the bar. "Roy!" When he looks my way, I point at the cash. "Gotta go!"

And then, I swear to God, Tyler marches me out of the club, his hand gripping the back of my neck as curious eyes follow us to the door.

The cool night air feels good on my hot face. And it's nice not to have to scream to be heard.

Tyler steers me to the right. "This way."

He walks me to a black BMW parked just a couple of blocks away, opens the front passenger door, and motions for me to get in. When I do, he shuts my door before walking around to the driver's side.

"What the hell do you think you're doing?" he says as he slides behind the wheel. He's staring straight ahead, his body rigid. His hands fist the steering wheel.

"This was one of Eric's regular hang-outs. I wanted to find out if he was here the night he was... you know."

"Murdered?" Tyler turns to glare at me. "And was he?"

"Yeah. I talked to the owner, Roy, who said Eric had been there a lot recently. He was pretty sure Eric was there Friday night."

Tyler's thumbs brush the leather steering wheel, and he sighs. "Ian, you shouldn't have come here tonight. You shouldn't be out at all right now. It's not safe."

I turn in my seat to face him. "Eric was my friend. I owe him."

He turns the key in the ignition, and the engine roars to life. "Buckle your seatbelt. I'm taking you home."

I feel a thrill at his words, even though he didn't mean them the way they sounded. *God, I wish.*

After he pulls out into traffic, he spares me a quick glance. "How did you manage to leave your townhouse undetected?"

I laugh. "That's my secret. If I tell you, it'll never work again."

He glares at me, clearly not amused. "This isn't funny, Ian. The police protection is for your own good."

I smile. "You called me *Ian*."

"Quit smiling," he says, still not amused.

"Sorry." But I can't help it. I love it when he's bossy. I'll bet he's domineering in bed. Just the thought raises my body temperature. "How did you find me?"

"I was making my rounds to all the clubs you listed, talking to the owners and the staff. When I arrived at this club, I spotted you at the bar."

He doesn't say another word on the drive to my house. When we arrive, he pulls into the driveway and parks behind the police cruiser. The officer on duty does a double-take when we walk past his vehicle up to the front door.

Tyler follows me inside, shutting the door behind us. Hard. He's still pissed. He runs his fingers through his dark hair. "Look, kid—"

I laugh as I switch on the lights. "*Kid?* Fuck, Tyler, I'm twenty-eight. I'm not a kid."

"You might as well be a kid, especially when you act like one.

You had no business sneaking out to Diablo's tonight."

He's dressed as I've always seen him, in a black suit and tie. I wonder if he's always so polished and professional. I'd give anything to see him let his hair down.

I walk right up to him, standing nose to nose, and he takes a step back, going up against the door. I catch a flash of something in his eyes. Was that panic? *Holy fuck.*

His nostrils flare as he sucks in a breath. His eyes are locked on mine, and he's staring at me like I'm something he doesn't quite understand. His eyes glitter beneath the lights of the chandelier, like sunlight dancing on water.

My gaze locks onto his lips, which are beautifully framed by his dark beard. Right now, those perfect lips are flattened in irritation. God, I want to kiss him, so damn badly. "Tyler."

He shakes his head as if answering *no* to a question I haven't even asked.

Do you like men?

Do you like me?

Do you even know what you like?

I suspect he doesn't.

I wonder how he'd react if I simply kissed him. Right now. Right here. Would he shove me away? Or would he kiss me back?

His eyes narrow. "Don't leave this house again." He's now firmly back in detective mode. "Don't sneak out, and stay the fuck away from those clubs until the murderer is caught. Is that clear?"

I'm desperate to taste those lips. I want to know if they're as soft as they look. Instead, I nod. Anything to make him happy.

"Good." He frowns as he scans my face, making no move to leave. His gaze lands on *my* lips, and he swallows hard.

I watch his throat muscles tighten and flex. Everything about him is tense, tight, completely unyielding. I've never in my life been so desperately attracted to someone.

His gaze returns to mine, holding it for just a heartbeat before he looks away.

"Lock this door behind me," Tyler says, reaching for the doorknob. "And no more stunts like the one tonight."

And then he's gone.

5

Tyler Jamison

My mind races on the drive home to my condo. I'm not focused on what I should be focused on—not on the countless interviews I did tonight with club owners and their staff. Yes, everyone knew Eric Townsend. No, no one knew anyone who had a problem with him. There was no disgruntled ex-boyfriend. No jilted lover. Nothing. Eric was a great guy, it was a terrible tragedy what happened to him, *et cetera*. That's all I got. Obviously, that's not the whole story. Someone bad came into Eric's life, and I'm going to find out who.

And then, to top off a less-than-productive night, I walked into the last club on my list to find Ian Alexander seated at the bar, drinking like he didn't have a care in the world. Like he wasn't possibly putting his life in danger by simply being there.

For fuck's sake! Does the guy not have any sense at all? He's at risk! It's entirely possible the killer might think Ian saw him the night of Eric's murder, or that he can identify him. Or, even worse, that Ian *knows* him.

When I spotted Ian at Diablo's, my heart stopped cold for a moment. I couldn't get him out of there fast enough. And when we got back to his place... the way he looked at me! Every cell in my body awakened, and I couldn't look away. When he stared at my mouth, I couldn't breathe.

I arrive home and park. My mind is racing as I head up the stairs to my second-floor condo. Once inside, I head straight for my bedroom, where I strip out of my suit and hang it in the closet. After making a quick pit stop in the bathroom to piss and brush my teeth, I crawl naked into bed. I've been up nearly twenty hours, and I'm exhausted. Or at least my body is exhausted. My mind is still racing, as is my pulse.

I've always known there was something wrong with me. Back in my school days, when the guys were crushing on girls and bragging about getting to first base, or second, or third, I always felt left out. I just didn't see what they did. The girls were nice enough, and certainly pretty, but that was all. Yes, they were soft and they smelled good, but they didn't send my pulse racing, not like they did for the other guys. And they never inspired hard-ons.

No, I got hard-ons at the most inappropriate times, like in the boys' locker rooms after gym class. It was all I could do to hide my physical reactions to seeing the other boys' bodies. Muscles and body hair made me sweat bullets. I was terrified of getting caught and being singled out as a freak, so I learned to temper my reactions. To hide them. To suppress them. And I got really good at it.

As I got older, I learned to play along so I could fit in with the other guys. I learned the art of camouflage. I dated girls in high school, but I was careful not to stay with any one girl too long. And I certainly never had sex with one. The girls thought I was being respectful, when in reality I just wasn't interested.

In college, I focused on my studies. And then I joined the police force and threw myself into training and conditioning. My dad, God rest his soul, was a Chicago cop, and more than anything, I wanted to follow in his footsteps. I loved him, and I wanted to make him proud—even after his death.

When my dad was killed, I felt his loss profoundly. His death created a giant hole in our family, a vacuum that I thought could never be filled. I did my best to step up. I helped my mom around the house, and I helped her take care of my little sister, Beth, who was just an infant at the time.

I channeled every bit of energy I had into being the best son I could be, the best big brother. I wanted to think my dad would have been proud of me. When my needs and wants didn't fit the role I thought I should play, I buried them deep. Really, really deep.

And now, over twenty years later, I'm still trying to be the best son I can be. The best brother. The best uncle to my nephew,

Luke. My identity is wrapped up in who I am for my family, and in who I think they'd want me to be. There's no room for anything else.

Over the years, I've considered marriage. And while I'm capable of performing sexually with a woman, it's not something I take any pleasure in. It's a task. On the rare occasions it happens, it's a chore I force myself to get through. It just wouldn't be fair to saddle a woman with me as a husband.

So, where does that leave me? Alone. Very much alone. There are no options I can live with. I can't bear the thought of being something less in the eyes of my family. It's not that they're homophobic, because they're not. One of my sister's best friends—Sam—is gay. Beth and her husband share their penthouse apartment with Sam and his partner, Cooper. Sam and Cooper are *family*. My mother adores them too. But I can't risk letting my family down.

When sleep doesn't come, I end up watching a bit of mindless TV. I need a distraction to keep me from obsessing over someone I shouldn't want and certainly can't have.

Tonight, when we stood inside the foyer of his townhouse, the two of us standing in a pool of light from the overhead chandelier, my heart hammered inside my chest. As he stood there staring at me, my world narrowed to that moment. I couldn't look away. My gut tightened, and my cock hardened. I couldn't prevent my body's reaction any more than I could prevent taking my next breath.

For a moment, I honestly thought he was going to kiss me.

And for a moment—a desperate moment—I wanted him to.

I have never in my life felt anything remotely like what I felt tonight. My skin was too tight for my body, and I was burning up inside. Even now, just thinking about it, my lungs feel like they're being squeezed and I can hardly catch my breath. *Shit.* I've never in my life felt so... *alive.* I've never felt such anticipation. Such exhilaration. All I could think was, why is this happening to me *now?* I'm forty-four years old. It's a bit late for me to start having crushes.

Dragging my fingers through my hair, I choke back a cry of frustration. I'm *finally* feeling desire, and it's for a man!

Eventually, I manage to doze off, but my sleep is fitful. Anxiety has me by the throat and won't let go. I can't stop thinking about Ian. I can't stop worrying about him. If he snuck out once, he could do it again. And the thought of anything happening to him... *Jesus*, I can't even contemplate it.

Maybe I should call Shane. My sister's husband is the CEO of a private security company that specializes in personal protection. I could arrange for someone to keep tabs on Ian and make sure he stays out of trouble. I have a sneaking suspicion that it's going to be impossible to keep him under house arrest for long.

6

Tyler Jamison

Monday morning arrives all too soon. I'm awake a few minutes before my alarm is scheduled to go off at six. I slept like shit, my mind racing nonstop, thinking about this case, about Ian, and wondering just how much danger he might be in.

No matter how hard I try, I can't get him out of my head. He's just a potential witness, nothing more. That's all there is to it. That's all there can ever be. But my brain keeps coming up with stupid excuses to see him again. I'm drawn to him, like a tree is drawn to the sun.

Shit! It's not supposed to be like this.

I haul my ass out of bed and head for the shower, stepping under a brutal spray of cold water to punish my body. The icy water does the trick. After my shower, I dress and fill a thermos with fresh coffee.

When I arrive at the office, there's a preliminary report from the coroner waiting on my desk. Eric Townsend had an alcohol blood level of 0.25, which is staggering. The killer must have been plying him with alcohol to keep him off-balance. And I know the forensics team found cocaine residue at the scene. Chances are Eric was high as a kite at the time of the murder. Maybe the killer was, too.

The forensics team collected hair, blood, and skin samples, and I'm waiting on an expedited DNA profile. The blood and skin samples were taken from the victim's fingernails, which means he did try to fight back despite the fact that he was bound at the time of the killing.

For the next two days, I follow up with additional interviews at the clubs. I talk to everyone I can find who knew Eric, to everyone who was in the clubs he frequented the night he was killed. No one saw him with anyone in particular. Apparently, Eric was a butterfly, flitting from man to man. But no one person stood out.

This isn't the first time I've dealt with a hate crime in the LGBTQ community. They get more than their share of violence directed at them. But murders like these? It's extreme.

The police protection detail watching Ian sends me periodic reports on his whereabouts. He's not staying put, as I'd asked him to, but I guess I can't say I'm surprised. He is, however, refraining from sneaking out of the house alone. At least he's cooperating with his minders.

This morning, Ian left his townhouse with an official police escort to visit his parents. He was at their house for two hours. Then he took his camera to Millennial Park, also with a police escort, and walked around the neighboring vicinity taking photographs of run-down, derelict buildings and crumbling back alleys.

He spent the afternoon and early evening alone on his yacht, down in the galley, out of sight from the police who stood guard on the dock. Then, as darkness fell, he headed back to his townhouse and holed up inside for the night.

By Thursday, I'm running out of leads. The few I had amounted to nothing, and I'm back to square one. This could go on indefinitely, and I know Captain Walker won't be able to justify the expense of a police protection detail on Ian for much longer, regardless of what Judge Alexander demands. Not without proof that Ian's in danger.

On Friday of that week, the police watch ends, and Ian is a free man, able to come and go as he pleases. To celebrate, he heads out after sunset. I know this because I'm sitting in my BMW just down the street from his townhouse when the police depart. He wastes hardly any time before going out.

An Uber driver picks him up at his townhouse twenty minutes later, and I follow them to Boystown.

When the driver drops Ian off at Diablo's, I park on a side street and debate whether to go in after him or not. It's a free country.

I can't tell him where he can and can't go. But still, I can't shake the feeling that he's putting himself in danger just by being here. If he insists on asking questions, he's going to open himself up to potential risk, and that I can't stomach. It's not his fault he was in the wrong place at the wrong time on the night Eric Townsend was murdered.

After sitting here debating with myself for nearly a half-hour, I get out of my car and cross the street. I walk right up to the front entrance and flash my police badge so I can skip the line that stretches two blocks.

The place is packed tonight, and I ignore the looks directed my way. Some of them are just curious, others are downright hostile. And still, others are blatant come-ons. Dressed in a suit and tie, I stick out like a sore thumb in this place. Clearly, I don't belong, and I see a lot of resentment coming my way.

Ignoring all the looks, I search the club for Ian, scanning the bar first, and then the standing crowd. Finally, I spot him on the dance floor, and I can't take my eyes off him. He's a really good dancer. His movements are so crisp and precise, perfectly choreographed to the beat of the music. No wonder he likes coming here. He's in his element on the dance floor.

He's also the center of attention, surrounded by men, like he's holding court and he's their prince.

I stand in the shadows, my pulse pounding in time with the loud music. I watch him move, feeling almost hypnotized by the way he gives himself over to the music. Right now, he's lost in the beat, his eyes closed, so he doesn't see me watching him. And that means, at least for the moment, I can look my fill.

One of the men dancing with him puts his hands on Ian's hips, clasping him tightly and drawing Ian back against his front. The two of them move together, perfectly synchronized, and their movements grow suggestive, blatantly sexual. And then the configuration changes, as someone else moves in between them, claiming Ian for a few moments until he too is replaced by yet another man.

Ian isn't the least bit self-conscious. He moves easily, confidently, as good as any professional dancer I've ever seen.

His ripped jeans hang low on his lean hips, exposing just the waistband of his black boxer-briefs. His t-shirt rides up, exposing his hip bones and the muscles narrowing down to his groin.

I stare, unable to look away.

Suddenly, he opens his eyes, and his gaze clashes with mine. His expression transforms instantly, from utter shock to surprise. And then he gives me this come-hither smile that throws my pulse into overdrive.

Ian breaks away from his friends and jogs over to me. "Tyler!" He's winded from dancing, and there's a fine sheen of sweat on his forehead.

"You shouldn't be here!" I practically shout to be heard over the music. *And neither should I.*

Grinning, he throws his arms wide. "I've been cooped up for days, just like you asked. And this evening my house arrest is finally over. I'm a free man, detective. I've got a lot of catching up to do."

I shake my head. "Let me drive you home."

He holds out his hand, beckoning me. "I have a better idea! Dance with me."

Shaking my head, I step back, trying not to look as horrified as I feel.

He frowns. "Your loss then." With a parting wave, he returns to the dance floor, quickly swallowed up by the crowd once more. A blond guy clutches Ian's hips and drags him close until they're practically chest to chest.

I tamp down a sudden surge of anger. Not at Ian, but at those men who think nothing of manhandling him, grabbing him and pulling him this way and that, like he's their play-thing.

Another guy steps forward and says something to Ian. This guy's clearly older than the others, and he carries himself with an air of confidence. His straight black hair is long enough to brush his shoulders, and he's a couple inches taller than Ian, his chest broader. He pulls Ian close and whispers in his ear. Then he turns Ian in his arms and plasters himself to Ian's backside. As the dancing continues, this guy practically *grinds* on Ian.

I force myself to look away. Not wanting to stand here gawking like an idiot, and not ready to simply leave him here to his own devices, without protection, I head for the bar and take a seat at the far end where I can see most of the room. A bartender approaches me, a guy with sun-kissed blond hair and blue eyes, a blatant smile on his face. He looks so young I doubt he's even old enough to work here. I'm tempted to card him.

"Hey, handsome," he says, winking at me. "What can I get

you?" He leans forward, resting his elbows on the bar. He acts like he has all the time in the world and my drink order is the only one that matters.

"I'll have a Guinness." I'm not on duty, and one beer won't kill me.

"You got it, sugar."

He brings me a glass, and I sit at the bar sipping my beer. I'm trying not to be obvious as I keep Ian in my sights. I tell myself I'm just watching out for him, but the truth is, I can't look away. I'm itching to grab him by the back of the neck and march him out of this place. I've done it before. I can do it again.

And then what?

I have no fucking clue.

I've accepted the fact that I feel no desire for women, but I also know I don't fit in this world either. I've seen more glitz and glam and leather here in one night than I've seen my entire life, and it's just not for me.

I watch Ian as he scans the club, a frown on his face. When he spots me at the bar, his lips curve into a pleased grin. He tears himself away from his entourage and joins me at the bar, where it's standing room only. He stands close beside me, his shoulder brushing against mine. I can smell his overheated body, along with his faint cologne, and my body responds instantly.

Ian reaches for my beer and helps himself to a healthy swig. "What's wrong, detective?"

"Nothing."

His hand is halfway to my glass again when he pauses to give me a questioning look. "D'you mind? I'm parched."

"Go right ahead." I watch his throat muscles work as he downs half my beer. I know I shouldn't feel this way, but I'm getting a kick out of the fact he's sharing my beer. It feels intimate. And out of all the guys fawning over him out on the dance floor, I'm the one he seeks out. "I don't think it's a good idea for you to be here right now, Ian. Please let me take you home."

As he sets the empty glass on the bar, the corners of his lips rise. "Okay."

"Okay?" I'm finding it hard to believe he's giving in that easily.

He nods. "Sure. Why not? Yours is the best offer I've had all night."

Before I can clarify my meaning—he makes it sound like I'm offering him a hookup—he winks. He's just playing with me.

He leans close, his lips brushing against my ear. At the feel of his warm breath on my skin, I stifle a shiver.

"I have a possible lead, detective," he says. "Let's go someplace where we can talk without having to shout."

A lead? Now Ian thinks he's an amateur investigator? I lay enough cash on the bar to cover my tab and a tip for the bartender. "Let's go."

We drive back to Ian's townhouse, and I park in the driveway. This time, when I follow him up the steps to his front door, it feels different. With the police presence gone, being here with Ian feels far more personal and far less professional.

While he unlocks the door, I quickly scan the immediate neighborhood, my gaze sweeping the line of cars parked along the curb. I peer into dark shadows across the street, looking for anything out of place. It's a deeply ingrained habit.

The truth is, I don't like the fact that he lives here alone, with no protection. There's still a chance he could be in danger, especially if he's nosing around dance clubs asking about Eric Townsend.

Ian opens the door and steps inside. I follow him in.

"So, what's your lead?" I say as I close the door and turn the deadbolt.

He switches on the foyer light. The crystal chandelier casts rays of fractured light on us, reflecting on the golden highlights in his hair. His eyes look even greener, and they're fairly glittering with excitement. "A friend told me Eric recently met someone, and that they'd been seeing each other pretty regularly, right up to the night of Eric's murder."

"Do you know who it is?"

"I do now. His name is Brad Turner." Ian walks into the parlor, turning on a lamp. "He was there tonight, at Diablo's. Can I get you a drink?"

"No, thanks. I'm fine."

"Well, I want one." Ian grabs a bottle of top-shelf whiskey from behind the bar, pops the top, and pours a shot of whiskey into a glass. He downs the entire shot, coughing as the liquor burns his throat. Once the coughing stops, he says, "I danced with him tonight."

Ian's words chill me to the bone. "You danced... why didn't you say something at the club?"

He pours himself another shot. "I didn't want to tip him off.

Besides, he might not be the guy we're looking for."

Ian downs the second shot, his hand shaking slightly.

"You should have said something, Ian."

He meets my gaze head on. "I'm saying something now."

I can tell he's shaken. "Are you all right?"

Ian slams his empty shot glass on the bar. "No, actually, I'm not! Someone practically *decapitated* a friend of mine, and I might have danced with the motherfucker tonight and pretended to like it. No, I'm not fucking all right!"

His hand tightens on the shot glass, his knuckles turning white. Afraid he might break the glass and cut himself, I take it from him. He's hurting.

Ian comes around to my side of the bar and plants himself right in front of me. We're standing practically nose to nose, and his chest heaves as he tries to catch his breath.

His eyes are bright, filled with emotion, his cheeks flushed. When he swallows hard, my gaze locks onto the tendons in his neck, to the rise and fall of his Adam's apple. His nostrils flare, and it's the sexiest thing I've ever seen in my life. My body reacts, my dick twitching in my boxers, lengthening as my blood rushes south.

Ian's gaze drops to my mouth, his tongue slipping out to graze his bottom lip. When he leans closer, staring at my mouth, his intent is clear.

My heart slams against my ribs, and immediately I step back, almost tripping over my own feet as I try to put some space between us. I shake my head. "No, Ian. I'm sorry, but I'm not—no."

There's a hint of a smile on his face. "You're not *what?*"

"I'm not... I don't..." *Shit!* I can't even bring myself to say the word. *I need to get out of here.*

He watches me, not the least bit offended by my reaction. If anything, he seems almost amused.

"I'm not," I repeat, shaking my head.

"Okay." He raises his hands in capitulation. "Whatever you say."

"Good." I release the tension in my shoulders. "I just didn't want you to get the wrong impression."

"Nope. No impression, none at all. My bad."

I need to go. I feel light-headed and overheated, almost feverish, and my pulse is still racing. My body feels like it's plugged into an electrical socket, my skin tingling.

I only make it halfway to the door when his next words stop me cold in my tracks.

"I made plans to see Turner again tomorrow night."

I turn back to face him. "What did you say?"

"I'm seeing him again. The guy Eric was seeing when he was killed."

My chest tightens, and a surge of panic nearly chokes me. "Ian, no, you can't."

"I can and I will, detective. I think Brad Turner might have killed Eric."

"Why do you say that?"

"Because when I mentioned I was Eric's friend, the asshole smiled at me... and it chilled me to the bone. He didn't show a shred of emotion over Eric's death. And when we danced, all he could talk about was Eric."

"I think I'll have that drink after all," I say, returning to the bar.

Ian pours me a shot of whiskey, and I knock it back. My hand is shaking, and I don't think I've ever felt so out of control. I can't let Ian do this. He can't put himself in harm's way.

7

Ian Alexander

Tyler is still here, but not because he wants to be. He's only here because he's afraid for me. He's totally on edge, and it's my fault. I shouldn't have pushed him tonight. He's a classic case of a man in complete denial about his own sexuality, and I'm not sure he's ready to face that fact.

After tossing back a shot of whiskey, Tyler sits on a barstool and lets my revelation sink in. Already I can see the wheels turning in his head as he works out an alternative plan. One where I'm *not* in close proximity to a possible serial killer.

"You can't see him again," Tyler says, shaking his head. "It's too risky."

I sit on the other barstool, facing him. It means a lot to me that he's trying to protect me, but it doesn't change anything. "I don't have a choice, Tyler. I have to do this for Eric."

"No. I'll send someone in undercover. Hell, I'll do it myself."

I laugh. "That won't work. I was Eric's friend, not you, and not some unknown undercover cop. If Turner was there that night, if he did kill Eric, then he probably knows my boat is moored next to Eric's. He might have seen me there that night. And if he did, then I'm a loose end he needs to tie up."

Tyler runs his fingers through the dark strands of his hair. "That's exactly what I'm afraid of."

"Then you know it has to be me." When he doesn't respond, I tell him, "I can do this, Tyler. I'm not afraid."

He meets my gaze. "That's the problem, Ian. You *should* be afraid." He doesn't contradict me, though, because he knows I'm right.

After he makes a phone call to his captain, my police protection detail returns and sets up a perimeter around my townhouse once more. It looks like I'm back under house arrest. He goes outside to talk to them, probably warning them not to let me sneak out again. I can just imagine him reading them the riot act for letting me pull one over on them before.

I've never met anyone like him. Not even close. Yes, he's a controlling SOB, but he's also exciting as hell. He's drop-dead gorgeous, and the thought of something possibly developing between us takes my breath away. I've never wanted someone as much as I want him.

If the way he watches me is any indication, I'm pretty sure he's gay. I see blatant hunger in his eyes. I catch him staring at my mouth. His chest rises sharply as his breathing kicks up. Damn, what I wouldn't give to be the one to introduce him to what he's been missing.

When he returns, he looks harried. "There will be officers guarding both the front and back doors. Please stay put, Ian."

I nod. "I will. At least until tomorrow evening. I'm meeting Brad at Diablo's at eleven."

Tyler's jaw tightens, his muscles flexing. "Then I'm going with you."

"Don't be silly. You've got *cop* written all over you. He'll make you in an instant."

"I'm not letting you meet him alone. That's out of the question, so don't bother arguing with me."

Damn. He's bossy. "Need I remind you this is a gay club? You just told me you're not gay. Therefore, you don't belong there. You'd stick out like a sore thumb."

Tyler moves in close, his long fingers circling my throat. "Do I need to remind you that three men have been strangled? Murdered?" He tightens his grip enough to make his point.

"*Gay* men, you mean," I say hoarsely. He's not choking me, but his grip is strong enough to make his point.

Tyler's gaze locks on mine, and he's breathing hard. My breath catches in my throat as my pulse starts racing. He's standing *so* close... I want to lean into him and brush my lips against his. I want to know if his lips are as soft as they look. I want to kiss his throat and feel his pulse pounding against my lips.

I'm guessing it would be his first kiss with a man. Desire tightens my belly. *God, I want it to be with me.*

He releases my throat, having made his point quite well.

"Fine," I say. "I'd rather not have my head severed from my neck, thank you very much. So, how do we do this, *detective?*"

"I'll go in with you so I can watch your back."

I chuckle. "I hope you have something to wear besides a suit, because you'll never fit in dressed like that." I give him a blatant once-over, scanning him from head to toe. "You might as well wear a neon sign that says *COP.*"

"I'm sure I can come up with something suitable."

I can't suppress my grin. I'm going clubbing with Tyler Jamison. Knowing he'll be watching me the entire night—knowing his eyes will be *on me*—makes me fucking hard as a rock.

* * *

At ten-thirty the next night, right on schedule, I step out my front door and jog down to the driveway so I can slide into the backseat of a taxi. Sure enough, there's a black BMW parked across the street from my townhouse. And there he is, my personal police escort, sitting behind the wheel. I catch only a glimpse of Tyler, but I can tell he's dressed casually.

I tell my driver where to take me, and we head out. The BMW follows closely, and I have to force myself not to turn and glance back at him. I'd make a shitty undercover cop.

My ride drops me off right in front of Diablo's. There's a line half-way down the block. I could skip the line, but that would leave Tyler outside waiting to get in. Otherwise, he'd have to re-sort to flashing his badge, and that would defeat the purpose of him trying to remain undercover.

So, I get in line like a good boy, along with everyone else, and shuffle along the pavement beneath the neon lights. Out of the corner of my eye, I track Tyler a few yards behind me in line.

He looks ridiculously hot in a pair of ripped jeans and a bad-ass black leather jacket. I thought he was hot in a suit and tie, but now he's off-the-chart gorgeous.

It's a little too warm out tonight to be wearing a leather jacket, but I imagine he's armed, and he's wearing the jacket to conceal his weapon. I find the notion of him carrying a concealed weapon to be a turn-on.

The guys are going to be all over him tonight. The fact that he's a new face here—not to mention hot as hell—means he's going to be on the receiving end of a lot of attention. I hope he's up for that.

The line moves pretty quickly, and within fifteen minutes, I'm inside. I know he won't be far behind me. I scan the crowded club, looking for familiar faces. When my friends spot me, they come over.

Chris puts his arm across my shoulders and gives me a side hug. "Hey, sweetie. I'm so glad you're here."

Trey pats my back. "It's about time you showed up. We were

just about to call you."

It's standing room only tonight. The dance floor is already in full swing and seeing quite a bit of action. The dancers on the raised pedestals are raking in the bucks, surrounded by eager admirers.

Chris grabs my hand and pulls me toward the dance floor. "Let's dance!"

I nod, but release his hand. "In a few minutes. I'm going to the bar first."

My friends offer to join me, but I shoo them to the dance floor. I head for the bar, grab a seat, and order a Cosmo. It'll be easy for Brad to spot me here, if he shows. I know there's a chance he might not show tonight. If he was involved in Eric's murder, it's possible he'll have second thoughts.

"Here you go," a bartender says as he hands me my drink. As I sip my citrusy-tart cocktail, I realize I probably shouldn't be drinking vodka tonight. I need to keep my wits about me. Tyler would definitely disapprove if I got tipsy.

Speaking of Tyler, I wonder where he is. He should have made it inside by now. I scan the bar from one end to the other, and it doesn't take me long to spot him. He's at the far end of the bar, where it makes a ninety-degree turn. From there, he can keep me in his peripheral vision easily, without being obvious about it.

I get a thrill knowing he's nearby—watching me. I have to look away. I'd much rather stare at him all night than wait for an al-leged monster to make his appearance.

Forty-five minutes later, Brad is officially a no-show, and honestly, I'm relieved. I'm ready to settle my tab and leave when I feel someone at my back. I know it's not Tyler, because he hasn't moved from his spot at the end of the bar.

I turn to look behind me, hoping it's Chris or Trey, but no. It's Brad.

"Sorry I'm late," he says, brushing up against my back. All the stools at the bar are taken, so he can't sit.

He lays his hands on my shoulders and leans in close. I smell alcohol on his breath, along with a whiff of Eric's favorite cologne. My stomach roils, and I swallow the hot surge of bile that threatens to choke me. It's entirely possible that this motherfucker killed Eric.

I let my irritation seep into my voice as I step off my barstool. "I'd given up on you. I was just leaving."

Brad is a bit taller than me, with a broad chest and shoulders to match. He's undoubtedly strong, and he easily could have overpowered someone like Eric, especially if Eric was restrained or drunk. I have to admit, he's good-looking.

His hand clamps down on my shoulder, and he presses me back down onto my seat. "Don't go." It's not a request. It's a command. His voice is sharp, matching his expression. But then his expression softens into a smile. "I said I was sorry for being late." He leans in and kisses my cheek, and his lips linger. "I promise I'll make it up to you," he whispers in my ear.

The guy seated next to me gets up, and Brad commandeers his seat. He starts massaging the back of my neck, his touch possessive, and it takes all I have not to pull away. I normally love being touched, but this guy makes my skin crawl.

I risk a glance down the bar. Tyler is facing forward, staring straight ahead and not directly at me. Still, I know he's watching. He's sitting ramrod straight, his shoulders set. There's a glass of beer on the counter in front of him, but I have yet to see him take a sip.

Brad's hot breath washes over my neck as he leans in close, his lips grazing my ear. "Let's go to your boat. I love fucking on the water."

Yeah, he knows I was Eric's neighbor.

An image of Eric lying in a pool of his own blood flashes through my mind, and my stomach turns. I glance at the stranger seated beside me. His shirt is half-unbuttoned, revealing a heavily furred chest. I'd guess he's in his late fifties.

I turn to face him, putting some space between us, mostly wanting to break his hold on my neck. I paste on a smile I don't feel. "I came to drink and dance. Let's hang out here for a while." I'm sure as hell not going anywhere with this guy.

His eyes narrow, and I can tell he's not happy. "I guess we can stay for a little while." He eyes my empty glass. "What are you drinking?"

"I had a Cosmo, but one was enough."

He winks at me as he waves at the bartender. "Two Cosmos! And keep them coming!"

Shit. He's trying to get me drunk.

8

Tyler Jamison

I t's all I can do to sit here and watch this guy drape himself over Ian. Ian's on his second drink, and Turner is already signaling the bartender for another round. I don't know how well Ian can hold his liquor, but I know one thing for sure. I'm not letting him leave this club tonight with Turner. *No way in hell.*

One thing I've noticed about these clubs is that a lot of the men are very hands-on. They like to touch and be touched. It's not unusual to see men embracing, kissing, or even copping a feel in public. And I know a hell of a lot more goes on in the bathrooms, dark hallways, and the alley out back.

Turner can't keep his God damn hands off Ian. He keeps grabbing the back of Ian's neck, rubbing his shoulders and biceps. Occasionally, his hand disappears below the counter, and God knows where that's going. I want to march over there and pull Turner off of him.

I know Ian isn't enjoying this any more than I am. I've seen the strained looks he's given me tonight, as if checking to make sure I'm still here. Still watching over him.

Don't worry, Ian. I'm not leaving you.

I'm searching for any pretense to arrest Turner and take him in for questioning, but I have absolutely nothing to go on right now. The fact that he was dating the victim at the time of the killing is not reason enough to arrest him.

After they finish their current round of drinks, Turner gets up and grabs Ian's arm, pulling him off his barstool. I tense, prepared to intercede if Turner tries to take Ian out of the club. But no, it looks like they're headed for the dance floor.

Ian is less than steady on his feet as he follows Turner into the pulsating crowd.

I watch as Turner manhandles Ian, pulling him close. From my vantage point, I can see Turner thrusting his hips against Ian's backside, simulating sex. Turner runs his hands up and down Ian's torso, stroking him blatantly. And all the while, Turner whispers into Ian's ear.

When Turner's wandering hands roam lower, Ian tries to pull away, but he's wavering unsteadily. Turner has no trouble hauling him right back where he wants him. Ian stumbles back against

Turner, his eyes closed as he sways on shaky legs.

Fuck! Ian's drunk.

I'm off my stool and halfway to the dance floor when Ian manages to break free of Turner and head for the restrooms. I wait to see what Turner's going to do. But instead of going after Ian, he returns to the bar and flags the bartender.

I follow Ian into the last of several bathrooms. Ian's standing at the sink, his hands braced on the white porcelain. His chest is heaving. I look around, checking the stalls. Thankfully, there's no one else in here.

I scan him from head to toe. "Are you all right?"

"Yeah." He turns on the faucet and scoops a handful of water into his mouth. He rinses and spits. Then he splashes his face. "Jesus, Tyler, he—"

The door crashes open and two inebriated men stagger inside. Ian immediately clams up, staring down into the sink.

"Let's go." I nod toward the door, and Ian follows me out. Once we're in the hallway, I steer him to the left and out the back door to the rear alley. It's dark out, and the air is heavy with the smell of cigarette smoke and the stench of ripe trash coming from a nearby dumpster.

Ian leans back against the brick wall and runs shaking hands through his hair. "He kept talking about Eric. He bragged about fucking him, about the things they did. Things he did to Eric. He went on and on about Eric's yacht, and he kept asking to see mine. He said he's seen me at the marina before, that he's been watching me for a while. He said—"

Abruptly, Ian turns away and bends over to vomit on the ground. When he straightens, he pulls up the hem of his shirt and wipes his mouth. "He said Eric liked pain, and he asked me if I did, too."

The police search of Eric's yacht on the night of his murder turned up a number of bondage implements specifically designed to cause pain. Nipple clamps, cock rings, whips... there was an entire chest filled with bondage gear. Many of the items had been left out and apparently used the night of the murder, and were therefore part of the crime scene inventory. It was the same MO with the other murders.

Ian looks at me, his eyes radiating pain. "I think I'm drunk, Tyler."

My jaw tightens. Even in the dim lighting, I can tell he's sickly pale.

"Please get me out of here," he says. "I can't face him another minute longer, let alone bear his hands on me. He makes me sick."

Usually so confident and sure of himself, Ian's anything but right now. The fact that he's admitting it and asking for help is telling. He's not as fearless as he'd like me to think.

I nod toward the street. "Let's get you home. This was a bad idea from the start."

He's not quite steady on his feet as we walk to the end of the alley and out onto the sidewalk. It's a couple of blocks to my car. I open the front passenger door for him. Ian sways unsteadily.

"Careful," I say, cushioning his head with my hand as he practically collapses onto the front passenger seat.

Groaning, he closes his eyes and leans back in his seat.

When I reach for his seatbelt, he brushes my hand aside. "I can do it."

By the time I walk around to the driver's door and slide behind the wheel, Ian has himself buckled in. His eyes are closed, and he looks miserable. I should never have let him do this.

I start the engine and head back to Ian's townhouse.

Quietly, he says, "Every time he touched me, all I could think about was Eric's throat split open, and all the blood and gore spilling out. He shoved himself against me from behind, going on and on about fucking Eric, and the more he talked about it, the harder he got." Ian covers his eyes with a shaky hand, his voice ragged. "God, it was awful. I'm not cut out for this."

"It's all right. You're not doing it again." I keep my eyes on the road, trying to remain calm for Ian's sake, but inside I'm raging that this motherfucker laid his hands on Ian.

He exhales a long breath. "Eric deserves justice."

"And he'll have it. But that doesn't mean you have to put yourself in harm's way. I won't allow it."

Ian grins. "You won't *allow* it?"

"That's right."

He chuckles. "Who made you the boss of me?"

I shoot him a brief glare before glancing back at the road. "I'm not going to let you get hurt, Ian. I'll apply for a search warrant in the morning."

When we arrive back at Ian's townhouse, I park in the driveway behind the patrol car belonging to the officer on duty. I help Ian up the steps to his door, just to make sure he gets inside all right. I hold him steady as he fishes his key out of his pocket.

I know I should leave. Now that he's home safe, there's no reason for me to be here. But then he turns in the open doorway and says, "Are you coming in?"

I want to say no, but the word dies on my tongue. Instead, I find myself stepping over the threshold.

Ian stands aside to let me enter, and then he locks the door. He points to the parlor. "Make yourself comfortable. I'll be right back."

I watch him climb the stairs to the second floor and disappear from view. Scrubbing my hand over my face, I exhale harshly. I really shouldn't be here. He's home; he's safe. It's clear after tonight that Ian needs to keep out of this investigation, no matter how much he wants to help get justice for his friend. Turner is our best lead right now, and I plan to pay him a visit soon. My hope is that I'll find *something* to justify taking him into custody.

The parlor is dark, so I flip on a light and head to the bar. I didn't drink anything at the club because I considered myself on duty. But now I'm officially off the clock, and after what happened tonight, I could really use a drink.

I grab a bottle of dark ale out of the mini-fridge behind the bar and pop the cap. Then I take a seat on one of the barstools while I wait for Ian to return. As soon as he does, I'll say goodnight and head home.

"Sorry about that," Ian says as he enters the room. He's changed his shirt, and he's steadier on his feet now.

"Not a problem. Are you okay?"

He walks around behind the bar and pulls a bottle of water from the fridge. After taking a long swig, he says, "Yeah. I'm better." He stands facing me, his eyes haunted. "Turner creeps the hell out of me. You should have heard the way he talked about Eric." He shudders. "The man is sick."

Ian takes another long pull on his water and sets the bottle down hard. "He described hurting Eric, and he said Eric liked it."

I set my bottle on the bar, a bit harder than I meant to. "You're not seeing him again. Is that clear?"

He smiles ruefully. "You can't keep me locked up, Tyler. I won't live in a cage, even a gilded one."

"I don't want this guy fixating on you."

"It's too late. He told me he wants to fuck me on my boat."

I lift my bottle to my mouth and down the last of my beer. "Jesus, Ian. Don't leave this townhouse without an escort."

"Who's going to escort me? You?"

I feel my face heat. "I'll make arrangements."

"A bodyguard? No thanks. Been there, done that. They cramp my style."

"It's only temporary. Until we arrest Eric's killer." I get up from my seat, needing to clear my head. "It's late. I should go. Thanks for the drink."

I'm halfway across the room when he calls out, "Tyler, wait!"

I turn to him, and he's almost caught up to me.

"Thank you," he says. "For tonight. For being there. As difficult as it was being around Turner, knowing you were there made all the difference in the world."

"You don't have to thank me. I was just doing my job."

Standing this close to him, I can see how long his eyelashes are. I notice a few faint freckles on his cheeks. He's staring at me, and I can feel the weight of the moment between us. It's heavy and... wrong.

And yet my heart's beating like I just ran a marathon, and I can feel my blood coursing through my body.

Ian's gaze darts down to my lips, then back up to meet mine. Then back to my lips. This close, I smell mint on his breath, and I realize he must have brushed his teeth when he was upstairs.

He takes a step closer.

I step back. "Ian, don't."

He moves with me. "Don't what?"

The way he's looking at me makes my body burn. My cock is throbbing. "I need to go."

I take a few more steps back and, like in a dance, he follows me, staying with me step for step, until I back into the wall and have nowhere to go.

Slowly, he reaches out to cup my cheek, his palm brushing softly against my beard. My breath is trapped in my chest.

"Say no, Tyler." His voice drops, and it's rough, full of heat. So damn seductive. "Tell me no." He says it like a dare.

"Stop it, Ian."

"All you have to do is say no. Can you do that?"

I open my mouth to say just that, but my breath stalls in my chest. I want to say no. God knows I do. It's on the tip of my tongue. *I can't do this.* But his fingers are in my hair now, his blunt nails scraping against the base of my skull, and his touch feels so damn good I could cry.

Ian has made me feel more in the past week than I've felt with anyone else my entire life. "I can't do this." My voice breaks, and I'm filled with shame. I'm a grown man, and I can't face this. I can't face my own needs and this yearning. And yet I can't walk away either. I'm trapped in my own version of hell.

"This is your last chance, Tyler. Tell me no, and I'll walk away. But if you don't, I warn you now, I'm going to kiss the fuck out of you. I'm pretty sure you want this as much as I do. Tell me I'm wrong."

I open my mouth to say the one word that will put an end to this, but nothing comes out. Not a damn thing. Because I can't bring myself to say it.

God help me, I don't want to say no.

9

Tyler Jamison

In a flash, Ian's mouth is on mine, hot and hungry, searching and demanding. His hand cradles the back of my head, cushioning it against the wall behind me. The bottom falls out of my world, and I'm left reeling, spinning out of control. My heart slams into my ribcage, and I can't breathe.

His hands frame my face, and his mouth eats at mine, drawing my ragged breaths out of me. It's all too much. I've never in my life felt anything like this. My body is on fire.

My hands shake when I move to push him away, but the moment I touch his taut shoulders, I end up pulling him closer. I drag him against me, chest to chest, hips to hips, and we kiss like starved lovers who are desperate for each other. I've never been so aroused. My dick throbs as my blood rushes south.

How can I want a man like this? How can this feel so damn good? It's wrong, and yet I can't bring myself to push him away. My mind is telling me one thing, but my body doesn't give a fuck. I just *want* him. And I'm so damn tired of fighting myself.

When his mouth dips down to my throat, sucking on my skin, I arch my back and groan roughly. His hand slides up beneath my shirt, his warm palm tracing the contours of my chest, skimming over my abs, my pecs. When he brushes his thumb over my nipple, pleasure knifes me, and I cry out, the sound low and guttural. "Ian!"

"It's okay," he says, his voice strained. He's breathing as hard as I am. Clearly, I'm not the only one affected.

Ian's hand slides down my torso and settles over my cock. When he presses firmly against my jeans, I let out a ragged groan and shove myself against his palm. I'm hard as a rock and aching, desperate for more, and he can feel it.

I've never been touched like this before—not by a *man*—and it feels so damn amazing I'm afraid I'm going to come right here in my boxer-briefs.

Blistering shame reminds me of all the reasons why I can't do this. Why I should never have let things get this far. "Ian, no! Stop!"

He breaks away from me, his chest heaving, his eyes wide and bright with arousal.

I lay my hands against his firm chest and push him back. "I'm sorry, but I can't do this."

He stands there looking both disappointed and dejected as I back into the hallway. "Tyler..." His voice breaks.

"Don't say anything, please." I unlock the deadbolt and turn the knob. "Make sure you lock this door behind me." And then I step out into the night and race down the front steps to the sidewalk.

Once I'm in my car, away from the curious eyes of his night-time security patrol, I start shaking uncontrollably. I can still feel his lips on mine. A shiver courses through me, and my cock throbs mercilessly.

I can still taste him, still smell him. It's like nothing I've ever experienced before. During all the times I hooked up with a woman, I never felt this all-consuming need. I had to fake my way through it, force my body to perform. I had to pretend to feel things I didn't.

But this time, I didn't have to fake a damn thing.

I take a deep, shuddering breath and lean my head back on the headrest. For the first time in my life, I feel real desire, real sexual need and yearning for someone, and it's for a *man*. I squeeze my eyelids shut, trying to stave off the tears pricking the back of my eyes.

Overriding my inner turmoil, though, is the knowledge that Ian's in danger. He's attracted the attention of a very dangerous man—possibly a murderer. I grab my phone and place a call.

My brother-in-law, Shane McIntyre, answers on the second

ring. "Tyler?"

From the sound of his voice, I know I woke him up. I hear him on the move, and I assume he's getting out of bed so he doesn't wake my sister.

I take a deep breath. "I'm sorry for calling so late."

"It's not a problem." His voice is low, quiet. I hear a door close softly, and then in a louder voice, he says, "What's wrong, Tyler?"

I choke back a laugh. Shane knows me well enough to know I'd never call him unless I had no other choice. There's no use beating around the bush. "I'm really sorry, but I need a favor. It's urgent."

"Sure," he says without hesitation. "Anything you need."

I can hear the undertone of surprise in his voice, and I don't blame him. Our relationship is tenuous at best. It started on rocky ground, and we've only recently become more comfortable around each other. But Shane loves my sister—I have no doubt about that—and he's proven himself time and time again. He'd do anything for her, including helping me.

I bite the bullet and ask. "I know it's late, but can I come over? I need your help with something."

"Of course you can. Come on over."

I end the call and start my engine. My hands are still shaking, but at least I have some direction now. I head straight for the apartment building Shane owns on Lake Shore Drive, just a few blocks from Ian's townhouse. I arrive minutes later, park in the underground garage, and take the private elevator up to the sprawling penthouse apartment, which occupies the entire top floor of the building.

I keep my eyes forward, locked on the doors, careful to avoid my reflection in the mirrored walls. My face is flushed, and my lips are still tingling from that kiss. I swear to God I can still feel the pressure of his mouth on mine.

A man kissed me tonight.

I can still taste him, still smell his cologne.

He wanted me. And I wanted him back.

The realization makes my breath catch.

The elevator doors open with a muffled chime, and I step out into the penthouse foyer. The floors are polished hardwood, and there's a crystal chandelier hanging high overhead, casting flickering lights throughout the space. In the center of the foyer is a round table holding a vase of freshly-cut peach and cream roses. I'm sure the flowers are my sister's doing. They're her favorite colors.

Ignoring my pounding heart, I take a deep breath and try to center myself before I face Shane. The man misses nothing, and I sure as hell don't want to explain more than I have to tonight.

I step through the doorway into the great room—the focal point of the penthouse—and immediately spot Shane seated on one of the sofas in front of a stone hearth. He's dressed in sweats and a t-shirt, and his short brown hair is a bit tousled from having been asleep. Looking at him right now, you'd never guess he's the co-founder and CEO of a multi-million-dollar security company.

The apartment is dark and quiet, the only source of light coming from two spotlights shining on the stone hearth. The exterior walls are glass, providing a million-dollar view of the Chicago night skyline and Lake Michigan.

Looking more than a little curious, Shane lifts his gaze from a tablet. "So, what brings you here this late? Beth's asleep."

I nod. "I figured she would be. Actually, it's you I need to see."

He nods toward the vintage bar in the corner of the room. He and his brothers bought the bar from an old tavern that closed years ago and reassembled it here. "Can I get you a drink?"

I take a seat on the sofa opposite his. "No. Thank you."

"All right. What do you need?" It's just like Shane to get to the heart of the matter.

"I need to arrange private protection for a witness to a homicide."

He lifts a brow in surprise. "The police can't provide protection?"

I shake my head. "This individual does have a police presence at his residence, but he's already snuck out once, right under their noses. I'm afraid he'll do it again, and I think he could be in real danger. You've probably heard about the three men who were murdered in this part of the city in the past couple of weeks. I'm afraid this... individual... has caught the attention of a serial killer."

"I assume you're referring to the strangulation and near decapitations of three gay men."

I nod.

"Does this individual have a name?"

"Ian Alexander."

Shane's eyes widen. "Martin Alexander's son?"

"Yes. The most recent victim was a close friend of Ian's, and I think Ian feels an obligation to help find the killer. He's been nosing around, asking questions in clubs the victim was known to have frequented. I have a primary suspect, and I'm hoping to get a search warrant in the morning. If this is the guy, then I'll just need protection for Ian for a few days, until I have enough evidence to detain the suspect."

"Of course, I'll help you," he says. "Text me Ian's address, and I'll get someone over there right away."

I do as he asks. "Thank you, Shane. I owe you."

"Not a problem," he says, brushing off my gratitude. "I'm happy to help."

"Tyler, what are you doing here? Is something wrong?"

Both of us turn our heads at the sound of a sleepy female voice. My sister, Beth, stands just inside the great room, dressed in a pink maternity nightgown. Her pale blonde hair hangs loosely over her shoulders.

Shane goes to her and pulls her into his arms. "I'm sorry we woke you, sweetheart. Please go back to bed. I'll be right there, I promise."

Beth peers at me from behind her husband. "Is everything all right?"

I stand. "Yes, everything's fine. I'm sorry I woke you. I needed to talk to Shane. It's work-related. Nothing for you to worry about."

Shane cups her face and kisses her forehead, their exchange

quiet and intimate. He lays his hand on her round belly and gently steers her toward their private suite. "Go back to bed, sweetheart."

She gives me a smile. "It's good to see you, Tyler. Good night."

"You too, kiddo," I tell her. "Sleep well."

Once he's sure Beth is back in their room, Shane returns to his seat. He switches instantly from doting husband to corporate CEO. "How about Miguel Rodriquez?"

I nod. "Miguel's a good choice." I've met Miguel on several occasions. In fact, he was Beth's first bodyguard when I hired McIntyre Security to protect my sister from an imminent threat.

Miguel Rodriquez is young—the same age as Ian—and easy-going. I can see the two of them hitting it off.

Shane makes a call, keeping the conversation brief and to the point. After he ends the call, he forwards Ian's address to Miguel. "All right. It's done."

Some of the tension leaves my body. "Thank you."

"There's no need to thank me." Shane meets my gaze head-on, as if daring me to contradict him. "We're family."

I nod. "We are," I say, amazed at how far he and I have come in our dealings with each other. I once provoked a fight with him. I punched him, and when he tried to defend himself, I had him arrested for assaulting a police officer. Admittedly, it was not one of my proudest moments.

But I realized soon enough that any animosity between Shane and me only hurt Beth, and I couldn't stand the thought. Not after what she has suffered.

I stand, anxious to be gone. "I'll see myself out. Let me know about the cost."

"That won't be necessary," Shane says, rising to his feet. "I'm happy to help."

As I glance around the multi-million-dollar apartment, I'm reminded of the kind of money Shane earns. Reluctantly, I swallow my pride. "Thank you, but I'm not looking for a hand-out. I'll pay."

As I head back to my condo, the streets are quiet. It's nearly two a.m. I'm exhausted, and my mind is still racing. No matter how hard I try to put that damn kiss out of my mind, it keeps coming back to me.

I want to be mad at Ian for pushing me like that, but I'm not. And now that he's opened that door, I don't know how to shut it. The world didn't implode on me because I kissed a man. The ground didn't open up and swallow me. I'm still here, but I suspect I'm not the same person I was before.

For the first time in my life, I felt the deep pull of sexual attraction. I felt alive, and my entire body burned with desire. Tonight, I kissed a man, and I liked it. More than that, I want to do it again.

If I'm being honest with myself, I can't claim to be surprised. The writing's been on the wall my entire life. I just didn't want to read it. Fact: I'm attracted to a man. And that makes me—*shit!* I can't even say it.

I am such a fucking disaster.

ꙮ 10

Ian Alexander

After Tyler stormed out of my townhouse, I watched him through my front window as he sat for the longest time in his car, gripping the steering wheel and looking very much like a man on the edge. The little bit of him I could see through his car window was enough to let me know he was shaken to the core.

I felt bad for pushing him like that, but God, I wanted to kiss him so badly! I had to fight the urge to walk outside and march right up to his car, open his door, and pull him out of the vehicle and back into my arms.

I know desire when I see it, and he was roiling with it. He liked our kiss. No, he *loved* it. His cock was hard as steel in my grasp.

Then he ran like the hounds of hell were on his heels. I just hope I didn't push him too far.

I turn off the downstairs lights and head upstairs to my bedroom. I can't resist the pull to look out my window to see if he's still there. But the spot where he'd parked is empty. He's gone.

I strip and climb naked into bed. My hand goes to my cock, and I grip myself hard, craving firm pressure.

How in the hell am I supposed to sleep now? Normally, on nights like this, when I'm feeling worked up, I'd go to the clubs and find someone to hook up with. But I'm tired of hooking up with strangers. I want more.

I want someone in my life, a constant, someone to fall asleep with every night and wake up to every morning. I want a partner, not just another random fuck.

As I lie there, I torture myself with the image of how Tyler looked when I backed him into the wall.

He didn't say *no*. Jesus, at that moment, when he refused to put on the brakes, the air rushed out of my lungs, leaving me light-headed. I fully expected him to tell me to fuck off. I never in a million years dreamed he would stand there silently, clearly conflicted, as if he was caught between a rock and a hard place, and there was no acceptable option for him.

Damn it, he'd wanted that kiss as much as I did. I gave him ample opportunity to walk away, to push me away, and he didn't. He *let* me kiss him. He could have stopped me, but he didn't. That kiss was hot and fierce, and I think it surprised both of us.

I honestly don't think he'd ever been kissed by a guy before. And I could tell by the way he kissed me back that he was just as hungry for it as I was.

I close my eyes and picture Tyler. That man is wound so tight, so in control. I know he'd be the same in bed, domineering and just as controlling. Just the thought of him pressing me into the mattress, thrusting deep inside me, riding me hard, his hands gripping my hips, my ass, his mouth devouring mine... *God!*

I come hard, spewing on my fist, on my abs. *Damn.* I don't think I've come that hard in a long time.

* * *

The next morning, I'm stir-crazy before I even open my eyes. I can't bear the thought of spending the day closed up inside my townhouse. I need to be outside. I take a cup of coffee up onto the roof and try to relax. I end up staring out at the lake, at the boats skimming over the water, and wishing I was out there instead of cooped up in here.

I need to be out on the water, feeling the wind in my hair and the sun on my skin. *Fuck this house arrest.*

Back in my room, I shower and dress in shorts and t-shirt. Then I head downstairs to the kitchen to grab a quick breakfast. I'm heading out. The cops can follow me if they want, but I'm not sitting inside another minute.

I load my backpack with protein bars and head out the back

door. As I'm walking to the carriage house, to get my car, the police officer on duty catches up to me, following me through the side door.

"Going somewhere?" he says.

I open the trunk and toss my backpack in. "Yep." I slide behind the wheel and push the button to open the garage door.

The officer frowns. "You're supposed to stay here."

I turn on him with a glare. "If you have a complaint, take it up with Detective Jamison."

And then I throw my Porsche into reverse and peel out of the carriage house, swerving to miss hitting the empty patrol car parked in my driveway. Once I'm on the street, I merge onto Lake Shore Drive and then I'm gone, quickly swallowed up in the fast-moving traffic.

This car practically growls as it tears down the highway toward the St. James Harbor. I'd give anything to be able to open up the throttle and hit top speed, but I can't do that here.

I take the harbor exit and follow the access road that leads to the marina. There's no sign of a police cruiser in my rearview mirror. After parking, I wait a few minutes to be sure they're not following. When the coast is clear—there's not a cop car in sight—I grab my backpack and head down the pier to the dock that leads to my slip.

When I reach Eric's boat, *Sassy Pants*, which is still marked off with bright yellow crime tape, I stop and stare at the pristine, empty deck. From the outside, there's absolutely no indication of the horror that took place down below in the stateroom. I saw the aftermath of what happened with my own eyes, and I won't ever be able to forget it.

Even now, I keep expecting Eric to come up from the galley to greet me. He always struck me as fearless, but maybe that was his undoing. He trusted someone he shouldn't have, and it got him killed.

I wonder if anyone has contacted his family back in San Francisco. I'm sure someone from the police department has—it's probably standard procedure—but I doubt his parents will even bother to come out here to claim the body or hold any type of memorial service for him. They wrote him off years ago when he came out to them. I don't even know his parents' names or how to contact them, or I'd do it myself. They deserve the right to know what happened to their son.

As much as my parents drive me nuts sometimes, I know they love me, and they'd never write me off no matter how much I might aggravate them. If anything, they've always been too protective.

I continue walking past Eric's boat to mine. The *Carpe Diem* is a sleek, 40-foot yacht. It's small, as far as yachts go, but mighty. It's my baby. *My escape.* The minute I step onto the swim platform and feel that gently rolling teak deck beneath my feet, the tension eases from my body.

I haul myself up the steps to the main deck, set my backpack on the aft bench seat, and stretch, letting my muscles loosen. The breeze, the smell of the water, the sunshine beating down on me... it's all good. Already I feel better.

I start preparations to cast off, priming the engines and checking all the power and fluid levels. I head up to the cockpit and check the dials, switching on navigation and comms. I start the engines and let them hum along while I go about preparing to disconnect the shore power and bring in the lines.

When I climb down onto the swim deck, intending to pull the lines, I notice a stranger watching me from the dock. He's about my age, Latino, a good-looking guy with dark hair and eyes. He's dressed casually in jeans and a t-shirt, and a black leather jacket.

He gives me a friendly wave. "Ian Alexander," he says. "Permission to come aboard?"

I catch a glimpse of a gun holster strapped to his chest, mostly hidden beneath his jacket. I know his type. He just screams *security*.

I cross my arms and glare, trying to look intimidating. "Who the hell are you?"

He doesn't seem to take offense. Instead, he grins sheepishly as he reaches into his back pocket and pulls out a leather wallet, which he flips open and holds up to me. "Miguel Rodriquez, McIntyre Security. I'm your new bodyguard, Ian."

"What the fuck? Did my parents put you up to this?"

He shakes his head. "No. My boss put me up to this. I'm supposed to be covert, but it looks like you're getting ready to set sail, and I can't very well protect you out on the lake if I'm stuck on shore."

"This is a motorized boat, not a sailboat. Who's your boss?"

"Shane McIntyre."

"Never heard of him."

"How about Tyler Jamison? Have you heard of him?"

I laugh. "Tyler did this?" Warmth spreads through my chest, and I can't stop smiling. He's worried about me. "Yeah, I know him." *Hell, I kissed him.*

"Permission to come along, then?" He points to the lines securing the boat to the dock. "I can help."

"Do you know anything about operating a boat?"

"Nope, not a thing. But I'm a real fast learner."

I point at one of the lines secured to the dock. "Untie that rope and toss it to me."

Miguel does as I asked. He moves with efficiency, seemingly pretty competent. I can operate this boat just fine on my own, but it's easier when I have help. Plus, it would be nice to have some company.

"All right, you can come aboard," I say. "Untie the remaining lines and toss them to me."

Once he's done, he steps onto the swim platform, swaying a bit as he adjusts to the rolling deck.

"Come on up to the cockpit." I wave for him to follow me.

I'm sitting in the captain's chair, double-checking the controls, when Miguel steps into the cockpit.

"Whoa," he says, eyeing the two gray leather chairs positioned in front of the command console. "This is pretty sweet."

I chuckle. "Yep. State of the art technology. She may not be big, but she's top of the line."

When I power on the radar console, lights come on. The

screen projects everything from local weather conditions to radar to GPS data. I power on the front and rear cameras, the side cameras. I have a three-sixty-degree field of visibility.

I nod at the seat next to mine. "Have a seat, Miguel. We're getting underway. If you're not used to cruising, you'll likely fall flat on your ass."

He sits, his gaze cycling between me, the dock, and the channel that leads to open water.

"You don't get seasick, do you?" I say.

He shrugs. "I have no idea. I've never been on a boat before."

I point toward the open doorway. "Please don't puke on my boat. If you're going to be sick, throw up over the railing."

"Got it."

When I rev the engines, Miguel white-knuckles the armrests of his seat.

Oh, this is going to be fun.

ℰ 11

Tyler Jamison

With the circumstantial evidence I had, it wasn't difficult to get a search warrant, even on a Sunday morning. By ten o'clock, I'm at Brad Turner's apartment with an escort of two uniformed officers. I knock on Turner's door, and a moment later he opens it, shirtless, wearing only a pair of black flannel pants. His shaggy mane of straight black hair is mussed from sleep, and his eyes are bloodshot, his pupils unfocused. He's probably coming off a night-long binge of alcohol and God knows what else.

"Brad Turner?" I say.

He narrows his eyes, glancing first at me, and then at the other officers. "What the fuck do you want?"

I pull the warrant out of my jacket pocket and unfold it, holding it out to him. "I have a warrant to search your apartment."

He pales, turning a sick shade of gray right before my eyes. "Fuck no! You have no right to come in here!" He tries to shut the door in my face, but I already have my foot wedged in the opening, preventing him from closing it.

One of the officers throws his shoulder against the door, shoving it wide open and sending Turner flying back. Turner falls on his ass, hitting the carpeted floor.

The three of us step inside, and one of the officers closes the door behind us. I quickly survey the small living room and kitchen combo. The apartment is sparsely furnished, and at first glance nothing seems amiss.

An officer hauls Turner to his feet and sits him down on a brown corduroy recliner.

I pick up the warrant, which ended up on the floor, and hold it up to Turner. "I have a warrant to search your apartment. Sit here. Don't move."

One of the officers stands guard over Turner, while the other officer and I begin a systematic search of the small apartment. It doesn't take long, as there are only three rooms to search: this living room and kitchen combo, a bedroom, and a bathroom.

The living room and kitchen are clean, as is the bathroom. My focus shifts to the bedroom. I pull on a pair of latex gloves and begin my search. His dresser and nightstands check out okay, but when I open the door to his small bedroom closet, my heart stops. The closet is a fucking BDSM shrine. Whips, canes, chains, and a whole slew of other implements hang from pegs on the walls. I don't even want to imagine what some of the more obscure items are used for.

Shelves hold a variety of cock rings, nipple clamps, ball gags, handcuffs, anal plugs, leather harnesses and collars, as well as some other items the purpose of which appears primarily for causing pain. On a small table is a display of photographs that depict a number of different men tied up, harnessed, clamped, and gagged.

I photograph everything, from the items hanging on the wall, to the accessories displayed on the shelves, to the individual photographs. Several of them depict Eric Townsend in varying poses of degradation, including one of Eric being choked. I recognize the other two murder victims as well. It's only circumstantial evidence, but it's pretty damning. Brad Turner had sex with all three of the men who've been murdered, and here's the proof.

"Shit." One of the officers is standing behind me, peering into the closet. "At least you have enough to bring him in for questioning."

I nod. I'll have a forensics team out here within the hour to catalog these items and process them as evidence.

"Let's go," I say, heading back to the living room.

Turner is still seated in the recliner, with an officer standing guard. He's not quite so confident now.

I stare down at him. "Brad Turner, you're under arrest for the murder of Eric Townsend." To the officer standing guard, I say, "Cuff him."

Turner jumps to his feet, his face beet-red. "I didn't kill Eric! I swear to God, I didn't!"

"That's for the courts to decide." And while the officer is putting Turner in handcuffs, I read him his rights.

As I walk out the door of Turner's apartment into the hallway, my thoughts immediately go to Ian. The idea of Turner getting his hands on Ian makes me sick. I can't get those photos out of my head, and the thought that Ian could have been one of those men shakes me to the core.

* * *

When we get back to the station, Turner is processed and booked.

As soon as I get to my desk, I get a phone call from one of the officers on Ian's home security detail. Officer Swanson.

"He took off in his Porsche. We lost him in traffic."

Fuck. Why am I not surprised? "All right. Thanks for the heads-up." But at least Turner is in custody. That gives me some peace of mind, although not enough, as it's not definitive that Turner is the one we're looking for. Circumstantial evidence is just that— circumstantial. Until we have corroborating DNA evidence, we don't know anything for sure yet.

I text Miguel.

Tell me you have Ian in your sights. – Tyler

A moment later, I get a return message.

I have Ian in my sights. – Miguel

The smart-ass.

I head to my office to see if there's anything new from forensics or from the coroner. I'm anxiously awaiting DNA results on tests from the crime scene on Eric's boat. I check, but there's nothing yet. I asked that the tests be fast-tracked, which means I can have the data in a matter of days, but still it takes time. And now we'll have to wait for the DNA testing on the BDSM implements we confiscated from Turner's little closet of horrors.

I go check on Turner, who's been stewing in an interrogation room for nearly half an hour. I watch him for a few minutes through a one-way mirror. He's clearly agitated, fidgeting in his chair and muttering to himself. His appearance is unkempt, his hair sticking up, his face covered in a scraggly two-day-old beard. It looks like he's had a rough few days.

When I walk into the room, Turner's head snaps up and he scowls at me. He's seated at a table, his wrists handcuffed together. There's a police guard outside the door.

I close the door behind me and take a seat opposite him, laying a manila folder on the table. "Mr. Turner."

He says nothing.

Without warning, he slams his cuffed wrists on the table. "You can't treat me like this! I didn't do anything!" He raises his wrists, threatening to slam them on the table again.

"If you'd calm down, we wouldn't need to cuff you. This is just an interview, Mr. Turner, but you're making it more difficult than it needs to be. Since you knew Eric Townsend, I'd just like to talk to you. That's all. You're not obligated to answer any of my questions without an attorney present. It's your call."

That shuts him up quickly. He sits there glaring at me. And then, shaking his head, he says, "I don't know who you're talking about."

I open the manila folder and pull out a grainy, black-and-white image taken from surveillance footage at Diablo's.

I slide the image toward Turner so he can see it better. It's not the best photo in the world, but it clearly shows Turner dancing with Eric, his hips thrusting against Eric's back side. "You were saying?"

Turner pales as he stares at the photo. "Is that his name?" He shakes his head. "I never got the guy's name. I danced with him at a club one night, that's all. We just danced."

"I see." I slip the photo back into the folder. "For someone who claims he's innocent, you sure are lying a lot."

Turner glares at me.

"Mr. Turner, I'd like to get DNA samples from you, if you don't mind. I can call in a technician to swab your cheek. It's a simple procedure and takes just a few seconds. Would you be willing to do that?"

He scowls. "Why in the hell would I agree to do that?"

"I'm trying to rule you out as a suspect, Mr. Turner. You were one of the last people to see Eric alive."

"Rule me out as a—hey, I told you I didn't kill him! I had nothing to do with that!"

"Then you won't mind if we collect a DNA sample, right? This is the fastest way to clear you of any wrongdoing."

I can almost see the wheels turning in his head as he thinks it through. We've collected DNA samples from the crime scene, from Eric's body, and from Turner's closet of horrors. Now we just need Turner's DNA to complete the circle. Once we have that, we'll know for sure if he's the perpetrator or not.

"What if I don't want to give it to you?" he asks.

"You don't have to," I tell him. "Not unless I obtain a court order requiring you to do so, which I will gladly do if you don't willingly cooperate."

Turner looks a bit green around the gills. He's certainly acting guilty as hell.

"You say you didn't know Eric Townsend personally? Other than dancing with him at Diablo's?"

Turner straightens in his chair. "That's right."

"Did you ever have sex with Eric?"

Turner freezes, his muscles tensing and his jaw tightening. "No!"

"Did you engage in bondage activities with him? Did you ever tie him up, gag him, or apply any sexual implements to his body?"

"No! I told you, I didn't know him."

I pull out a second photograph and slide it across the table. "I found a photograph of the murder victim in your bedroom closet. It was just one of many."

Turner glances down at my snapshot of a photograph depicting Eric naked, his bent legs attached to a spreader bar. There's an elaborate metal cock ring around the base of Eric's erection and his testicles, and red stripes visible on his thighs from where he'd been caned. His genitals are red and swollen, and his eyes radiate pain. If the man was in pain, no one would have known, as he was also silenced by a ball gag.

"You're lying, Mr. Turner," I say, eyeing him directly as he glances at the photo and then looks away.

Turner's shoulders fall and his cuffed wrists drop to his lap. "We fucked, sure," he admits. "But that's it. We fucked and had a bit of fun, but I didn't kill him."

I've seen enough for now. I stand and collect the photographic evidence. "I have enough evidence to hold you for further questioning. And in the meantime, I'll get that court order requiring you to provide a DNA sample."

Turner is silent as I walk out of the interview room. I tell the officer standing guard outside the room to return him to his holding cell.

As I'm walking to Captain Walker's office to update him on the case, my phone chimes with an incoming message from Miguel.

My cover is blown. I'm on Ian's yacht, and we're heading out to sea. Nice guy, btw. Cool boat. – Miguel

I chuckle as I send Miguel a reply.

Michigan is a lake, not an ocean. Stay with him. – Tyler

I'm relieved Brad Turner is in custody. If he's cooling his jets here in jail, he's not out there posing a risk to Ian's safety. Or to anyone else's.

Now I just need proof we've got the right guy.

In the meantime, I've got eyes on Ian, and he's safe.

12

Ian Alexander

If I'm going to be stuck with a bodyguard, this one's not too bad. He's pretty chill, and he's my age, not some cranky old asshole. I had some real gems when I was younger.

Once we're past the no-wake zone, I open up the throttle and let my baby fly over the waves. It's windy, and the water is a bit choppy.

Miguel has a death grip on the armrests of his seat as he divides his attention between me and the horizon. "How long have you been operating boats?" he says, loudly enough to be heard over the sound of the engines and the spray.

"For as long as I can remember. When I was little, my parents would take me out on their yacht. Even though they had a full crew, my dad would take over the helm sometimes and let me sit on his lap and operate the controls. I was hooked. I wanted to be a pirate, and being out on the water was about as close as I was ever going to get."

"This boat must have cost a pretty penny."

I shrug. "Well, it wasn't cheap."

I head farther away from shore, out into the open water where there are far fewer boats. I like being out here past the tourists' stomping grounds. I like the solitude.

When we're far enough out, I lower my speed until we're cruising at an easy pace. Miguel relaxes his grip on his chair. After a while, I lower speed until we come to a stop and drop anchor.

Miguel follows me out of the cockpit to the rear of the deck.

"Want something to drink?" I ask him as I step behind the bar and open the mini-fridge. "I've got water, soft drinks, juice, and beer."

He frowns. "Beer?"

"Not for me, silly. I don't drink when I'm operating the boat. But you can have one if you like."

Miguel shakes his head. "Not while I'm working. But I'll take a water."

"Still or fizzy?"

"Still's fine."

I grab a chilled bottle of spring water and toss it to him. Then I grab a bottle of sparkling water for myself. I like the burn.

"So." I sit on a barstool and swivel to face Miguel, who's seated on one of the padded aft benches. "You're a bodyguard."

The corners of his lips turn up slightly. "Yep. And… you're a client. I'm glad we got that established."

I lift my water bottle in his direction. "Touché. Cheers."

"Cheers." He guzzles a third of the bottle in one swig.

"My parents started hiring bodyguards for me and my sister when we were kids. I gave mine up when I dropped out of University of Chicago."

"Why?"

I shrug. "It drove me nuts having someone shadowing me constantly, looking over my shoulder all the time."

Miguel laughs. "You're a free spirit. That's okay. Not everyone has to play by the same rules." He nods as if he gets me. "Why did you drop out of college?"

"For the same reason, I guess. Rules and schedules drive me batty. I guess I'm ADD." I take a drink of my fizzy water. "So, this was Tyler's idea." The thought makes me want to smile.

Miguel nods. "Yep. He asked Shane for a bodyguard, and Shane assigned me. I'm good with free spirits."

"I see. So, you didn't just pick the short straw?"

Miguel rests his arms along the chrome railing behind him and looks around at the unbroken expanse of water as far as the eye can see in every direction. Some people might be unnerved when they can't see land, but I find it liberating.

"The way I see it," he says as he leans back against the railing, "this is a cushy assignment. I get to follow you around, chase after your shiny blue sports car that probably cost more than I make in a year, and now I'm riding the waves, literally, and enjoying the good life."

I laugh and then take another drink. "I'm glad you approve."

"If I'm lucky, I might even get to hitch a ride in the Porsche."

We both look up when a seagull circles overhead, screeching at us. Finally, when it gets bored, it flies away.

"So, what's on the agenda today?" Miguel says.

"Nothing specific. I just needed to get out. I've been cooped up in my townhouse for too long. I don't do well inside for long periods. I need to be out in the fresh air and sunshine. We can sit here awhile. I'll grill some burgers and we can just relax, maybe swim or take the jet ski out for a spin."

Miguel's phone chimes, and his lips curve up as he checks the screen.

"What's so funny?"

He lifts his dark eyes to me. "Tyler's checking up on you." As he keys in a reply and hits send, he regards me curiously.

The thought makes me smile. "Do you know him well?"

Miguel shrugs. "As well as can be expected. Tyler is a bit of a loner. He pretty much keeps to himself. What about you? How well do you know him?"

Not as well as I'd like to. My cheeks grow warm, and I chalk it up to the sun. Stepping off my barstool, I peel off my t-shirt and head down to the swim platform. "I'm changing into swim trunks and taking the jet ski out. Do you want to join me?"

Miguel hops up and follows me down the steps, patting his

jacket pockets. "I'm afraid I didn't pack any swim wear."

"I've got clean spares down below in the stateroom. Help yourself. Or, stay on board. It's your call. Do you know how to swim?"

"Yeah, I can swim." He hesitates. "What's a stateroom?"

I laugh and point behind him. "The bedroom. Go down the steps by the bar, walk straight back past the galley—the kitchen— to the bedroom. You'll find clean swim gear in the closet."

"Great. Thanks."

While Miguel is getting changed, I haul out the jet ski and a pair of lifejackets. We take turns on the jet ski, churning up the water. After all our horsing around, we climb back on board, and I pull out the protein bars I brought with me and a bag of chips I find in the cupboard.

"So, what do you do for a living?" Miguel asks me as we eat at the bar.

I hate it when people ask me this. "Nothing really."

His eyes widen in surprise. "*Nothing?*"

"My sister and I both inherited sizeable trust funds from our paternal grandfather. Neither one of us needs to work. Besides, I wouldn't know what to do anyway. I have trouble sitting still for long. I could never do an office job."

"What about your sister?"

"She's a student at UChicago, currently majoring in psychology."

"What do you like to do?" he says.

I shrug. "I like being outside. I like the water and my boat. And photography."

"Well, there you go. You could be an outdoor photographer."

"I suppose. What about you? Do you like being a bodyguard?"

"Yeah, I do. I like protecting people. I'm not afraid to get between my client and someone who means them harm. It's very rewarding work because I *know* what I do makes a difference in someone's life. Sometimes it's the difference between life and death. Not everyone can say that."

I can hear the conviction in his voice, the passion. He means what he says. He's selfless.

After we finish eating, Miguel checks his phone again. "We'd better head back. Tyler wants to talk to you."

My heart skips a beat at the thought of seeing Tyler again. I don't know what he wants, but it must be serious if he's willing to face me after last night's kiss.

Miguel helps me stow the jet ski. Then we change back into our clothes and return to the marina. I'm wired with anticipation, and I can't stop wondering how he'll act. *Will he pretend it didn't happen? Will he want a repeat?* I'm not going to hold my breath.

By the time we get back, it's mid-afternoon. I dock the *Carpe Diem* in her slip, and with Miguel's help I secure the boat. I hop in my car, and Miguel follows me in his vintage black Ford Mustang. When I arrive back at my townhouse, I spot Tyler's BMW parked in my driveway. The patrol car is gone.

As I pull into my drive, I realize Miguel is also gone. He was right behind me a few minutes ago, but now he's nowhere to be seen.

By the time I park my Porsche in the carriage house and shut off the engine, my pulse is racing.

Tyler's appears at my door, his expression sober as he opens my door. "We need to talk." He's all business, his tone direct and professional.

My dream of a repeat kiss goes right out the window. "Hello to you, too."

He scowls. "This isn't a personal call, Ian. It's official business."

"Let's go inside." I nod toward the house, and Tyler follows me through the back door into the kitchen.

"All right, so talk," I say once we're inside.

He looks like he'd rather be anywhere but here. He certainly doesn't look like a man who wants to be kissed again.

"I got a search warrant this morning and paid Brad Turner a visit," he says, getting right to the point. "We searched his apartment and discovered a shrine—there's no other way to describe it—of BDSM toys, implements, and photographs. I arrested him on suspicion of murder and brought him in for questioning. He denied knowing Eric, let alone having sex with him. Then I showed Turner photographs that proved otherwise. I requested a DNA sample from him, and he refused."

"Can he do that? Flat out refuse?"

Tyler nods. "If he hasn't been charged with anything yet, yes, he can refuse. But I have enough circumstantial evidence to get a court order to force his compliance. That court order is in process. We'll get our sample soon."

Tyler stands in my spacious gourmet kitchen—amidst cherry cabinetry with hand-cut, black granite countertops and stainless steel appliances—looking uncomfortable. He eyes me warily, like a man facing a firing squad.

I'm not in the mood to discuss murder suspects or DNA samples. I want to talk about last night, about the fact that our lips *touched*. "Thanks for the new bodyguard. I like him. So, how was your day?"

Tyler's expression tightens. "Ian, don't."

"Don't what? You want me to stick to the script and talk about murderers and DNA? You want me to pretend the last time I saw you, I didn't have my tongue in your mouth?"

Tyler flinches as if I slapped him, and I feel like a total shit.

He sighs. "I'm trying to keep things professional," he says, motioning from himself to me. "Can we do that? Please?"

The pain I see in his eyes makes my chest hurt. "I'm sorry. I can be a real shit sometimes."

He looks away. "It's all right."

"No, it's not." I take a step closer, wanting so much to reach out and touch him. He's dressed in his detective uniform, so fucking handsome I could cry. And right now, he's utterly untouchable. I'm afraid he might snap if I push. "Tyler—"

He raises his hand to cut me off. "There's something I need to say, so I'm just going to come right out with it. Last night was a mistake. I shouldn't have done that."

"Done what? Let me kiss you?"

He nods, struggling to meet my gaze. "Yes. It was a mistake."

My heart sinks.

As he swallows hard, his Adam's apple rises and falls, his neck muscles straining.

I take another step forward, half-expecting him to step back, but he doesn't move. "You didn't enjoy it? I sure as hell did."

He frowns. "It's not... look, I can't do this, okay? I just can't."

"Tell me you didn't enjoy it." I close the distance between us, and he eyes me warily. "I gave you a chance to say 'no' last night, Tyler, to walk away, and you didn't. Now tell me you didn't enjoy it."

He opens his mouth to speak, but nothing comes out except for a shaky rush of air. He's tied in knots, and it's killing me because I think he does want this.

He just won't let himself have it.

I approach him slowly, giving him plenty of time to protest, to back up or walk away. Hell, to even shake his head. But he doesn't do any of those things. He stays rooted to his spot. His posture is rigid, his face flushed, and he's breathing as hard as I am. He looks away, avoiding my gaze.

I lay my hand on his chest, my palm right over his heart. "Look at me, Tyler."

He closes his eyes and sucks in a breath. "Ian, please..."

Please don't. That's what he's telling me. *Please don't do this to me.*

Reluctantly, I pull my hand back. "I think you want this as much as I do."

He meets my gaze with a pained expression. "It doesn't matter what I *want*. I can't."

"Why not?"

He shakes his head, as if he believes I couldn't possibly understand what he's feeling.

"Try me, Tyler. Talk to me."

"You have no idea—"

I laugh, but the sound is bitter. "You think I don't know how hard it is? You think this is easy for me? For any of us? It's *never* easy, Tyler! We face it every single day! But you know what? It's worth the struggle, because living a fucking lie sucks!"

His jaw tightens and his eyes narrow. "Just stop! I told you, I can't do this."

"Why not?"

"Because I can't!" he yells in my face.

As he starts to walk away, I grab his hand and press it to my chest, right over my thundering heart. I want him to know I'm just as affected by this as he is.

I'm wearing a t-shirt, and I'm hot and sweaty from being out on the water. When his nostrils flare, I realize he can smell me— my skin, my sweat—and his reaction is visceral. His eyes are wild, the blue-green deepening to teal. A shudder rocks him.

"It's okay for you to want a man," I tell him, my voice breaking. "Hasn't anyone ever told you that?"

Tyler swallows hard and shakes his head.

His honesty breaks my heart. "Have you ever been with someone you truly wanted?"

He shakes his head.

My throat tightens painfully. "Have you ever been with a man?"

"No."

"Just women?"

Tyler nods.

"Did you enjoy it?" I ask him.

His jaw tightens again, a muscle flexing violently. "No. It never felt right."

Shit. He's lived his entire life without ever feeling sexual fulfillment.

I move into his space, my hand slipping gently behind his head, my fingers sifting through his short, dark hair. I grip the back of his neck, and he stands perfectly still, now frozen to his spot. "It's okay," I say quietly, as if I'm gentling a wild animal.

He watches me cautiously, as if he's still debating between flight or fight. I hope he picks neither.

"I'm going to kiss you again," I tell him, keeping my voice low. "You're free to walk away, but if you decide to stay, just remember it's okay for you to like it."

～ 13

Ian Alexander

Another step brings me face to face with Tyler. I lean in, gauging his reaction when I whisper, "I want to kiss you so badly."

His eyes search mine, almost desperately, and my heart breaks a little. He's not running this time. Not from this, and not from *me*. I've pushed him so many times to get to this point, but I don't want to push him anymore.

I want him to meet me halfway. He has to *choose* this.

I brush his hair from his forehead. "Please tell me *yes*."

He swallows hard and nods. He doesn't actually say the word, but it's close enough.

As I press my lips to his, gently, just testing the waters, he sucks in a sharp breath. But he doesn't pull away.

I slide my fingers through his hair, gripping the back of his head. My lips cling to his, moving over his, *with* his. I nudge his lips open, and he complies—*yes!* I groan, the sound loud and raw.

Abruptly, he turns the tables on me, taking over without warning. His hands come up to cradle my head, his fingers digging into my scalp, and he backs me into a wall. The air leaves my lungs in a heated rush as he crushes his mouth to mine. He presses me into the wall, his strong hands gripping my head and angling me for his kiss.

"Fuck, Tyler," I gasp against his mouth. I clasp his wrists, not to fight him or to control him, but to relish in his strength. Blood rushes hot and furiously straight to my groin, and my cock hardens. My balls draw up tight as desire rages through me, stealing my breath. My chest heaves.

He leans into me, eating at me, his lips devouring mine. His tongue slips into my mouth, searching and seeking, and when it strokes mine I groan again, feeling completely undone.

The change in him is so swift and so sudden that my head spins. It's like a damn has burst inside him and years of pent-up need are breaking through.

His hand slides down my side, to my hip, and then his fingers slip around to my backside. He grips my ass hard and pulls me against him, our erections aligned, both of us hard as hell. He grinds against me, and the friction feels so damn good my knees go weak.

Jesus, I could come like this. God, I want to. I want him to make me come. Now I'm the one shaking.

With a harsh moan, he releases me abruptly and steps back as if he's been burned. If it weren't for the wall behind me, I think I'd be on the floor right now, sitting on my ass.

His chest heaves the same as mine, as he tries to catch his breath. "Fuck."

I laugh. "No kidding. Damn, Tyler."

There's the barest hint of a grin on his lips right before his expression falls. "I'm sorry, Ian. I shouldn't have done that."

"For fuck's sake, don't apologize." I take a step toward him, wanting more, but he steps back.

His next words take the wind right out of my sail.

"I have to go."

I'd beg him not to go, but I can see the resolution in his eyes. He just stepped over a line he thought he'd never cross. He's probably reeling inside. I laugh, the sound rueful. "You're your own cockblocker, aren't you?"

"I shouldn't have—"

"If you say you shouldn't have kissed me, I'll punch you."

He gives me another fleeting half-grin just before his expression sobers. "I've always known I was... different. I've never been attracted to women. I'd force myself to go through the motions, time after time, pretending, hoping that one day I'd meet a woman and it would finally click for me. But it never happened and I'm tired of trying. I'm so damn tired of failing."

My heart hurts for him. "You haven't failed, Tyler. You've just been looking in the wrong place."

This time he doesn't look away. "Maybe."

Maybe. I'm shocked at his admission. "What are you so afraid of? That your family won't accept you?"

"No. They're not like that."

"Then what is it? Work? Are you afraid of what your colleagues will think?"

"I..." His explanation stalls, as if he doesn't know what's holding him back.

I reach for his hand and stroke the back of it with my thumb. "It's okay to want, and to be wanted."

Despite the fact that his erection is clearly visible beneath his trousers, his expression transforms into a cool, emotionless mask. My heart sinks. He's withdrawing again.

"I came to tell you that Turner is in custody," he says, his voice level, matter of fact. He's completely closed himself off. "There's a lot of circumstantial evidence pointing to him as the killer, but until the DNA results are in, we can't be sure. Don't get complacent. I'll keep following up with any other leads I find. In the meantime, I want Miguel to stay on the job. He's outside in his car right now, watching the townhouse. I'd rather him be inside with you. He can protect you better from the inside."

Disappointment—as well as rejection—rides me hard, and I want to lash out at him. I want to yell and scream and show him the door. But I don't, because no matter how much he's hurting me, I know deep down that he's hurting himself even more.

My throat tightens, and I want to wail with frustration. "You're going to shut me out, just like that? Is it so easy for you?" When his expression darkens, I know I've hit a nerve. And I feel like an ass for doing it. "Fine, go!" I snap. "Send in the bodyguard."

Tyler frowns, and for a moment I think he might relent. But then he's back to being Mr. Professional again. "Please stay away from the clubs until we know more. I'll send Miguel in. Don't go anywhere without him. He's your 24/7 bodyguard until further notice. Let him do his job."

Then, he walks out of the kitchen and down the hallway to the front door.

I follow, my stomach sinking as I watch him walk out the front door.

* * *

It's not long before there's a knock at my front door. I open it, knowing who's on the other side.

Miguel Rodriquez, with a worn duffle bag thrown over his shoulder, stands on my front stoop, a grin on his handsome face. "Tyler told me to come inside. Is that okay?"

I nod, stepping back to let him enter.

Miguel stands in the foyer and scans the immediate area, taking in the parlor to the right, the living room to the left, and the staircase leading upstairs. "Nice place."

"Thanks."

He eyes me with concern. "Are you okay?"

I try not to think about what just happened in the kitchen. Tyler gave me a taste of what I've been craving, and then he walked out. Again. *Am I okay?* "No, not really."

"If this is a bad time... if you want me to stay outside..." Miguel points at the door. "I can do my job outside, if you want your privacy."

"No, you're fine. If I'm going to be under house arrest, it'll be nice to have someone to talk to. Come on. I'll show you to your room."

There are four bedrooms upstairs, each with its own private bathroom. Mine is the master suite that spans the entire front of the house, with a street view to the front and a lake view to the east.

I show Miguel the three guest rooms. "Take your pick."

He chooses the one closest to the top of the stairs, I guess for tactical reasons. He drops his duffle bag at the foot of the bed and whistles in appreciation as he looks the room over. "You've got a *really* nice place, if this is where the help sleeps."

I laugh. "You're not the help."

"You really don't mind me being here?"

"Nah, I grew up with staff and bodyguards in the house. It's no big deal."

Like a typical bodyguard, he checks out the vantage points from all windows in his room.

"Unpack and settle in," I tell him. "Then we'll figure out what we want to do for dinner this evening."

He unzips his duffle bag and pulls out a few things. I leave him to it.

* * *

That night, I lie in bed wide awake, replaying my conversation with Tyler. I keep reliving our kiss. Right now I'm so hard I swear I could come without even touching myself. I feel like I've been reduced to a teenager with a fantasy crush. I have a massive hard-on for a guy I can't have.

The idea of going out and hooking up with some random guy doesn't interest me anymore. I don't want a nameless fuck. I want Tyler. I want his hands on me, his mouth. I want his cock inside me.

Fuck. Would he even want anal sex? If he did want it, I'm certain he'd want to top, which would be fine with me. He strikes me as a giver, not a receiver. I can go either way, but I'd prefer bottoming, especially with him. I'd want to feel all that strength and power coming at me, pouring over me, washing through me.

I grab some lotion and lube my palm. There's no way I'm getting any sleep tonight with this raging hard-on. The whole time I'm stroking myself, I picture Tyler. When my orgasm comes, I grit my teeth and bite back a hoarse cry. I'm not alone in my townhouse tonight, and it wouldn't do for my bodyguard to hear me shouting my fool head off over a hand job.

If jerking off to thoughts of Tyler feels this good, I can't imagine what it would be like to actually have him in my bed.

I suspect that man might just rock my world.

14

Tyler Jamison

Sitting out on my balcony, I nurse a tepid bottle of beer and try not to think about Ian.

I'm failing miserably.

I've been out here for over an hour, just staring off into space, listening to the night sounds of the neighborhood—people talking as they walk by, dogs barking, car horns. I live in an upscale, residential section of Lincoln Park, but it still has the vibe and soundscape of an urban environment. Off in the distance, an ear-splitting siren shatters the night. It's the normal backdrop of city life.

I don't know what got into me this afternoon. I promised myself I wouldn't let things get personal between us again. I swore I'd keep things professional, stay focused on the case and Ian's safety. But he has a way of turning everything upside down—of making me forget my resolutions. And when he touches me, I lose all sense of self-preservation, and I just want *more*. I want him to touch me. Hell, I like it when he pushes my buttons. He exhilarates me like no one ever has.

I can't believe the things I told him tonight—admitting that I'm not attracted to women. I've never said that to another living soul. He's got a way of making me open up. Tonight, he made me face something I thought I'd never be ready—or willing—to face.

I know what I am. But if I can't even admit it to myself, how in the hell can I admit it to anyone else? For a split second, I imagine telling my sister or my mom. My heart stops cold, and a crushing sense of panic sets in.

It's not that they're homophobic. They're not. Beth and Shane live with a gay couple, for God's sake. But the idea of telling my family—risking their disappointment or somehow being seen as somehow *less* in their eyes—terrifies me. And my dad? If he were still alive, what would he think? Would he be ashamed of me? I couldn't bear that. And then there's my career. What would Captain Walker think? My colleagues? I know it would affect how they see me, how they treat me.

I finish my beer and toss the empty bottle into the recycling bin. Then I head into the spare bedroom where I've got a treadmill, and I run. I run long and hard and fast, as if I could possibly outrun my pain. By the time I've worn myself out, I take a quick shower and fall into bed.

But instead of falling asleep, I review the Townsend murder case methodically, retracing my steps to make sure I haven't missed anything. I think Turner's guilty, but until I have the DNA report, I can't afford to lose sight of other potential suspects.

The common denominator in all three murders is Diablo's. All three of the murder victims frequented that club in the weeks leading up to their killings. That has to mean something. It's the only thing they had in common besides their sexual orientation.

Tomorrow I'll pay the club another visit and talk the owner, Roy Valdez. I'll review the video surveillance footage again, to make sure I haven't missed any potential connections. Someone's life might depend on it.

Ian's life might depend on it.

* * *

The next morning, I have my court order requiring Brad Turner to provide a DNA sample. He's swabbed right away, and the sample is sent to the lab for testing. Now I just have to wait for the results. I'm not the only one trying to get my requests pushed through the overworked and understaffed department.

I'm in my office looking through my interview notes, searching for new leads I can follow up on, when the captain walks in. He looks haggard, with shadows beneath his dark eyes. I know he works long hours and carries a lot of responsibility on his shoulders. When I see him, I imagine what my father might look like now. They were the same age.

"How confident are you that Turner's the killer?" he says.

"It doesn't look good for him, I'll say that." But I've been at this job long enough to know that things aren't always as they first appear. "But all we have right now is circumstantial. Without a DNA match, something concrete, we're just making assumptions. So, not confident enough."

Walker nods. "How about Judge Alexander's son? How's he taking all this?"

"In stride." I don't dare tell Walker that I hired a bodyguard for Ian. There's no way I can justify arranging protection for him on my own—not without drawing unwanted attention and a lot of uncomfortable speculation.

"I'll let you know as soon as we get the DNA test results back," Walker says as he turns toward the door. "I'll make some calls, see if I can speed things along. We can only keep Turner for forty-eight more hours without pressing charges, and I don't want to press charges until we have something concrete."

"Understood." The clock is ticking, and I need proof one way or the other.

Walker pauses in the doorway, glancing back. "We've had three high-profile murders in our district in two weeks. I don't want another one."

"Neither do I." Especially when Ian might have a target on his back.

Walker shakes his head. "Heaven help us all if anything happens to Judge Alexander's son."

* * *

Midmorning, I return to Diablo's with the intention of reviewing the surveillance footage from the past two weeks again. As Diablo's is the common denominator, there has to be something here that ties these cases together.

The club's front door is locked when I arrive, but after I pound on it a few times, Bruno grudgingly opens the door. He towers over me, looming like Mt. Vesuvius dressed in tight black jeans and a black leather vest, sans shirt. His muscular arms are covered in tattoos, from shoulder to wrist. Even the backs of his hands and fingers are tattooed.

Nodding curtly, Bruno crosses his massive arms over his chest. "Detective," he says in his deep voice. Despite his intimidating physical appearance, his demeanor is relatively friendly. "What can I do for you?"

"Is Roy Valdez in?"

Bruno steps back and motions me inside. "He's in his office."

During the daytime, this club is unrecognizable. The place is well lit, from its polished black vinyl floor to the industrial rafters high overhead. There's not a single neon light to be seen. The air is heavy with lemon-scented floor cleaner, which is clearly attributable to the young man mopping the floor. Instead of pounding club music, someone's got a local pop radio station playing over the sound system. And except for a handful of employees wiping down the tables and bar, the place is otherwise deserted.

Bruno points to the hallway left of the bar, which leads past the restrooms to the offices at the back of the club. "That way," he says. "Last door on the right. It's marked."

I nod. "Thanks."

When I reach the door marked OFFICE, I knock.

"Come in!"

I open the door and walk inside, my gaze sweeping the cluttered room. Roy Valdez looks up from his desk, his eyes widening in surprise before he quickly recovers. I have that effect on people. Even when they haven't done anything wrong, people tend to freeze in the presence of a cop.

"Come on in, detective," Valdez says. He gives me a welcoming smile as he motions toward the old wooden chair parked in front of his desk. "What can I do for you?"

I approach the desk, but remain standing. "I'd like to review your surveillance video from the past three weeks again."

His leather office chair creaks when he leans back. "Sure. Anything you want." He throws his arms wide. "I'm an open book, detective. I'll do anything I can to help you find this motherfucker. These deaths have been bad for business."

He seems more concerned about his bottom line than he is about the fact that three men who frequented his club in the past three weeks were brutally murdered. "I appreciate your cooperation."

"No need to thank me." He rises from his chair and walks over to a computer workstation where the surveillance video is archived. He cues the footage I'm interested in. "Take your time. I'll leave you to it."

Then he vacates his office, leaving me alone to work, which I appreciate. I spend the next several hours reviewing the footage again, painstakingly attempting to piece together the various feeds and timestamps from multiple cameras.

I identify the first two victims and trace their steps through the club, from the moments they each arrive to the time they leave. I do the same for Eric Townsend, making note of everyone he came into contact with, whether on the dance floor, at the bar, or mingling in the crowd.

All three men spent time sitting at the bar, drinking. They all danced. They all mingled. Not surprisingly, the obvious common denominator is Brad Turner. He talked to all three men. He danced with all three men. I have good reason to believe he had sex with all three men.

I let the footage continue, focusing on Brad Turner.

My heart stops when I come to the video footage from the other night, when Ian came here specifically to meet up with Turner. I skim through the footage, tracing Ian's movements from the moment he entered the club until we left together. I see Ian talking to his friends. I see Ian seated at the bar, drinking and interacting with the bar staff.

Turner was slow to turn up that night, and I'd almost decided he was standing Ian up. But then he's there, looming behind Ian. He wraps his fingers around the back of Ian's neck, startling him.

I slow the replay down and watch more carefully as Turner

takes the seat beside Ian. It's difficult watching them together. Turner's hands are all over Ian, massaging his neck and shoulders, stroking his arms. Turner's interest in Ian is intense, and Ian looks more than a little uncomfortable. It's obvious that Turner is trying to get Ian drunk, plying him with drink after drink.

Turner flags down one of the bartenders to order yet another round of drinks. My gaze is so closely focused on Ian and Turner that I almost miss it. *Jesus.* The look on Roy Valdez's face as he glares at Ian and Turner from the far end of the bar is nothing short of seething. *Holy shit.* My gut tightens.

I rewind the footage to the exact moment Ian took a seat at the bar. Valdez pays him hardly any attention at all. But once Turner shows up, joining Ian, Valdez's demeanor changes abruptly. His body tenses, and his expression hardens. *What the hell?* That's jealousy, plain and simple. But what's driving his jealousy? Ian? *Fuck.*

Or maybe it's Turner.

I watch the scene several more times in an effort to catch every little nuance. I let the footage play until Turner heads to the dance floor, practically dragging Ian with him. But instead of focusing on Ian and Turner on the dance floor, I keep my focus on Valdez, who watches them intently as they dance. Valdez pours himself a generous shot of what looks to be vodka and slams it back.

I continue through the footage, past the point when Ian disappeared to the restrooms and I went after him. Shortly after that moment, we left the club through the rear door leading into the alley out back.

Turner leaves the dance floor, heading toward the restrooms. I figure he's going to look for Ian. But just seconds after Turner disappears from sight, Valdez exits the bar and heads after him.

I switch feeds and match up the timestamp on the hallway footage. Sure enough, Turner appears, walking down the hallway toward the men's room. A moment later, Valdez enters the frame, hot on Turner's tail.

Without warning, Valdez grabs Brad Turner from behind and throws him up against the wall, fisting the neckline of Turner's shirt as he pins him in place. Valdez is livid. He gets right up in Turner's face, gritting his teeth as he practically growls something at the man. Turner shakes his head, apparently denying whatever Valdez is saying. In response, Valdez wraps his fingers around Turner's neck and squeezes, hard. Turner's complexion darkens as he fights Valdez's chokehold.

Just before he releases Turner, Valdez gives him a hard, possessive kiss. And then he lets go and walks back the way he came. Turner sinks to the floor, his hand on his throat as he catches his breath.

I watch their exchange over and over. And while I can't tell what Valdez is saying to Turner, it's clear that the two men have an intense connection.

I lean back in my chair and run my fingers through my hair. There's a hell of a lot more going on here than I realized... and Brad Turner is definitely at the center of it. The problem is, he's not the only one. Roy Valdez is somehow involved, too.

When I've seen enough, I leave Valdez's office and find him behind the bar inventorying the liquor.

"Detective," he says with a smile, waving me over. "All done? Can I get you a drink? It's on the house."

I shake my head. "Thanks, but I'll have to pass. I'm on duty."

"No problem. Another time, then."

"I'm heading out," I tell him. "Thanks for the assistance. I appreciate it."

"Anything to get to the bottom of these senseless killings."

I turn to go, then pause and pivot back to him. "How well do you know Brad Turner?"

His brow rises in surprise. "Brad Turner?" He pauses, as if he has to think about it. "Not very well. Why?"

"Just curious. Thanks again for your help."

As I head out of the club, one thought keeps looping in my head. *Roy Valdez is lying.*

That means I need to have a heart-to-heart talk with Brad Turner and reassess everything.

✎ 15

Ian Alexander

I pick up my phone, immediately recognizing the ringtone, *Let It Go* from *Frozen*. It's my sister, Layla. "Hey, sis," I say, as I slather strawberry cream cheese on my bagel. "What's up?"

"Ian?" Her voice cracks, and then she goes silent, until I hear a muffled sob.

I instantly go on red alert. I have a soft spot for my sister. Life has saddled her with more than her fair share of challenges, and I'll do whatever I can to ease her way. "Layla? What's wrong?"

Miguel looks up from the kitchen table where he's drinking coffee and reading on his phone. He eyes me sharply, as if he's on alert too. I shake my head and point at my phone, mouthing *my sister* to him. He goes back to what he was doing.

"Layla, talk to me, hun. Tell me what's wrong."

She struggles not to cry. "My sugars crashed in the night, and Mom and Dad were so upset they fired Rob first thing this morning."

"I thought you didn't like Rob."

"I don't. Didn't. But I hate breaking in a new bodyguard even more."

"How low were your sugars?"

"Forty-eight."

"Are you kidding me? Yeah, I'd say Rob fucked up. He's lucky he only got fired. He's supposed to monitor your levels, not let you slip into a diabetic coma."

"It wasn't *that* bad," she says, sounding far from convincing. "I was conscious. The alarm woke me. It woke Mom and Dad, too."

"And where was Rob while the alarm was going off?"

"Asleep. He had a lot to drink last night. He was sort of out cold."

"Shit, Layla. He's not supposed to be drinking at all."

"I know. We went to a party. He met this girl—"

"That's unacceptable. You need a new bodyguard—one who knows what the fuck he's doing and can be trusted to do it." I can hear her sniffling. "Don't you have class this morning?"

"Yes. That's why I'm calling. I have a psych exam in an hour, but Mom and Dad said I can't leave the house without a bodyguard. The agency is sending a new one, but he won't get here until later this afternoon. I can't wait that long."

"Can't you make up the exam?"

"No. This professor doesn't allow makeups. Not for *any* reason." She muffles a sob. "Ian, I can't miss this exam. I have an A in this course right now, but if I miss this exam, the best I'll be able to get is a C."

Shit. My sister takes her classes seriously. It's the only thing in her life she can actually control. Between her health issues and our parents' suffocating oversight, her life isn't her own. "Hold on, Lay." I glance across the kitchen at Miguel. "How do you feel about going back to school?"

He chokes on his coffee. "What?"

"I need to escort my sister to UChicago this morning so she can take a psych exam. Are you coming with me or not?"

Miguel downs the rest of his coffee as he rises from his chair and wipes his mouth on a napkin. "You're sure as hell not going without me. Of course I'm coming."

I return to the phone. "We'll be there in twenty minutes, Layla. Be ready."

"Oh, God, thank you! You're the best, Ian! I mean it."

We both race upstairs to get dressed, and five minutes later we're heading out the front door and climbing into Miguel's Mustang.

I give him the address of my family's home, and he plugs it into his GPS. Fifteen minutes later—right on time—we arrive.

"This is it," I say. "Pull around to the back."

Miguel gazes up at the two-story white building that takes up an entire city block. "Which house is hers?"

"What do you mean, which house? This is it."

"I mean, which unit?"

I laugh. "Dude, it's all one house."

His eyes widen. "Are you shitting me? This is just one house? That *entire building* is your parents' home?"

"Yep."

"Jesus Christ. How many bedrooms does it have?"

"Twelve."

Miguel shakes his head.

"Yeah, I know," I say. "It's overkill."

Looking at it from his perspective, I admit it's overly ostentatious, but to me, it's just my family home. It's the place where I grew up, where my father grew up. *His* father—my paternal grandfather—built this house at the turn of the last century.

I direct Miguel to the end of the block, and then he turns right and takes another immediate right, which leads to an access lane behind the house. I'd call it an alley, but it has a six-car garage and separate living quarters for the household and security staff.

"Rich people," Miguel says, shaking his head in dismay.

"At least my parents aren't home. Be glad for that. They won't take kindly to me busting Layla out of home detention."

"How old is your sister?"

"Twenty-one."

"And they keep her locked up?"

"Not exactly." I debate how much to tell him. "She can leave with her bodyguard. It's complicated. She's what they call 'medically fragile.' She's a type 1 diabetic, and she has other... issues."

Miguel turns to me. "Care to elaborate?" When I hesitate to offer more, he says, "Hey, man, I need to know. If I'm going to be responsible for her today, I need to know what I'm dealing with."

I hate telling him, because I know how people react when they hear her diagnosis. They jump to conclusions before they know the facts, and they fear her. It's completely unnecessary, and it's not fair. My sister wouldn't hurt a fly. But he has a point. "She's also schizophrenic."

Miguel's eyes widen, but he doesn't say a word.

"It's nothing to worry about," I tell him. "You'll realize that when you meet her."

"Hey, I'm not worried. Who said I was worried?"

We park in the back and walk up to the rear door. Layla's there already, waiting for us just inside, her backpack slung over her shoulder. She looks like a typical co-ed, dressed in ripped jeans, knee-high boots, and an off-the-shoulder, slouchy gray sweater with a black tank top underneath. Her long black hair is pulled up in a high ponytail.

Standing behind Layla is Margaret, my parents' middle-aged housekeeper, who is currently glaring daggers at me. Margaret runs this household and everyone in it. She's dressed in her typical uniform: a navy blue skirt and white blouse. Her gray hair is pulled back in a severe bun, and her only accessory is a pair of small gold studs in her pierced earlobes.

"Hi, Margaret," I say, trying to head off a lecture. We don't have time for that. I smile at my sister as I point a thumb at Miguel, who's standing behind me. "Layla, this is Miguel. He's *my* bodyguard, and today, he's kindly offered to fill in as yours."

Layla's dark eyes, enhanced with kohl cat eyeliner, widen. "You have a bodyguard?"

"Yeah, well, it wasn't exactly my idea. But he's actually a really great guy, so it's not too bad."

"Gee, thanks," Miguel says, bumping my shoulder with his.

Layla laughs, instantly at ease. She turns a hopeful expression to Margaret.

I face off with the housekeeper. "Layla has an exam this morning that she can't miss, and since her bodyguard hasn't been replaced yet, we'll escort her to campus. We'll bring her straight home after her test, I promise."

Margaret doesn't look impressed. "Ian, your parents would never agree to this."

"I know. That's why we're not going to tell them. She'll be fine, I promise. Miguel and I won't let her out of our sights for an instant."

Layla turns her puppy dog eyes on the housekeeper. "Please, Maggie."

Margaret releases a heavy breath, her lips tightening into a thin line as she assesses Miguel. "You're a professional bodyguard?"

"Yes, ma'am." He pulls out his wallet and shows her his identification. Then, when Margaret doesn't seem impressed, he unzips his jacket and gives her a glimpse of the black handgun tucked into his chest holster.

"Fine." Margaret's glare shifts to me. "But you'd better bring her back to this house as soon as her class is over, or I'll call your father."

"Deal," I say.

Layla goes up on her tippy toes to hug Margaret. "Thank you!" Then she follows us to Miguel's car, giving me a grateful smile as she climbs into the back seat.

As Miguel drives toward campus, I turn to face my sister. "What happened last night? How did your sugars get so out of whack?"

She sighs. "I went to a party last night and I might have had a beer or two."

I frown. "Rob shouldn't have let you drink alcohol."

"He was too busy flirting with a girl at the party to notice what I was doing. Besides the beer, I had a *tiny* sliver of cake." She holds up her index finger and thumb, just half an inch apart. "And maybe half a scoop of mint chocolate chip ice cream."

"Jesus! No wonder your blood sugar levels got out of whack! Your insulin pump was working overtime trying to compensate for all that sugar. Rob didn't check your levels during the night, did he? He was supposed to."

Layla's attention drifts out the window, and she stares at the passing traffic.

"Layla?" I wave at her, trying to get her attention, but she doesn't respond. Then I snap my fingers. "Layla!" Still no response.

"What's wrong?" Miguel says, shooting me a quick look of concern.

"She's hallucinating," I tell him.

Miguel watches her in the rearview mirror.

"She suffers from auditory hallucinations, and she's easily distracted by them. The voices—mean girls, all of them—make it hard for her to pay attention to what's going on in the real world." I reach back and gently pat her leg. When she still doesn't respond, I shake her. "Layla! Look at me."

She turns to look at me. "Sorry."

"Put your earbuds in," I tell her.

She digs into her backpack and pulls out her earbuds and phone. She sticks the earbuds in, puts on some music, and closes her eyes.

I turn forward in my seat, noting Miguel's curious gaze. "Music helps her block out the hallucinations."

I'm furious that her bodyguard would let her consume that much sugar. No wonder her blood sugar levels plummeted dangerously overnight. She has a pump that injects insulin directly into her bloodstream as her blood sugar levels rise, but it's not fool-proof. Her levels still need to be closely monitored. That was Rob's job, and he clearly fucked up. "Fucking incompetent prick," I mutter.

Miguel shoots me a look.

"Her bodyguard. He was supposed to monitor her blood sugar levels in the night, and he fucked up."

"Your sister needs a medically-trained bodyguard."

"Is that a thing?"

"Sure, it is. We have bodyguards who are former paramedics. That's what your sister needs. Tell your parents to call my boss,

Shane McIntyre. Our guys would never fuck up like that."

Miguel parks in the university's visitor lot, and we escort Layla across campus to her psych class. I can't help noticing all the looks she gets from guys. They're practically drooling. I guess I can't blame them; she's stunning, a breath-taking beauty who draws attention wherever she goes.

We reach her classroom with eight minutes to spare. Gratefully, she slips inside and takes a seat near the back of the room.

Miguel and I stand guard outside Layla's classroom while she takes her exam. It's dead quiet in the classroom while all the students have their noses to their desks, pencils scribbling madly. Toward the end of the class period, students start filing out as they finish their tests.

Layla's the last one out, but that's not a surprise. It takes her longer to complete assignments because she has to fight to block out the auditory distractions. She'd qualify to have special testing conditions, but she doesn't want special treatment. She wants to be treated just like every other student on campus.

"How'd you do?" I ask her.

She gives me a big grin. "I kicked ass!"

I open my arms to her, and she steps close for a hug. "Good job, sis. Now let's get you home before we get busted."

ᵒ 16

Ian Alexander

On the drive back to my townhouse, Miguel says, "Your sister needs a bodyguard just to keep the guys off her. She's seriously gorgeous."

He's right, of course. In fact, she's too attractive for her own good. Nice guys are way too intimidated by her looks to even approach her, let alone talk to her or ask her out. Instead, she tends to attract the attention of egotistical, narcissistic bastards who think they're somehow entitled to her.

When we get back to the townhouse, I feel restless. Seeing my sister does that to me. I worry about her. Because she has health issues, both physical and mental, I worry what will become of her if she doesn't have good care. My parents worry, too. They provide her with everything she needs, but the incident last night with an incompetent bodyguard only highlights how fragile she is. All it takes is one fuckup.

I do what I usually do when I'm worried about something: I head downstairs to the workout room. Miguel comes with me, and he lifts weights while I run on the treadmill. Then we switch places, and I work on my shoulders and arms, while he runs. I do a little bit of abdominal work, too, because... well, you know... just in case. *I can always dream of having a certain homicide detective's hands on my body, can't I?*

* * *

That evening, while Miguel and I are playing a video game, my phone chimes with an incoming text.

I'd better see you ad Diablo's tonight, or I'm coming after you. – Chris

I laugh.

"What's so funny?" Miguel asks.

"A friend of mine is threatening to come after me if I don't go clubbing tonight."

Miguel frowns. "You're supposed to stay away from the clubs."

I shrug. "The suspect is cooling his jets in a prison cell right now. I don't think I need to worry."

"Ian, they have *a* suspect. That doesn't mean he's *the* suspect."

"Tyler said he found incriminating evidence at Turner's apartment. It's practically a confession." I look at the time. It's already after nine. I set my game controller down and make a split decision. "I'm going out. You can come or stay, it's your call."

With a sigh, Miguel shuts the game down. "Of course I'm coming. But I warn you, Tyler's not going to be happy."

"Only if he finds out—and don't you dare tell him. Besides, I don't give a shit what Tyler thinks." *Well, that's a lie.* "If he's not happy, he can come tell me himself. In person."

After we both shower and change, Miguel meets me downstairs in the parlor. He's dressed for work in black jeans and a form-fitting black t-shirt that hugs his lean muscles. His gun is holstered to his chest. I watch him shrug on his leather jacket.

I'm standing at the bar nursing a bottle of beer. "Want one?"

He rolls his dark eyes at me. "I'm working," he says drolly.

"Right. Sorry, man. No alcohol for you tonight. I, on the other hand, feel like getting plastered."

"You know," Miguel says, twirling his keychain on his index finger, "if this was a horror movie, someone luring you to the nightclub where the killer finds his victims would simply be a ploy to draw you out. You'd get killed because of your own stupidity."

I laugh. "Then it's a good thing I have you watching my back, isn't it?" I swig the last of my beer. "I've got a bodyguard *and* a designated driver, all in one. What could possibly go wrong?"

Watching Miguel fight a grin makes me smile. Of all the bodyguards I've had in my life, he's hands-down my favorite. I grab my phone, keys, and wallet and walk out the front door, Miguel close on my heels. He locks up behind us.

"Let's take my car," I say as I head for the carriage house. "I'll drive us there, and you can drive us home, when I'm semi-plastered."

His eyes light up. "I'm totally cool with that."

We arrive at Diablo's just after ten. I park on a side street, and we walk toward the club entrance.

"So, what's the plan tonight?" Miguel asks.

"I'm going to drink, dance, and get laid, in that order."

Miguel eyes me curiously like he's trying to decide if I'm serious.

"Well, at least the first two," I say. "While I do want to have sex, I don't want to have it with just anyone. As stupid as it sounds, I'm saving myself for someone special. And I guess that makes me an idiot, as that someone special doesn't seem to want me."

"That's not stupid at all," Miguel says. "So, who's your someone special?"

I give him a look. "That's not public knowledge."

"Will he be here tonight?"

"I seriously doubt it."

Feeling impatient, I bypass the long line—which wraps around the building—and walk right up to the front doors. I wave at Bruno, and he unclips the velvet rope and motions me forward.

"Hey, Ian," Bruno says. He eyes Miguel with more than a little curiosity. "Who's your friend?"

"This is Miguel. He's with me."

The bouncer gives Miguel a heated once-over.

"Don't waste your time, Bruno," I tell him. "He's not your type or mine."

I swear Miguel is blushing as Bruno lets him through.

As we walk inside the club, I study Miguel's reaction. Inside, it's dark and raucous with flashing lights and pounding music. The floor literally shakes to the beat. The air is electrified with anticipation and an overload of testosterone.

I point at the bar across the room. "I'm going to get a drink!"

He nods, not bothering to answer me over the loud music.

I lead the way through the crowd to the bar, and we find two empty stools at the far end.

Roy spots me immediately and comes over, standing directly across from me. He gives me a big smile. "Ian! Hey, sweetie, what can I get you?"

"I'll have a beer, and my friend here will have a—" I turn to Miguel. "What do you want?"

"I'll have a Coke," Miguel says as he methodically scans the customers seated at the bar and the staff working behind it.

Roy eyes Miguel appraisingly, just as Bruno did, before he walks away to get our drinks.

"They're trying to figure out if you're gay or not," I tell Miguel.

He chuckles. "Afraid not."

"I think it's mostly wishful thinking on their part. You are pretty hot."

Miguel bats his eyes at me. "Gee, thanks."

Roy returns quickly with our drinks. He sets Miguel's glass on the bar in front of him. As he hands me my beer, his fingers graze mine, lingering a second longer than necessary. Surprised, I meet his gaze.

He leans closer to be heard over the din. "How are you doing? I mean, after Eric's death. You two were friends."

At the mention of Eric's name, my stomach knots. "I'm okay. Eric didn't deserve that."

Roy frowns. "No, he didn't." Then he reaches out and takes my hand in both of his, turning it over to run his thumb down the center of my palm.

Although he's always been friendly, Roy's never paid this kind of attention to me before, and I'm not enjoying it now. I pull my hand back and force a smile.

Roy's gaze darts over to Miguel, who appears to be preoccupied with his phone, but I know better. Miguel doesn't miss a thing.

When I glance back at Roy, he gives me a heated look. "Do you have plans later?"

In other words, *How about a hookup?*

Roy's a good-looking guy—muscular, about five-ten. His blond hair is buzzed short, and he's got a lot of tats visible on his neck and arms. He's well-liked by his customers and employees, from what I can tell. Before meeting Tyler, I probably would have taken Roy up on his offer. But not now. I'm not ready to give up on Tyler.

Before I can pass on Roy's offer, my buddies Chris and Trey join me at the bar, both of them flushed and breathless from dancing.

"There you are!" Chris says as he throws his arm across my shoulders.

Miguel casually shifts on his stool to face me as he evaluates the new arrivals.

"It's okay," I tell him. "These are my friends."

Roy gives me a tight smile as he eyes Chris and Trey. "We'll talk later, Ian." And then he walks away.

Chris eyes Miguel, not very subtly. He leans close to whisper in my ear. "Who's the hottie? Should I be jealous?"

"No. He's just a friend. Chris and Trey, this is Miguel."

They exchange greetings as Chris tightens his hold on me and says, "I'll forgive you if you come dance."

I finish off my beer. "Time to go shake my booty," I tell Miguel. "Try not to miss me." I figure he's not going to follow me out onto the dance floor in a club full of guys who might make a grab for his mighty fine ass, but I'm not entirely sure. After all, he's obligated to keep me within view.

Miguel gives me a look that speaks volumes. *Don't go far. Stay where I can see you.* He swivels on his bar stool and watches me follow the guys out into a sea of gyrating bodies.

My friends and I meet up with a few other guys we know on the dance floor, fortunately on the edge of the dense crowd of partiers. I greet the others, and then easily step into the rhythm of the diva classic playing loudly on the sound system. I make a point of keeping myself on the periphery, within Miguel's sight.

"Oh my God, Ian," Trey says as he glances back at Miguel. "Your friend is seriously hot." He rolls his eyes. "Who is he, and why isn't he dancing with us? Why isn't he dancing with *me*?"

"He's not here to party. He's actually working."

When Trey's eyes get big, I laugh. "Not that kind of working.

He's my new bodyguard."

"Oh, fuck me," Trey says, as he fans himself. "I think I need a bodyguard, too. Want to share?"

We've been dancing long enough that I've worked up a sweat when I notice Miguel's no longer sitting alone at the bar. *Shit.* At the sight of Tyler seated beside him, my belly does a little flip. *He's here?*

Both Tyler and Miguel are sitting with their backs to the bar, facing the dance floor, arms crossed over their chests. They're both wearing black leather jackets that I know conceal holstered handguns. It's hot, the pair of them, in a *Men in Black* kind of way. No, actually it's hotter. Especially Tyler.

Suddenly, I feel like the belle of the ball, because the hottest guy in the room is watching me like a hawk. Miguel says something to Tyler, and Tyler shakes his head, looking a bit rueful, but he never once takes his eyes off me.

Chris comes up behind me, his hands on my shoulders. He leans close and says, "You're awfully popular tonight, sweetie. The cop's staring at you. And who's the hottie who came in with you?"

"Miguel. He's my new bodyguard."

Chris laughs. "I thought you said no more bodyguards."

"It's just temporary, until the murder investigation is over."

"But the cops arrested Brad Turner, right? I thought they got the guy."

I shrug. "They're still waiting on the DNA results. Nothing is official until then."

Chris links his arm casually around my throat and pulls me

back against him. He murmurs in my ear, "The cop looks like he wants to eat you alive."

Laughing, I duck out of Chris's hold. He flirts a lot, but he doesn't mean anything by it. We've never hooked up. "I'll be back," I tell him.

I walk over to the bar, stepping right in front of Tyler. "What are you doing here?"

Dressed down in jeans and a graphic tee beneath his requisite black leather jacket, Tyler looks incredible. With his dark hair and trim dark beard, he looks like he just stepped off the cover of a men's fashion magazine. Seeing him dressed casually for a change just adds to my torture.

His expression tightens. "I could ask you the same thing, Ian. I told you to stay away from the clubs."

I shrug. "I can't stay cooped up. I needed to get out and let off steam." I grab the front of his jacket and pull him a couple of inches toward me before he starts to resist.

"*Ian.*" There's a lot of warning in that one word.

"*Tyler.*" I just want to be closer to him. I want to feel his body against mine, his arms around me. But clearly, he doesn't feel the same way. "You shouldn't have come, Tyler."

Tyler's brow furrows. "Ian, it's not safe—"

"I have Miguel. I don't need you to keep me safe."

I turn to Miguel, who's pretending not to listen to the exchange between us. "I'm going to the john," I tell my bodyguard. "And then we're leaving."

Without waiting for a reply, I head for the restrooms. I'm halfway down the hall when I realize someone's hot on my tail. I assume it's Miguel, but I don't bother looking. It doesn't really matter. I came out tonight for a distraction from my problem, but it appears my problem followed me here.

There are two large unisex restrooms in this club. I can hear a lot of voices coming from the first one, so I pass it by and opt for the second. I walk inside, glad to find it empty. Except for the four white porcelain urinals lined up against the wall, the room is almost entirely decorated in black, from the floors to the walls to the stall doors.

The door opens behind me, and I glance back out of habit. I'm expecting Miguel, come to keep an eye on me, but it's not him. It's Tyler. I'm already in a pissy mood. I don't need to hear any more shit from him. "What do you want?"

After checking to make sure we're alone in the bathroom, Tyler faces me, his hands on his hips. He looks as exasperated as I feel. "We need to talk."

If all he's going to do is tell me again how he's not interested, I don't want to hear it. "Tell it to my bodyguard."

"I don't want to talk to Miguel. I want to talk to you."

I take a step toward him. "Well, maybe I *don't* want to talk to *you*." I know I sound like a petulant brat, but I can't help it.

And then Tyler grins at me. The son-of-a-bitch actually smiles, as if my shitty attitude amuses him. And that only pisses me off more.

"Fuck you!" I tell him. "You think any of this is funny?" My chest is tight, and my fucking heart hurts. I've never wanted someone like l want him. l've never felt like this before, and it fucking hurts. But he doesn't seem one bit affected, while l feel hot and breathless and needy. To hell with it. Maybe l should hook up with someone tonight. Maybe l should get laid and move on.

Tyler takes a step forward, his expression softening. He reaches out for a split second before pulling his hand back. "We do need to talk," he says, his voice gentler now. "l need to ask you some questions about Roy Valdez."

Pain knifes through me, searing my chest. This isn't about me or him, this is about the fucking case. This is strictly work. My chest deflates. Why in the hell do l have to want someone who doesn't want me? Someone who can switch off his emotions and his needs at the drop of a hat?

"What about Roy?" l say. l think back to Roy's bizarre behavior earlier tonight, asking me if l had plans this evening. "He hit on me tonight."

Tyler's expression changes instantly, sharpening as his jaw clenches. "He *what?*"

"He. Hit. On. Me. l thought l was pretty clear the first time."

Tyler presses the heels of his hands to his eyes and exhales harshly. "Roy Valdez lied to me this morning about the nature of his relationship with Brad, and now l've got all kinds of alarm bells going off in my head. As far as l'm concerned, Roy's now a suspect."

l frown. "But you arrested Brad."

"l know l did. Did you know they were involved with each other? Roy and Brad?"

I shake my head. "Are you sure? I've never even seen them talk to each other, let alone anything more."

"Yes, I'm sure. I caught them on video surveillance, kissing in the hallway. Not only that, but Roy choked Brad. When I asked Roy if he knew Brad, he said he didn't." Tyler scrubs his hand over his jaw. "Tell me exactly what he said to you tonight."

"He told me he was sorry about Eric, and then he asked me if I had any plans tonight."

"What did you say?"

"I didn't say anything. I didn't get a chance to. My friends dragged me off to the dance floor."

"Stay clear of him, Ian. He's a suspect now. I'll know more once Turner's DNA results are in."

"Thanks for the update, *detective*," I say, unable to keep the scorn out of my voice. I have to remind myself he's just doing his job. None of this is personal to him. This isn't about me. This is about the case. "Excuse me while I collect my bodyguard and head home."

I stalk past Tyler, my shoulder brushing against his, and he remains frozen to the spot. When I open the door, I see Miguel standing in the hallway. I don't know whether he's guarding the restroom or waiting for me. "I'm ready to go," I tell him.

He nods, falling in step beside me as I head for the exit. He motions back to the restroom. "What was that all about?"

I look back, expecting to see Tyler, but there's no sign of him.

"The fuck if I know," I say as we step outside. "Let's go home."

"I get to drive, right?" Miguel says as we head toward my

Porsche.

I only had two beers, so I'm not really that impaired, but I did promise him he could drive my car. I'd hate to disappoint him.

"Sure. You can drive." I dig the keys out of my pocket and hand them over.

Miguel slides into the driver's seat, and I get in the front passenger seat.

"Try not to get caught speeding, will ya?" I say.

Miguel laughs as he pulls into traffic. "Hey, by the way." He glances at me. "Is there any chance Tyler Jamison is your *someone special?*"

I glare at him. "Don't ask."

17

Tyler Jamison

Tuesday morning, I walk into an interrogation room at the precinct headquarters. The room is sparsely furnished with a square metal table and two metal chairs, all bolted to the floor. Brad Turner is the only occupant of the room. He's seated at the table, his cuffed wrists resting on his lap.

I stand behind the chair opposite his.

He glares up at me, looking worse for wear. Jail time doesn't seem to agree with him. "What the hell do you want?" he says.

I'm running out of time. We have to charge him or release him. "I have some questions, Mr. Turner."

"Too bad. I'm all out of answers." His complexion is pasty white, his dark hair greasy. "I told you, I didn't kill those men."

"I just want to ask you some questions."

"Why should I answer any of your questions? Why the hell should I help you?"

"Because, if you're innocent, wouldn't you want to help me find the killer?"

His posture relaxes a bit, but his tone is still defiant. "What kind of questions?"

"Tell me about Roy Valdez."

Turner grows even paler, if that's possible. "What about him?"

"Are you, or have you ever been, involved with him? Either romantically or sexually?"

Turner studies me, his shoe tapping the hard floor. "What does Roy have to do with anything?"

And that's when I know my growing suspicions might have some validity. There is a connection between Turner and Valdez. "Because Roy lied to me about knowing you. I asked him if he knew you, and he said he didn't. But I came across video surveillance footage from the club that says otherwise. I saw him throw you up against the wall in the hallway. I saw him choke you and then kiss you."

Turner looks away, staring a hole through the door. His chest rises as he inhales sharply, and then he sighs.

"What aren't you telling me, Brad?"

"We were together for about a year."

"Were?" I say.

"Yeah. We broke up a couple months ago."

"Who ended it?"

"I did," he says.

"Why?"

"Because he was so fucking controlling! He was smothering me. When I told him I wanted to see other guys, he threw a fit. He started getting physical with me, and it got out of hand. He choked me once, to the point I passed out. When I came to, there was a leather collar around my throat, cinched so tight I could barely breathe. That's when the threats started."

"What kind of threats?"

But Turner doesn't answer.

"You had sex with each of the murder victims, Brad." It's a statement, not a question. That much has already been established. The sexually-explicit photographs I found in his apartment are confirmation of that fact. I just want to make a point—connect the dots for him.

Turner nods. "After that time Roy choked me, I broke it off with him. For good. I started seeing other guys."

"Do you think it's a coincidence that the men you had sex with ended up dead? You never questioned that?"

He stares down at his cuffed hands.

"Do you think Roy Valdez is capable of murder?" I say.

Turner lifts his tortured gaze to me and nods. "He told me I'd regret leaving him." His eyes redden. "I did *not* kill those guys, detective," he says, his voice shaking. "I swear to you."

"You didn't answer my question. Did Valdez kill them?"

Turner shrugs. "I have no idea."

"Did Valdez ever talk to you about the men who'd been murdered?"

Turner winces. "After Eric died, Roy cornered me in the back hallway at Diablo's. That's what you saw on the video footage. He grabbed me by the throat and squeezed hard enough I couldn't breathe. He said, 'Who's next?' It never occurred to me that he might have had anything to do with the murders until he said that."

"And you didn't say anything to the authorities? You didn't report what he'd said to you?"

Turner shakes his head. "At that point, I was too afraid to say anything."

My stomach knots. "Thank you, Mr. Turner. That's it for now."

When I leave the interrogation room, I fill out an affidavit for a search warrant for Valdez's apartment. The one thing I have yet to find is the garrotte used to strangle the murder victims. If I can find that, I'll have enough for an arrest warrant.

* * *

Two hours later, after getting my search warrant signed off by a magistrate, I'm on my way out of the office to Valdez's apartment with police backup to execute the warrant. If we're lucky, Valdez will be there, and we can pick him up too, assuming I find something at his apartment that ties him to the murders.

Captain Walker intercepts me in the hallway and hands me a

sheet of paper. "The DNA results on Brad Turner just came in. It's not a match."

I glance down at the report.

NEGATIVE

Brad Turner was telling the truth.

Shit.

I take a steadying breath in an effort to rein in the anxiety threatening to overwhelm me. *We have the wrong guy.* The killer is still out there. And so is Ian.

"I'm releasing Turner," Walker says. "We have no grounds to hold him."

I nod, distracted as my mind races through all the implications. Valdez is now my primary suspect, and Ian said Valdez came on to him at the club.

Fuck!

Valdez had to have seen Ian dancing with Turner.

I hold up my search warrant. "I'm on my way to search Roy Valdez's apartment. He and Turner were lovers."

"Good luck." Walker steps back as I walk past him and out the door.

* * *

Half an hour later, we arrive at Valdez's apartment building.

Accompanied by uniformed officers, I lead the way up to the second floor, to Valdez's door. I knock. "Roy Valdez, open up! Chicago PD!" There's no answer.

I try again and get the same results.

One of the officers goes down to the ground floor to obtain a master key from the building's maintenance supervisor. We open the door and, after confirming that Valdez isn't home, we begin a thorough sweep of the apartment.

"Spread out," I tell the other officers. I'd already briefed them, so they know what we're looking for—evidence of homicide, particularly the smoking gun, which in this case, is a garrotte. Or, anything related to the murder victims.

While they search the living area, I head straight to the bedroom. Most criminals hide incriminating evidence in there so they can keep a close eye on it.

After pulling on a pair of gloves, I search his dresser and nightstand. Nothing there. Then I search the small walk-in closet. Along the perimeter of the closet are shelves high up, above the clothing rods. The shelves are stacked with a multitude of cardboard shoeboxes. I pull down the boxes, one at a time, and search them thoroughly. It wouldn't be hard to hide a slender, flexible wire in one of these boxes.

Most of the shoeboxes contain shoes. A few hold old family photographs and mementos from high school. One box is filled with photographs of Brad Turner—the two men together on vacations, at the beach, camping, hiking, on a cruise, photos of them engaging in sex. There are a couple of flash drives in the box, too, and I'm pretty sure they contain videos of the two men having sex.

When I search the last box in the back corner, I hit gold. Inside, lying beneath a red silk handkerchief, is a gruesome display that warrants Valdez's arrest for the murder of three men.

Three different Polaroid photographs of three different men with a garrotte cinched around their bloodied necks. The three murder victims.

The garrotte in the photographs looks to be about eighteen inches long, a razor-thin wire with wooden handles attached at each end.

The idea that Ian could have been a victim number four makes me sick. My stomach churns, and bile shoots up into my throat, burning me.

The photographs are enough evidence to arrest Valdez on suspicion of murder, but the key piece of evidence I'm looking for is missing.

The garrotte.

And that worries me more than anything.

I photograph the contents of the box and call for a forensics team to come process the evidence.

"I found what I was looking for," I call out to the other officers as I return to the living area.

The officers stay behind to wait for forensics to arrive. My plan is to return to the precinct and file a request for an arrest warrant for Roy Valdez. But first, on my way to my car, I text Miguel. The killer is out there somewhere, possibly with a garrotte in his pocket, and I need to know that Ian's safe.

℮ 18

Ian Alexander

I 'm going to the marina," I tell Miguel as I polish off the last bite of my salmon fillet.

We stopped for a late lunch at Tavern on Rush, one of my favorite local restaurants. Out in front of the eatery, we're seated at a sidewalk table. It's a beautiful day, with clear blue skies and a nice breeze, and I need to be out on the water. I'm feeling antsy and I need physical activity. I need the sun beating down on my skin and the wind in my hair. I need to forget about Tyler.

As Miguel polishes off the last of his burger and fries, I lean back in my chair and study him. I can't hang out with someone and not get to know them—it's way too impersonal. He may be a bodyguard, but he's not a servant or some nameless, faceless employee. "So, what do you do when you're not working?"

He looks a bit surprised by my question. "During my down time—which is pretty rare—I work on my car. It takes a lot to keep a classic in tip-top shape." He wipes his mouth on a napkin. "I ride my motorcycle out in the country, play basketball with my brothers, and on Sunday afternoons, my whole family gathers at *mi abuelita's* house for supper."

"*Abuelita?* That's your grandma?"

"Yeah." He nods. "I'm a pretty simple guy, living a pretty simple life. I work a lot and play whenever I have the chance. I can't complain."

"What did you do before becoming a bodyguard?"

"I did a stint in the military—six years in the Army right out of high school. After I got out, I came back here to Chicago and started messing around with kickboxing and MMA. That's how I met Liam McIntyre. He told me about his brother's company, McIntyre Security, and I applied for a job. Shane hired me. One of my first clients was Beth McIntyre. Well, she was Beth Jamison back then."

"Jamison?" My heart rate picks up. "Any relation to Tyler?"

He nods. "She's Tyler's younger sister. Now she's the boss's wife."

After I settle the bill—I insisted on paying for both of our meals—we walk the few blocks to my townhouse to grab some gear. Miguel offers to drive us to the marina in his Mustang.

Half an hour later, we pull into the marina parking lot. Miguel pops the trunk so we can grab our gear.

A silver SUV parks in the spot next to us, and the driver lowers his window. "Hey, Ian!"

I'm surprised to see Roy Valdez here. He opens his door and steps out.

"Fancy meeting you here," I say. I didn't know he was into boats.

Miguel closes the trunk and casually positions himself beside me.

Valdez laughs. "Yeah, what are the odds?" He eyes Miguel. "I remember you from the club."

"Miguel's a friend," I say. "Miguel, this is Roy Valdez. He's the owner of Diablo's."

Roy nods curtly at Miguel, but he doesn't offer to shake his hand. Instead, he turns his attention back to me, nodding toward the clubhouse at the far end of the pier. "I'm meeting a friend for lunch." Roy looks out toward the rows and rows of boats moored in the harbor. "Are you taking your boat out?"

"Yeah. The weather's too nice to pass up an opportunity to go cruising."

He nods. "Sure is. Have a good time. I hope I'll see you again soon at the club."

Miguel watches Roy as he heads toward the clubhouse. Once Roy is out of earshot, he says, "Have you ever seen him here before?"

"No."

"Huh."

"What's that supposed to mean?"

"I heard him hitting on you last night at Diablo's, and now he just happens to show up at the marina the same time you do? That seems a little too unlikely to be a coincidence."

"It's a free country." I pat Miguel on the back. "Come on, dude. Forget about him. Let's go boating."

We walk down the dock to my boat and step aboard. Then we climb up to the main deck and head down into the galley. Miguel does a thorough sweep of the galley and stateroom while I stow our gear in a closet. Then he follows me up to the cockpit while I begin prepping the boat.

Miguel shadows me as I go through the process of getting the boat ready. I check the electronics and fuel levels, and I prime the engine.

As we climb down from the cockpit, I nudge him with my elbow. "Do you think you can manage the lines?"

We're standing at the railing overlooking the dock, where black nylon ropes secure the boat to the dock.

"Sure." Just as he's about to climb down, his phone chimes with an incoming message, and he glances at the screen. "It's Tyler, asking where we are." He pauses to respond.

His phone rings almost instantly, and he takes the call. "Hey, detective." He listens for half a minute, then says *Tyler* in a sharp tone that catches my attention.

I can tell from Miguel's stiff posture that something's not right. "Miguel? What's wrong?"

He shakes his head at me as he continues to listen. Then he says, "Valdez is here at the marina. He pulled into the parking lot right behind us not twenty minutes ago." He pauses, listening. Then he says, "Yes, he could have followed us here. I wasn't watching for a tail."

Miguel's expression tightens as he glances at me and puts his phone on speaker. "He's right here beside me, Tyler. Go ahead, you're on speaker."

"Where exactly are you guys?" Tyler asks in a clipped voice.

Miguel meets my gaze. "We're on the deck of Ian's boat."

"Miguel," Tyler says. "I want you to get Ian below deck right now. He's the target. Secure him in the stateroom and stand guard. I'm on my way, with backup."

"Roger that," Miguel says as he grabs my arm and steers me toward the steps that lead below deck.

"What's going on, Tyler?" I say trying not to trip over my own feet as Miguel hustles me along.

"Roy Valdez killed those men, not Brad Turner." His words are direct, matter of fact. He sounds breathless, as if he's running. "I'll explain more later. Right now, get below deck and stay there. I'm on my way."

After ending the call, Miguel gives me a gentle shove down the steps into the galley. He follows me down and points toward the stateroom. "Get in there and lock the door." Then he pulls his handgun from his holster and loads a round. "I'll wait up on deck for Tyler."

"Miguel, no! If Valdez is out there, I'm not going to let you put yourself at risk for me."

"Ian, this is my job."

"No!"

He's interrupted by a shout from the dock. "Hey, Ian!"

I meet Miguel's sharpened gaze. "That's Valdez."

"Fuck." Miguel pushes me through the galley and into the stateroom. "Lock this door and don't come out for any reason! Do you hear me? No matter what you hear, don't come out!"

My heart hammers as my adrenalin spikes. "Miguel—"

"Don't argue," he says as he pulls the stateroom door shut. "Lock it!"

I do as he says, hating the fact that he's putting his life on the line for me.

I hear Miguel's heavy steps as he runs up the steps to the main deck. After that, I can pick up only fragments of his conversation with Valdez.

Valdez says, "Where's Ian?"

Miguel sounds perfectly at ease when he says, "He's changing. He'll be up in a minute."

Valdez says something else, but I can't quite make it out.

"How about a beer?" Miguel says.

"Yeah, sure."

I search the stateroom for something I can use as a weapon, but the only thing I find is a spare lifejacket and a pair of canvas boating shoes. Neither is promising as a weapon. I do own a handgun, but it's at home in a safe. It won't do me any good here.

I step into the bathroom and quickly search the drawers.

Nothing. Then my gaze lands on the shower curtain rod. I rip it off its brackets and remove the curtain. It's no match for a gun, but I could use it to club someone over the head.

Sirens wail off in the distance. Then I hear the thud of footsteps as someone walks across the deck. The sirens grow louder, the sound shrill and piercing, until suddenly they shut off. I hear shouts on deck, thundering footsteps, and then the tell-tale sound of a scuffle. A shot rings out, and the yelling escalates as more voices enter the fray.

My heart pounds as I listen to what sounds like an all-out gun battle taking place on the deck of my boat, while I'm stuck down below with nothing but a curtain rod as a potential weapon.

Damn it!

I can't let Miguel get hurt because of me, so I unlock the stateroom door and ease it open, just enough to see if the coast is clear below deck. The noise above escalates as people yell over one another, their shouts punctuated by the deafening cracks of multiple gunshots in rapid succession.

I hear a sharp cry, and then there's a heavy thud on the deck.

The gunshots stop.

The shouting stops.

Suddenly, it's deadly quiet on the deck above me.

With the curtain rod braced in my hands like a weapon, I head for the steps leading up to the main deck. A tall form appears at the top of the steps, blocking the light. I glance up at Tyler, who looks like a kickass avenger holding a handgun at his side.

"You can come up now," he says. "It's over."

I charge up the steps and push past Tyler to survey the scene. Roy Valdez lies on his back, a pool of blood slowly spreading out beneath him. He's clutching a silver handgun.

Miguel is sitting on the deck, his gun lying at his side. He's cradling his left shoulder with a bloody hand and grimacing in pain. Two uniformed police officers stand over Valdez's body, one speaking quietly into his radio.

Hesitantly, I approach the body, staring down at Valdez's lifeless eyes. Blood oozes from three holes in his chest, soaking into his white shirt and spreading.

"Who shot him?" I ask numbly.

Tyler and Miguel both say, "I did."

Tyler pulls on a pair of gloves and crouches beside Valdez. He rifles through the man's inside jacket pockets and pulls something out. It's a coiled wire, caked with dried blood and gore, worn wooden handles at each end.

Jesus, is that Eric's blood?

I feel sick knowing Valdez came here to use that thing on me. I don't even realize I'm holding my throat until Tyler walks up to me and gently pries my hand from my neck. I glance at him, and the look on his face confirms my suspicion. Valdez came here to kill *me*.

My stomach turns as I drop down onto one of the padded benches and lean forward, putting my head down and breathing through my mouth. If not for Miguel and the cops arriving when they did, I might have ended up just like Eric. And Miguel might have been killed.

I feel a gentle hand on the back of my neck, just a brief, comforting touch.

"It's all right," Tyler says. "You're safe. Slow your breathing, or you'll hyperventilate."

I hear more sirens in the distance, getting louder by the minute. We all wait quietly, a bit dazed by what happened here.

I stare at the dark red pool spreading out beneath Valdez's body and wonder how hard it's going to be to get blood out of the teak boards. "Jesus." *I'm losing it.*

Miguel joins me on the bench, clearly favoring his shoulder. "You okay?"

I laugh shakily as I meet his concerned gaze. "I should be asking you that."

He shrugs, grimacing. "It's just a flesh wound. It's nothing serious."

"You were shot! How is that not serious?"

He smiles through the pain. "Just doing my job."

"Your job sucks!"

A crowd begins to form along the dock as curious onlookers congregate.

I cover my face with shaking hands and focus on my breathing. It's hard to take this all in. *Someone wanted to kill me.*

I don't really know how much time passes before a forensics team and the coroner arrive. My boat is swarmed by law enforcement technicians who document the scene and collect evidence. Meanwhile, the crowd of onlookers on the dock grows.

Tyler bags the garrotte and hands it over to one of the forensics people. Then he comes over to sit beside me. To Miguel, he says, "You're going to the hospital. An ambulance is on its way, and I've already notified Shane you were injured."

Miguel glances at me. "What about Ian? I drove him here."

"I'll take Ian home," Tyler says, eyeing me. "You take care of yourself, and then take a well-deserved break."

"All right," Miguel says. But he looks to me for confirmation.

I nod. "I'll be fine. You worry about yourself."

Miguel smiles. "This is nothing. I've had worse."

19

Ian Alexander

The ambulance arrives soon after to transport Miguel to the hospital.

There will undoubtedly be an investigation into the shooting, since there was a fatality. Fortunately, there were several witnesses who came when they heard the shouting. They saw everything, and they can corroborate what happened, that Valdez struggled with Miguel, who stood guard at the steps leading below deck. When Tyler and the cops arrived, the scene deteriorated quickly, followed by gunshots. A few of the bystanders filmed the whole thing, and of course the cops had bodycams on them to record what happened.

Tyler and Miguel both shot Valdez, and I wonder if either of them could get in trouble because of it. I know Tyler will be investigated, simply because he's a cop and that's standard procedure anytime a police officer shoots a suspect. Miguel's a private citizen, but he was also acting in an official capacity as my bodyguard.

It's another hour before Tyler and I are cleared to leave. The scene was processed, and the body was taken away to the morgue. Officers put crime tape around my boat to keep out curious gawkers. I look at the bloody mess on the deck of my boat and figure that section will have to be replaced. I make a mental note to contact my shipbuilder.

"Ian, let me take you home," Tyler says gently.

It takes me a moment to realize he has his hand on my back. I'm sure he can feel me shaking. He may be used to this kind of thing, but I'm not. "Thanks."

I walk with Tyler to the parking lot and climb into the front passenger seat of his BMW. He observes me closely but doesn't say anything.

"Don't worry," I say as I buckle my seatbelt. "I'm not going to flake out on you. I'm just a bit shaken."

"Anyone would be."

Neither one of us says anything more on the drive to my townhouse. He pulls into my driveway and shuts off the engine. Then he turns in his seat to face me. "I'd like to come inside. We need to talk about what happened tonight. And I'll fill you in on what I found out about Valdez today."

I nod, still fighting a pervasive sense of numbness. I'm so cold. I wonder if I'm a little bit in shock.

We get out of his car and walk up the front steps to my door. My hands are shaking so badly that Tyler takes my keys from me and unlocks the door, pushing it wide and motioning for me to walk inside.

Once I'm in, I head right into the parlor, straight for the bar. I grab a glass and a bottle of whiskey and pour myself a shot. I knock it back, coughing as the liquor burns my throat. "Do you want one?" I ask him, without meeting his gaze.

"No."

"Right. You're working." I pour myself a second shot and toss it back, nearly choking this time. My hand shakes as I slam the empty glass on the bar. "Fuck!"

"It's all right," Tyler says. "Your adrenalin is on overload. It'll pass."

I finally bring myself to face Tyler, fully aware that I've been avoiding looking at him all evening. "So, it's over? It was Valdez all along?"

He nods. "He and Brad Turner were lovers until Brad broke it off a couple of months ago. When Brad moved on, Valdez snapped. I found plenty of incriminating physical evidence at his apartment. The only piece missing was the garrotte."

"Poor Eric. He died because he hooked up with Turner." I reach once more for the whiskey bottle, but Tyler captures my hand.

"You've had enough, Ian," he says, his voice low as he gently squeezes my hand.

I yank my hand out of his grasp and pour myself a third shot. "So, I guess Miguel's out of a job, right?"

Tyler frowns as he watches me swallow a mouthful of liquor. "Looks that way."

When I grab the bottle again, Tyler takes it from me and sets it out of reach. "I know you're upset," he says, "and you have every right to be, but self-medicating with liquor won't help."

I turn to face him, my chest on fire, and take a step closer so that we're standing just inches apart. My eyes lock onto his, and I want to lose myself in those beautiful blue-green depths. "Do you know what *will* fucking help?"

His expression grows wary. "What?"

I reach for his belt buckle and unfasten it roughly. "A good fuck."

"*Ian.*"

There's a sharp edge to Tyler's warning, but I don't give a fuck right now. My blood is burning, my heart is racing, and I feel like I'm about to come undone. I need something to ground me. I need... *him.* I drop to my knees on the plush rug and hastily unfasten his black trousers. He's already hard, so hard I have to use care as I lower his zipper past his thick erection. I tug his slacks down to his knees.

"Ian, for Christ's sake!" He grabs my arms and tries to haul me to my feet, but I resist.

I want him.

I fucking want him in my mouth. I stare at the impressive outline of his cock beneath his gray cotton boxer-briefs. He's thick and long, so long my belly clenches in anticipation. I know I shouldn't push him like this, but he's a big boy. If he wants to tell me to fuck off and walk out the front door, he's perfectly capable of doing so.

I press my open mouth against the ridge of his erection and blow on his hot flesh, right through the soft fabric. And then I trace the outline of his length with my tongue, from root to tip.

"Fuck!" he cries, his voice ragged. He reaches down and grips my head firmly, his fingers digging into me.

I fully expect him to pull away from me, to shove me or even punch me, but he doesn't do any of those things. Instead, his fingers tighten on my skull.

I lift my gaze to his, shocked at the heat and fire I see in his. *My God, he's gorgeous.* My mind is spinning, and my gut clenches tightly with desire. "I want you so badly." My voice is so hoarse, I'm not even sure he understood me.

When he doesn't push me away, I lick the length of him right through his briefs, wetting the fabric, and he groans low and harsh. When I mouth the head of him through his briefs, he moans. "*Fuuuck!*"

I run my nose along the length of him, breathing him in, loving his smell, the heat and muskiness of him. My dick hardens and my balls draw up tight. I'm so fucking aroused, I groan loudly, desperate for more. I mouth him through the fabric, my lips caressing his length, and he wavers on his feet.

I grip the waistband of his boxers and lower it, finally freeing his erection. He lets out a heavy breath, his chest heaving as he sucks in air. His thick cock bobs in the air, defying gravity. I grip him in one hand while my other hand reaches behind him, to cup an ass cheek and gently squeeze it.

His knees nearly buckle, but he manages to catch himself on the bar counter, gripping the edge with a white-knuckled fist. "Ian," he chokes out. "Shit! I can't do this."

He says he *can't* do it, not that he doesn't want to.

My gaze returns to his, and the sight of him looking down at me, towering over me with a dark, hungry expression, his blue-green eyes on fire, makes me crave him with a desperation I've never felt before. My own cock throbs, pulsing with need, and I *ache* for him, so badly it hurts.

"There's the door, Tyler," I say roughly, nodding toward the foyer. My voice is raw. "You're welcome to leave at any time."

When he remains in place, his feet rooted to the spot, I smile up at him, taking his response—or rather his lack of response—as tacit permission. I lick the length of him from root to tip, once, twice, my tongue worshipping his heated flesh. I wrap my fingers around his cock, reveling in the heat of it. A thick vein pulses beneath my fingers, and I moan in approval. He smells like sex, and I can't begin to get enough of him. I want to eat him alive.

I lick the crown of his erection and swirl my tongue around the head, teasing the rim. I taste him on my tongue, salty and warm, and it only makes me want more. I'm desperate to make him come. Desperate to take him inside me and swallow every drop. His hands return to my face, and he cups my cheeks firmly, his fingers digging roughly into my jaw.

He's not pushing me away. He's *letting* me, and the realization is heady. It emboldens me. I draw the head of his cock into my mouth, my tongue circling it, teasing him, stroking him, worshipping him the way I've dreamed of doing.

I draw him in deep. *Damn, he's a lot to take!* I don't think I've ever had such a big cock in my mouth before. I take him all the way to the back of my throat, my face almost pressed against his groin, his wiry hair teasing my nostrils. The heat and scent of him make me want to weep.

I start moving on his cock in earnest, my lips dragging along the taut length of him. I grip the base of his cock with one hand, and with my other hand, I reach down and unfasten my jeans, easing my zipper past my own throbbing erection. Frantically, I shove my jeans down, and my briefs, just enough to free my cock. I grip myself hard, stroking my length and wishing it was Tyler's hand on me instead.

"Fuck!" Tyler cries when I take him deep once more. I alternate between sliding my mouth up and down his length, then my tongue, to taking him as far back as I can. The animal sounds coming from him only spur me on, the groans and the cursing only drive my own arousal higher.

His hands cage my skull, and suddenly he's holding me where he wants me. Without warning, he starts thrusting into my mouth, hard and fast, like a wild man who's lost all control.

His body has clearly taken over, and there's no shred of reticence left in him. He holds me firmly in place as he fucks my mouth, his strokes long and hard, hitting the back of my throat over and over. I will myself to relax and breathe through my nose, loosening my throat muscles so I can take all of him, give him what he needs.

He grimaces like a man who's been starved for so long he doesn't know what to do when offered sustenance. His thrusts quicken, his hips bucking into me, his breath rushing out of him in harsh grunts. One hand grips my jaw hard enough to leave bruises, and the other hand slips behind my head and fists my hair, pinning me. As if I'd move a muscle!

I've never been so fucking aroused in my life. *God, I want him!* I want him inside me, I want him in my ass, thrusting with abandon like he is now. I stroke myself hard and fast, matching his driving rhythm. My balls draw up tight, and with a rush of heat and mind-numbing pleasure, I come in hot spurts into the palm of my hand.

Tyler throws his head back and shouts a hoarse "Fuuuck!" as he comes in a blistering rush, filling my throat. He freezes, lodged deep in my throat, his cock spasming with each pulsing release. He milks his orgasm, spilling down my throat, and it's perfect. *He's so damn perfect.*

Suddenly, Tyler pulls out and staggers back, his eyes wide with shock. He stares down at me as I swallow his spunk, his gaze locking on the ribbon of jizz that clings to my bottom lip. As I lick it up, his gaze snaps to mine, making my heart sink. I see it all clearly in his eyes—horror, disgust, fear. *Guilt?*

I stand and reach for him, but he stumbles back, shaking his head frantically as tears stream down his face into his beard. "I'm so fucking sorry."

He pulls his boxers up with shaky hands, tucking his limp cock inside, and then he drags his trousers up and swiftly fastens them. "Jesus, I'm sorry," he mutters, no longer meeting my gaze. He looks gutted.

I shoot to my feet and scramble to right my own clothes, wiping my wet hand on my jeans. "You have nothing to be sorry for, Tyler." But before I can get another word out, he's halfway to the door. "Tyler, wait!"

The door slams shut behind him, the sound echoing ominously in the silence of my empty townhouse.

He's gone.

What the fuck have I done?

ᒲ 20

Tyler Jamison

I drive blindly away from Ian's townhouse, frantically wiping tears from my eyes. My heart is pounding and my lungs can't keep up. I find myself heading toward home, on autopilot. But I can't go home right now. Not like this.

I need... hell, I don't know what I need. But I need someone. I can't go on like this anymore. I'm coming apart at the seams. My insides are shredded, my heart gutted. I'm going to implode. I have a death grip on the steering wheel, and still I can't stop my hands from shaking.

At the last minute, I make a sharp U-turn and head back toward my sister's place. I need to talk to someone, and she's the only one I can imagine confiding in. I park in the underground garage, in one of the spaces reserved for the penthouse, and use my personal code to summon the private elevator.

As the elevator swiftly ascends, I catch my reflection in the mirrored walls, shocked by what I see. I look as lost and desperate as I feel. *God, I'm a wreck.*

After the elevator glides to a smooth stop, the doors open to the foyer. They have to know I'm here. Shane's state-of-the-art security system alerts him any time someone summons the penthouse elevator. And there are surveillance cameras in the elevator as well as in the foyer.

When I step through the foyer doorway into the great room, I immediately spot Shane and Beth seated on one of the sofas in front of the fireplace. Luke is standing on Shane's lap, on wobbly legs, while Shane supports the baby's weight and helps him practice walking.

Shane and Beth glance up at me in unison, surprise evident on both their faces. Of course, they're shocked to see me like this, with no warning and looking so disheveled.

"I'm sorry for barging in." My voice is shredded. As I meet my sister's frantic gaze, fresh tears begin to fall. I know I look like shit, and I'm scaring her. "Beth—"

Shane rises to his feet, the baby in his arms. "I'll let you two talk," he says quietly, reaching down to touch Beth's face. "Call if you need me."

I watch Shane until he's out of sight, having disappeared into the nursery down the hall. Once we're alone, I turn to face my sister. She's already on her feet, running to me. She's dressed for bed, in a nightgown and robe. I didn't realize how late it was.

"I'm sorry, Beth. I shouldn't have come." My voice breaks, and I start sobbing. It's like a dam has burst inside me—a wall I've been shoring up for decades has finally crumbled—and I can't hold back the flood of emotion.

She wraps her arms around my waist and holds me tight. "My God, Tyler, what's wrong?"

She's crying now, too, I realize. I'm rooted to the spot, unable to move. Right now, she's the only thing keeping me grounded. My life is falling apart all around me, the broken pieces lying at my feet, and I'm lost.

Beth's hot tears soak my shirt. I know I'm scaring her, and that's the last thing I wanted to do. I brush the tears from my face, but try as I might, I can't get the words out.

She pulls back to look up at me, anxiety clouding her pale blue-green eyes. "Tyler, what's wrong? Is it Mom?"

Shit, this is all wrong. I'm the big brother. I'm the one who should be taking care of her. I should be the one drying her tears. It shouldn't be me who needs comforting. "It's not Mom. She's fine. I'm sorry, Beth. I didn't mean to scare you."

She grabs my hand and leads me to the sofa. "Come sit down."

I do as she says, sitting beside her on the couch. I lean forward, propping my forearms on my thighs, my head in my hands. I'm wracked with shame, disgusted by my own loss of control. I can't believe I did that to Ian, *used* him like that. It's inexcusable.

Beth lays her arm across my back and leans into me, her head on my shoulder. Her voice is no more than a whisper. "Please talk to me."

I press the heels of my hands to my eyes, trying to stem the tears. But they keep coming, streaming down my face hot and furious. The only other times I cried like this were the day I buried my father and the day my little sister was abducted.

I blow out a heavy breath, as if releasing pressure on a keg that's about ready to blow. I don't know how to tell her. I don't know how to say the words. Once they're out, I can never take them back. "I..." *God, I can't.*

"Just say it, Tyler," she says, hardening her voice. "Whatever it is, just say it."

She's right. I need to get this off my chest once and for all. I need to trust someone. I turn to face her, gazing into eyes that are so like my own. She's fair, like our mom, whereas I'm dark, like our dad. Even though our respective genes come from opposite ends of the spectrum, we share our mother's eye color.

Fresh tears spill out, scalding my cheeks as I take a deep breath and just come out with it. "I was with a man tonight."

She stills, watching me closely, and I don't think she gets my meaning.

I try again. "I had sex with a man."

Her eyes widen in understanding, and then her lips curve up in a gentle smile. She reaches out to brush the tears from my cheeks. "Okay."

I laugh shakily. "Is that all you're going to say? Just *okay?*"

Her smile widens. "Well, I was going to ask if you like him."

A snort escapes me, followed by a hollow laugh. "Yeah, I do. I like him." God, just saying that relieves so much pressure. But then reality returns in a vengeful rush. The way I treated him tonight... the way I *used* him, it's shameful. He has every right to hate me.

She takes my hand and squeezes it. "I love you, Tyler. I just want you to be happy. Nothing could ever change that."

I shake my head. "Honey, it's not that easy."

She squeezes my hand. "Yes, it is. Have you been with a man before?" Her voice is soft, hesitant, as if she's afraid to pry.

"No."

"So, this is new for you?"

I laugh again. I can't believe she can make me laugh at a time like this, when my life feels like it's careening out of control. "Yeah, it's new. I met someone recently who—" I stop.

"He's gay, I take it?" she says.

I nod. "Yes."

"And you like him? You want to be with him again?"

I scrub my hand across my face, exhaling hard. "I walked out on him, Beth. I don't know if he'll want to see me again after the way I behaved tonight. I really fucked up."

She cradles my hand in hers, drawing it to her chest. "If he likes you, he'll understand. He'll give you another chance. You just have to ask for one."

"I have to tell Mom. She needs to hear it first from me. Will you come with me tomorrow to see her?"

"Of course." She links her arm through mine. "Stay here with us tonight. We'll go see Mom together first thing in the morning."

I kiss her temple. "That sounds like a good idea." I don't want to go home alone tonight anyway. I stand. "I really need a drink. Do you mind?"

I cross the room to the bar, grab a bottle of whiskey, and pour myself a double. Beth joins me at the bar, taking a seat on one of the barstools. "Can I get you something?" I ask her. "Water? Or maybe some fruit juice?"

She shakes her head. "I'm fine."

As I take a sip of the smooth, top-shelf liquor, the elevator chimes.

Shit. Sam and Cooper must be coming home. I'm not exactly ready to face company.

A moment later, two men come through the foyer door, their arms wrapped tightly around each other. Sam laughs as Cooper pulls him close and plants a kiss on the younger man's temple. When they notice me across the room, standing behind the bar, their laughter fades.

"Hey, Tyler," Sam says as they head our way. He shares a quick look with my sister. "Is everything okay?"

Sam reminds me so much of Ian. They're nearly the same age—late twenties. They've both been out since they were young. Sam's confident and outgoing, fearless. Nothing fazes him. His personality is as fiery as his red hair, which is gathered up top in a man bun.

Cooper, on the other hand, is in his fifties, short iron-gray hair and trim silver beard. He's a retired Marine Corps sniper, now a shooting instructor for McIntyre Security, a company he co-founded with Shane.

Cooper is old school and a bit of a hardass. He only recently came out as gay, practically kicking and screaming, when Sam gave him an ultimatum and forced the issue.

"Hey, Sam." I knock back the rest of my drink and pour another. I'd really like to get hammered tonight, and since I'm not going anywhere anytime soon, I can. "Everything's fine."

Sam grabs a bottle of beer from the fridge beneath the bar and pops the top. "You don't look fine."

I know my eyes are bloodshot from crying. "It's been a rough day." Actually, it has, and not just because of what happened tonight with Ian. "I shot and killed a man today."

Sam takes a seat beside Beth. "Shit. What happened?"

At that moment, Shane returns to the great room and joins us at the bar, taking the empty seat on Beth's other side. He leans in to kiss the side of her head. "Baby's asleep." Then, to me, he says, "Miguel's doing well. He was released and sent home to recuperate."

"What happened to Miguel?" Beth says, looking concerned for her friend.

"It was just a flesh wound," Shane says. "He's fine, I promise."

"He was shot?" She sounds horrified.

"Yes." Shane looks to me. "Tyler caught the serial killer targeting gay men here in Chicago. There was an altercation. Shots were fired. Miguel's shoulder was grazed."

"And the killer?" Sam says.

"He's dead," I say, and then I swallow the last of my drink.

"Whoa," Sam says, his eyes widening. He goes to pour me another shot, but then hesitates. "Are you driving?"

"No, I'm staying here tonight."

"Good. Then let me buy you a drink." Sam pours another shot of whiskey into my glass and offers me a toast. "Way to go, detective!"

"Thanks."

Cooper takes his rightful place behind the bar as the official family bartender.

I envy Sam and Cooper. They're so in sync with each other. They're happy—engaged to be married even. It wasn't always smooth sailing for them, but they managed to work through their differences. They make it look so easy. I'm afraid it'll never be easy for me.

Cooper pops open a bottle of beer and hands it to Shane, and then he offers a toast. "To Tyler, for putting an end to a hellish nightmare." Cooper lifts his own beer bottle, and we toast. "Was it the guy you arrested?"

I shake my head. "No. The killer turned out to be that guy's former lover, the guy who owned Diablo's."

"Holy crap," Sam says. "Roy Valdez?"

I nod and take a sip of my whiskey. "You knew him?"

Sam shakes his head. "Not personally, but I remember him from the club. He was often behind the bar. I used to hang out at Diablo's quite a bit before settling down with this guy." He tips his head to Cooper and gives his partner a smile.

I realize I will never find a more sympathetic audience than this one. "There's something I need to say."

Beth meets my gaze, fresh tears forming in her eyes as she gives me an encouraging smile.

I swallow hard and take a deep breath, probably one of many to come. "This isn't easy for me to say." Everyone's still, waiting for me to explain. If I can't be honest with my family and with two gay men who might as well be family, I'm screwed.

Patiently, they wait.

Beth reaches for my hand and squeezes it. "It's okay. I promise."

I stare down at my tumbler, swirling the amber liquid in my glass, avoiding eye contact. Finally, I lift my gaze to Cooper. If anyone understands where I'm coming from, he does. It wasn't that long ago that he came out publicly. "I'm gay."

My announcement is met by stark silence.

Cooper is the first one to break it. "Well, I'll be damned. I didn't see that coming. You'd think I would have, but I didn't."

Sam laughs as he raises his bottle to me and winks. "Oh, hell, I knew all along."

"You did not," Cooper says in exasperation. He reaches across the bar to grab Sam's t-shirt and pull him close for a kiss. Then, to me, he says, "Welcome to the club, pal."

Shane eyes me with a curious expression. I have no idea what he's thinking, but clearly his response isn't hostile.

I breathe easier as yet another weight is lifted from my chest. But a more difficult announcement will come tomorrow, when I face my mother and tell her the truth. And after that—I have to face the hardest task of all.

I have to apologize to Ian and hope he forgives me.

༄ 21

Tyler Jamison

As the early morning light filters into my room through floor-to-ceiling windows, I lie awake and stare at the ceiling. I have a bit of a hangover from last night, but it's nothing more than I deserve.

I hardly slept last night. I lay in bed for hours, reliving the encounter with Ian over and over in my head. Without a doubt, that was the most intense sexual pleasure I've ever experienced in my life. Lots of women have given me head, but it never felt anything like that.

I remember gazing down at Ian, mesmerized by the sight of

his long fingers wrapped around my cock, his hot tongue and lips stroking me, his chiseled jaw covered by a trim beard. I remember gripping his head hard, holding him in place while I fucked him without mercy.

I was fully aware every second that it was a man who'd taken me into his mouth. And dear God, he took me all the way to the back of his throat. I don't understand why it was so different when it was a man on his knees in front of me, instead of a woman. His touch was different than a woman's. Harder, rougher. I nearly lost my fucking mind. Hell, I *did* lose my mind.

All I could think was that I wanted *more*. So damn much more.

My mind bounces back and forth between memories of exquisite pleasure and feelings of abject shame for how I treated Ian. I wouldn't blame him if he never wanted to see me again.

I'm numb. There's no other way to describe it. The ground is falling out from beneath my feet, and everything I thought I knew is now in question. I'm in a freefall.

I'm gay.

There's no point in denying it any longer. I had oral sex with a man, and it was the most earth-shattering sexual experience of my life. I think it's fair to say Ian rocked my world last night. As cliché as that sounds, it's the truth.

And how did I treat him afterward? I walked out on him. I used him, abused him, and then I disrespected him in the worst way possible. I don't know if he'll ever forgive me. I wouldn't blame him if he didn't.

Just thinking about what I did with Ian last night has me hard as a rock. And it was only a blow job! I can't imagine what it would be like to do more—to hold him, touch him, kiss him.

Damn it, I want more.

I head for the bathroom and, after emptying my bladder, I step into the fancy walk-in shower with its Italian travertine marble tiles and multiple shower heads. The water is instantly hot, and as I step beneath the spray, I close my eyes and groan.

What I remember most from last night is Ian's grip on my cock. It was a man's grip, and it blew my mind. Everything about him blows my mind—his touch, his scent, the texture of his skin, his hair, his jawline covered in scruff, his muscles and tendons. Everything about him is *masculine*. And why does that make such a big fucking difference to my brain? To my body? What makes me crave him and his touch, when the touch of a woman does nothing for me?

I close my eyes and let the hot water beat against my body. Steam rises around me, shrouding me in a private world where I can admit these feelings.

After showering, I dress in my slightly rumpled suit and head to the great room. Shane and Sam are already seated at the dining room table. Luke sits in his highchair, his little fingers chasing bits of scrambled egg across the tray. Shane offers him a spoonful of baby cereal.

My nephew is almost a year old. His birthday is in a few weeks, and there's going to be a big family celebration here at the penthouse. I'll be here for the event, of course. I wouldn't miss his birthday for anything. For a moment, I wonder how everyone would react if I brought someone with me to the party.

I've never brought a date to a family event. I always knew that if I did, they'd mentally have us engaged and ready to walk down the aisle. I could never have done that. I never wanted to give any woman the impression that we were more than what we really were. For a second, I imagine bringing Ian. The thought makes me smile. Ian would be thrilled.

Luke picks up his sippy cup with both hands, takes a noisy sip, then bangs it against his tray. He gazes up at Shane, waving his cup. "Dada! Dada!"

Grinning, Shane cups the back of Luke's pale blond head. "I'm here, buddy."

Luke hands his cup to Shane, and Shane pretends to take a sip before handing it back.

I owe my brother-in-law a huge apology. When I first found out he was involved with my sister, I was furious. I accused him of taking advantage of her. She's so much younger than he is, and she was so emotionally fragile when they first met. To be honest, I was an ass to him. But now, seeing how he is with her, and how he is with their son, I realize how wrong I was.

Beth approaches the table holding two cups of coffee. She sets one down in front of Shane and takes a sip of the other one. "Good morning," she says, smiling at me. "I hope you slept well."

I nod. "I did. Thanks." *Not really.*

"Can I get you some coffee?"

"Coffee would be great."

Sam rises from the table. "Sit down, Beth. I'm heading to the kitchen. I'll get his coffee." Then to me, he points at the open seat beside Beth. "Sit, detective. Relax."

As soon as I sit, Beth eyes me curiously. "How are you *really*?"

I shrug. "As well as can be expected, I guess."

She reaches over to squeeze my hand. "You have nothing to worry about. Mom loves you, and nothing could ever change that. Believe me, she just wants you to be happy. Same as I do."

Luke reaches for Beth. "Mum-mum-mum!"

She cuts the leafy stem off a fresh strawberry and dices the fruit before placing the pieces on his tray. Immediately, he grabs the tiny bits and crams them into his mouth.

Beth laughs. "I don't know why I bother to cut up his food because he shoves everything into his mouth all at once." She watches him chew, making sure he doesn't choke. To me, she says, "Joe will be here at eight-thirty to drive us to Mom's. I figured we should drive separately so we can go on to Clancy's afterwards, and you can go to work."

By *us*, she means herself, Sam, and Luke. As her full-time bodyguard, Sam goes wherever Beth goes, unless she's with Shane. Beth brings Luke with her to Clancy's Bookshop—the downtown Chicago business she owns and manages. She has a nursery attached to her office and a full-time nanny to take care of Luke. Joe Rucker is my sister's chauffeur.

I ask her, "Have you talked to Mom this morning?"

Beth nods. "I called a little while ago and asked if we could come over this morning. She said yes, of course, but the request put her on alert. She asked me what was wrong."

"What did you tell her?"

"I told her nothing was wrong. We just wanted to stop by for a visit."

Of course she suspects something is wrong. We never stop by on a weekday morning, out of the blue, for a social visit. Especially not both of us at one time.

A cup of black coffee appears on the table in front of me. I glance back to see Cooper standing behind me. "Thanks, Cooper."

He nods. "No problem. Can I get you something to eat?"

"No, thank you. My appetite is shot to hell."

Cooper clasps my shoulder and gives me an encouraging squeeze. "Stop worrying. It's going to be fine."

Sam carries in two plates of food, one for himself and one for Cooper. They sit on the opposite side of the table. Sam steals a piece of bacon from Cooper's plate, earning a look of amused reproach from his partner.

"Ingrid loves you," Cooper says to me. "She doesn't care about your sexual orientation. She just wants both of her kids to be happy."

Just as we're wrapping up breakfast, the elevator chimes. Joe Rucker walks into the penthouse apartment. The man is intimidating, I'll give him that. He's nearly six feet tall, broad shouldered, with arms that haven't gone soft since he retired from heavyweight boxing. The man clearly still works out. His white hair is buzzed short, contrasting dramatically with his brown skin.

He walks over to the table just as Beth rises from her seat. "Hi,

Joe. I'll be ready in a minute. I just need to brush my teeth."

As she races off, Shane washes Luke's hands and face and lifts him out of his highchair. He kisses the baby's temple, nuzzling him for a moment as the baby grips Shane's shirt. Shane laughs as Luke makes a grab for his face. Then Shane makes a comical face, which in turn makes Luke laugh. "If you'll excuse us, somebody needs a diaper change. We'll be right back."

"Hello, Detective," Joe says to me in his deep, resonant voice.

In his late fifties, Joe is old school, respectful, with southern charm and manners. He's almost old enough to be my dad, but he treats me with deference. I stand, and we shake hands.

His grip is firm and confident. "Miss Beth told me we're taking a detour this morning to the family compound, to see your mother. I hope Miss Ingrid is well."

"Yes, she's fine."

He nods. "I'm glad to hear it."

Sam rises from the table, wiping his mouth on a napkin. "I'll be ready to go in a minute." And then he disappears down the hallway that leads to the suite he shares with Cooper.

I help Cooper clear the dirty dishes from the table and carry them to the kitchen sink.

It's not long before everyone's ready to go. I head down to the parking garage with the others. Everyone loads into the Escalade, and I follow them to Lincoln Park in my car.

Shane bought a brand-new residential development a while back, a private, gated community that currently consists of four homes, all belonging to McIntyre family members. The only exception is my mom. She lives here as well, certainly considered to be part of the family.

Shane's parents have a house here, as does Shane's brother, Jake, along with his wife and three young children. Shane's pain-in-the-ass little sister, Lia, lives here with her fiancé, heart-throb and singer-songwriter Jonah Locke. And lastly, my mother has a small bungalow here.

Since the community is gated, with security guards monitoring the only entrance twenty-four/seven, the family members have more freedom here than they would elsewhere. Even Jonah can move about freely in this compound without fear of being swarmed by mobs of hysterical teenage girls.

The guard lets us in, and Joe pulls up to the curb in front of Mom's house to let everyone out. I park behind them. Sam and Luke head across the street to visit Jake's wife—Annie—and the kids, while Beth and I walk up to Mom's front porch.

Mom meets us at the door, opening it before we have a chance to ring the bell. She has a wary smile on her face. "Hello, my darlings," she says, opening the door wide and motioning us inside. She hugs Beth first, holding her daughter carefully, so as not to put pressure on her burgeoning belly.

Mom releases Beth and eyes me with concern. "Hello, honey." She pulls me into her arms. When she releases me, her gaze goes from me to my sister, then back to me. "All right, what's wrong?"

I smile. "Does something have to be wrong for us to visit you?"

She motions for us to follow her down the hallway to the rear of the house, where a small kitchen and sitting room are located.

The rear windows look out over a small duck pond and a white gazebo. "It's nine o'clock on a weekday morning, when both of you would normally be at work. I'd say something is wrong."

"It's nothing for you to worry about, Mom," Beth says as she sits on a sofa.

Mom stands hovering. "Can I get either of you something to drink? Coffee? Or tea? Anything?"

Beth shakes her head. "We just ate. I'm fine."

My chest tightens at the thought of telling my mother the truth. "Nothing, Mom, thanks."

Mom sits next to Beth and reaches out to tuck my sister's hair behind her ear. "Luke's okay?" And then she glances down at Beth's rounded belly. "The baby's fine?"

"Yes, they're both fine," Beth says.

"I heard the news this morning," Mom says, directing her attention back to me. "I heard about what happened at the marina last night. I'm glad you caught that awful murderer. Is that why you're here? You didn't get hurt, did you?" She scans me from head to toe, looking for signs of an injury.

Clearly, my mom knows something's up, so I can't draw this out any longer. It's just making her more and more anxious. I brace myself because there's no going back. "Mom, there's something I need to tell you."

I glance at Beth, whose eyes are glittering with unshed tears.

Mom notices too, because she takes Beth's hand in hers. Her voice shakes when she says, "Come on, guys. Please tell me what's wrong."

As I stand facing my mother and sister, I feel like I'm facing a firing squad. My eyes sting as tears form. "Mom, I..." I take a steadying breath as my throat tightens into a tight knot. I meet her pained gaze head-on. "This isn't easy for me to say."

She swallows hard, her own eyes tearing up. I'm sure she can count on one hand the number of times she's seen me this emotional. "Just say it, honey. Whatever it is, just say it. You know I love you."

"The last thing I want to do is disappoint you."

"Oh, honey, you could never disappoint me."

Tears are streaming down her cheeks now, and I feel like shit for upsetting her. There's no easy way to rip this band-aid off. I just need to say it.

"Mom, I'm gay."

22

Tyler Jamison

My mom's eyes widen, and it's pretty clear I took her completely by surprise. She stares at me for a moment, and then she shoots to her feet and rushes to me, enveloping me in her arms. She holds me tight, her arms like iron bands around my waist, and she sobs into my shirt. As I hold her, I look over at my sister who's quietly crying, a sofa pillow clutched to her chest.

I lean down and kiss the top of my mother's head. "Mom, I'm so sorry."

She pulls back to look at me. "Why are you apologizing?"

"For upsetting you. For disappointing you."

"Tyler, sweetheart, I'm not upset. And I'm certainly not disappointed! I was *scared*, honey. Scared that something bad had happened to you, or to Beth, or to my grandbabies." Her expression falls. "Tyler, if anyone should apologize, it's me."

"You? What for?"

"Honey." She sighs, like mothers do. "I've always suspected you were gay, since you were a teenager. Your father and I both suspected it."

Her admission knocks the wind out of me. "You did?"

She nods. "Yes. But then, later in high school, you started dating *girls*, and we just assumed we were wrong."

"I've—" I stop and swallow hard, squeezing shut my burning eyes. Taking a deep breath, I forge ahead, wanting to get it all out there. "I've always struggled with relationships. I've dated so many women in my life. I tried so hard to make it work, but it just didn't. I always felt so alone, even when I was with someone. I finally decided I'd rather be alone—I'd rather be *lonely*—than be with someone and feel nothing."

She reaches up and brushes my hair. "You know I love you, and your sexual orientation could never change that." She takes my hands in hers and brings them to her lips, kissing my knuckles. "What changed? Why are you telling me this now?"

"I met someone."

She smiles through her tears. "Really?"

I laugh shakily. "Yeah. He's... pretty amazing."

"That's wonderful, honey. I just want you to be happy, Tyler.

That's all I've ever wanted. That's all your father wanted, for you two kids to be happy."

She's so sincere, so accepting, I am floored. I shudder in relief, overwhelmed by my emotions. She pulls me into her arms again and holds me, and I can feel her shaking. Beth joins us, and the three of us embrace.

Finally, Mom releases us and says to me, "So, who is this gentleman friend of yours, and when do I get to meet him?"

I laugh. "I'm afraid that's a bit premature. I only just met him recently, and well, I think I screwed up my chances with him. I'm not sure he'll want to see me again."

"Of course he'll want to see you again," Mom says, reaching up to touch my face. "You're an amazing man, Tyler. If he has half a brain in his head, he'll realize that."

Chuckling, I lean down and kiss my mom's temple. "You're a formidable ally, Mom. Thank you."

She smiles. "So, when do I get to meet him?"

"Sometime soon, I hope. If he's still talking to me."

She laughs. "Don't be silly. You're a catch. Now, where's my grandson? I need some cuddling."

Beth wipes her damp cheeks and gives us a watery smile. "Sam took him across the street to visit Annie and the kids."

"Well, call them over. I want to see my grandbaby."

Beth texts Sam, giving him the all-clear to join us. A few moments later, there's a knock at the front door. I follow Mom to the door, and when she opens it, Sam and Luke are there, along with Joe Rucker.

"Is the coast clear?" Sam says, winking at me as he carries Luke inside.

I roll my eyes at the smug grin on his face. "Yes. It's safe to come in."

Joe stands on the front porch, his hands stuffed into his pockets. He nods hesitantly at my mother. "Miss Ingrid," he says in a quiet, deep voice.

As Mom finally turns her attention to Joe, her cheeks flush. "Hello, Joe. Won't you please come in?"

He steps inside. "Yes, ma'am. Thank you."

Mom turns and follows Sam into the house, anxious to get her hands on her grandson. Joe remains at the door, his gaze locked on my mother's retreating form. I observe him watching my mother, and there's no mistaking the hint of adoration in his eyes.

I can see how he'd be taken by her. She is a beautiful woman. Age has only accentuated her beauty. Tall and willowy, like Beth. It's a shame she never found love again after my dad died. But I think that was her choice. She could never move past the memory of my father.

"I told you there was nothing to worry about," Sam says to me as he rejoins us in the foyer. He fist-bumps my shoulder. "Your mom is da bomb."

While Mom coos and cuddles with the baby, I continue to observe Joe, who's still keeping a low profile. Pretending not to, he watches my mom intently as she loves on her grandson. The heat in Joe's watchful gaze is palpable, and I wonder if my mom is aware of his interest.

When he catches me observing him, he smiles, looking a bit sheepish. "I'll wait in the Escalade," he says as he opens the front door. "Let Miss Beth know I'm ready whenever she is."

"Leave Luke with me today," Mom says to Beth. "I'll watch him while you're at work."

While they work out the childcare details, I say my goodbyes and take my leave. There are things I need to handle at work before I'm free to see Ian again. I have reports to write and file. I should have done that last night, immediately after the shooting, but life got in the way, and I had a bit of a melt-down. I've got to take care of that now before Captain Walker sends the troops out after me.

* * *

I head to the precinct office and hole up in my office with the door closed. I write my reports, documenting everything that happened yesterday, from executing the search warrant at Valdez's apartment to the events that occurred at the marina. I check on the disposition of the evidence that was obtained yesterday at Valdez's apartment. I review the witness statements. There were three civilian witnesses who offered statements at the scene last night. Fortunately, two of them used their phones to record the events that occurred on Ian's boat.

I'm anxious to get out of here, so I can talk to Ian. But Captain Walker asks me to hang around for a departmental review meeting on the shooting death of Valdez, scheduled for early after-noon. There are processes that have to be followed, procedures, an internal investigation. It's all standard operating procedure.

According to the coroner's report, Valdez was struck three times in the chest. A forensics exam has concluded that two of those shots were mine, and one was Miguel's. It was one of my bullets that hit Valdez directly in the heart and ended his life. I was justified in taking that shot—he was actively firing at fellow police officers as well as at me and Miguel—but still, there will be an investigation. That's fine. I'm not concerned about that.

All afternoon, my thoughts drift to Ian, and I wonder what he's doing today, what he's thinking. I wonder how he feels about last night and the way I treated him. When I think about how rough I was with him, I'm ashamed by my loss of control.

Finally, after the incident review meeting, after all the reports have been written and submitted, and after all the questions have been asked and answered in triplicate, Walker clears me to leave the building.

It's early evening now and there's only one thing on my mind. Getting to *Ian*. I need to see him. I need to face him. And I hope to God he accepts my apology.

I head home first, to shower and change into clean clothes. I dress casually, in a pair of ripped jeans my sister got me for Christ-mas last year. She said they were *cool*, and that I needed to *let my hair down once in a while*. I guess now is as good a time as any.

I dab on a bit of cologne and a form-fitting black tee that I've been told looks good on me. I laugh at myself when I realize this is the first time I've made an effort to look good for someone.

I reach for my gun holster and my jacket, and then I'm out the door. Tonight, I'll do whatever it takes to make things right with Ian.

Ian's house is dark when I pull into the driveway. I shut off my engine and sit there for a moment, trying to psych myself up for this. My hands are shaking. *Shit, I'm actually nervous.*

I walk up the stone steps to his door and knock, but there's no answer. I guess I'm not entirely surprised as the house is dark. I knock again. I suppose he could be inside and simply ignoring me. I wouldn't blame him if he was. There's still no answer.

I walk around to the carriage house in the back and peer through the windows. It's empty. He's not home. I could leave and come back later, or I could come back tomorrow. But instead, I end up back at his front door where I take a seat on the top step. I'm not leaving until I see him. I'll wait as long as it takes.

I have a lot of time on my hands to think, which isn't good. I try not to speculate on where he might be, or what he's doing. Or, God forbid, whom he might be with. He's young and headstrong and a bit impetuous, and I imagine he's fed up with me. I worry that the combination of those things might drive him to seek attention elsewhere.

If he's out clubbing tonight, I'm sure he's not lacking for offers. He attracts men like moths to a flame. The thought of him being with someone else sucks the air right out of my lungs, leaving me feeling more than a bit panicked. It almost feels like... *jealousy.*

Finally, just as it's getting dark, he pulls into his driveway, the headlights of his Porsche flashing across the front lawn and momentarily across me. He continues on back to the carriage house, and I hear the garage door opening and then closing. I remain fixed to my spot on the top step, my heart pounding as I wait for him to appear.

When he steps into view, at the base of the stoop, my heart lurches painfully. He stares up at me with a guarded expression. I can't tell what he's thinking, and that unnerves me. I've finally found someone who makes me feel something, and I'm afraid it might be too late. I have no idea what I'm doing, and I'm scared shitless.

I stand and face him, my hands in my pockets, my heart in my throat. I'm not sure what to say.

I'm sorry I was an ass?

I'm sorry I walked out on you last night?

I have no idea what I'm doing?

I have no idea how to do this. "Hello, Ian."

He nods, still looking wary. "Tyler. What are you doing here?"

There's no use beating around the bush, so I plow ahead. "I came to… can we talk?"

His eyes widen a bit in surprise, and I think I caught him off guard. Maybe he assumed I was here on official police business.

"Sure, we can talk," he says. But he makes no move to climb the steps.

"Inside?" I say, nodding toward the door.

23

Ian Alexander

Tyler looked so fucking lost sitting there on my stoop. Seeing him like that, I could have cried. He looked nothing like his usual bossy, opinionated self. I didn't know what to think.

Now, I'm trying not to let myself get too excited about why he's here. *Can we talk?* That isn't something cops say when they want to discuss a case or interview a witness. No, this sounds *personal*. Personal, as in between the two of us.

As I climb the steps, his gaze remains locked on me, wary, unsure. How the hell can this guy be unsure about anything? I've never met a more charismatic, dominant personality in my life.

Once I reach the top step, I fish my keys out of my front pocket and unlock the door. He pushes the door open and holds it for me, motioning for me to enter first.

My mind is reeling because I have no idea why he's here. He made his feelings known last night. Is he here to lecture me on sexual harassment? Or better yet, arrest me for assaulting an officer?

I shouldn't have done what I did last night. "I owe you an apology." I throw that out quickly before he has a chance to say anything.

He shuts the door and throws the dead-bolt. His brow furrows in confusion. "You have nothing to apologize for."

"How about for taking advantage of you last night after you'd just shot and killed a man on my behalf? Does that ring a bell?"

He fights a grin. "Ian, no—"

"I'm sorry for what I did last night. It was a shitty thing to do."

Looking bewildered, Tyler shakes his head. "Ian, I'm the one who's sorry."

"You?" I thought he was here to read me the riot act. Now he's apologizing?

He stands ramrod straight, stiff and uncomfortable. "Yes. For the way I behaved last night. For the way I used you and then walked out. It was inexcusable."

Tyler looks utterly disgusted with himself, and I can't stop smiling. He's apologizing for using *me? Oh, dear Lord, the sweet fool.* "No, Tyler. You didn't *use* me. You *fucked* me—well, you fucked my mouth. I wanted you to. I wanted exactly what you gave me. I pushed you into it. You have nothing to apologize for."

The look on his face is priceless—a little bit shocked, a little bit surprised, and a whole lot of hopeful. I step closer and take hold of the edges of his jacket so I can pull him closer. I lower my voice. "Baby, you didn't *use* me." I watch his expression shift as my words sink in. "I loved every minute of it."

"I—" He stops, clearly shaken. "I did, too."

My chest seizes at his unexpected admission. I never dreamed he'd say anything like that. Maybe there's still a chance. "Tyler, I've never wanted anyone as much as I wanted you last night."

I stare at his lips, which part on a quick breath. His nostrils flare, and I'm pretty sure he's remembering last night and *letting* himself feel arousal, and it's such a turn-on. I want a repeat of last night. Hell, I want a whole lot more than what we did last night. I want *everything* with him.

As I gaze into a pair of eyes reminiscent of a deep Caribbean pool, I'm lost. He's so beautiful. Midnight-dark hair and beard, sun-kissed golden skin. And he looks so damn nervous. I can't believe I have this kind of effect on him.

My heart starts pounding, and my nerve endings tingle. We stand face-to-face, just the two of us alone in the house. I press my hand to his chest, right over his sternum, and I swear I can feel his heart pounding. Just like mine.

I want him so badly.

But I learned my lesson last night. I don't want him freaking out on me again. *Baby steps with this guy,* I remind myself. *Baby steps.* "Can I get you a drink?" I nod toward the parlor. "I'll even break out the good stuff, just for you."

He nods. "I could sure use a drink right now."

You and me both, gorgeous. I release his jacket and head for the bar to grab two glasses and a bottle of my best Glenfiddich. He sits on a barstool across from me and watches me pour a neat shot into each glass. I hand him one and lift mine for a toast.

"What are we toasting to?" he says.

"How about a fresh start? A do-over."

He smiles as he touches his glass to mine. "I'll drink to that." And then he takes a biting sip. I watch his Adam's apple bob as he swallows. When he licks his bottom lip, my belly tightens, and my cock throbs.

Baby steps, I remind myself. *Don't fuck this up!*

I lean forward on the bar. "So, Tyler..." I pour him another shot. "Have you ever been attracted to a man?"

He gives me a *duh* look.

"I mean, besides me. Surely your body reacted in the past when you saw men... in movies, in magazines, in the locker room at school? Or maybe at work? Hell, when I was a teenager, I'd get a hard-on watching shaving commercials on TV. Guys with beards really do it for me." I give him a pointed look.

He stares down at his glass. "I tried not to think about it."

"That's a shitty way to live."

He shrugs. "I was used to it."

I'm dying to walk around to his side of the bar, pull him into my arms, and kiss the hell out of him—show him what he's been missing.

I do walk around the bar, but not to jump him. He watches me intently, his gaze so damn wary it kills me. He turns on his barstool to face me.

I stop just inches away from him. "In case you haven't noticed, I'm really attracted to you, Tyler."

He fights a grin. "I've noticed."

I reach out and gently cup his face, my thumb brushing across his cheek. "I'd really love to kiss you right now."

He blinks in response, and I can't help smiling. We *are* starting over. I'm going to get another chance to do this right. I hold my breath as I wait for his reply.

He swallows hard. "I don't know how to do this."

"You don't know how to kiss?" I laugh. "You've kissed women before, right?"

"Yes, but that was different."

"I know. That's the whole point."

He smiles as he runs a hand through his hair, clearly nervous as hell.

I take the final step which brings me to stand between his spread knees. "Well, it pretty much works the same way when it's two guys. My lips against yours. Yours against mine. It's that simple."

Tyler's gaze goes to my mouth, and he sucks in a shaky breath. "You make it sound so easy."

"It is." I reach out and run my fingers through his hair, loving the feel of the strands sliding between my fingers.

He closes his eyes and groans.

When his eyes open again, I search his gaze. "Can you trust me? Can you do that?"

He rises to his feet and, we face each other. I swear to God he looks like he's about to face an execution.

I slide one hand around to the back of his neck, my fingers threading through his hair. When I scrape my nails along his scalp, he shivers.

Slowly, I lean in until our lips brush lightly. He sucks in a sharp breath, his body tensing. My lips gently coax his open, and I press closer. I nudge his lips wider apart, and my tongue slips inside, just barely grazing his. I taste whiskey and spice. Our tongues meet timidly, our lips sliding over each other's.

When he closes his eyes and moans, my cock swells.

Baby steps. I step back with a pleased smile. "See, it *is* that easy."

He lets out a heavy breath.

"Let's start over, okay?" I say. "We're just two guys getting to know each other." I reach for his hand, his fingers warm and rough against mine. "Have dinner with me tonight."

He nods. "I'd like that."

"Do you cook?"

"Just the basics. I know enough not to starve."

He's still so damn nervous. Reality hits me. *He's a virgin.* No matter how many women he's been with, right now he's a virgin. *Jesus.* The thought of being his first is heady.

I want that. I want to be his first. "Let's cook dinner together. We can eat up on the roof, beneath the stars. How does that sound?"

"That sounds great."

I lean in and kiss him again, simply because I can't resist looking at that face and not kissing it. This time he eagerly kisses me back.

A weight lifts off my chest.

Maybe there's hope for us after all.

* * *

"How about pasta?" I say when we're in my kitchen.

"Sure. That's one thing I do know how to make."

He's already removed his leather jacket and hung it in the hall closet, along with his gun and holster. His t-shirt hugs his torso, outlining how fit he is and showcasing biceps that strain against the fabric. My gaze follows the veins that snake down his arms to his wrists. *Fuck.* I'm a sucker for arm porn, and he's got it in spades.

"Red sauce or white?" I ask him.

"Red."

"Garlic bread? Salad?"

"Yes to both."

"And a bottle of red wine."

He smiles. "I didn't realize you were such a culinary expert."

"My mom made me and my sister take cooking classes when we were teens. She said she'd sleep better at night knowing we knew how to feed ourselves."

"Smart lady."

"How about your mom?" I ask him. "Does she like to cook?"

"She's an amazing cook. I learned out of necessity—being a bachelor and all—but my sister can't boil water. Her husband can't cook either, but they don't have to. They have someone who does all the cooking for them. They're spoiled rotten."

"They have a cook?"

He laughs. "Not exactly. Cooper is my brother-in-law's best friend and business partner. My sister and her husband share the penthouse floor of their apartment building with Cooper and his partner, Sam."

My brows rise. "A gay couple?"

"Yeah." Then he sobers. "Last night, after I left you, I went to my sister. I told her I was gay."

"Whoa."

"Yeah. After last night—after what we did—I couldn't deny it any longer. And this morning, she and I paid a visit to our mother. I told her."

"How did they take it?"

"They were great. I knew my sister would be okay with it—Sam and Cooper are like family to her. I was more worried about my mom's reaction." He shakes his head. "She said she and my dad always suspected I was gay, but when I started dating girls in high school, they thought they must have been wrong."

"Why did you date girls, if you weren't into them?"

He shrugs. "I wanted to fit in. And because I couldn't contemplate any other alternative, especially after my dad died. I was eighteen. My mom needed me, as did my baby sister. I couldn't let them down." He runs his fingers through his hair. "I couldn't let my dad down."

"So, instead you carried the weight of the world on your shoulders for...what? Decades?"

He nods. "Pretty much."

"What about what *you* wanted? What about your needs?"

"That didn't matter."

I put a pot of water on the stove to boil and then join him at the kitchen island, where he's cutting up veggies for a salad. I stand close, my shoulder brushing against his. When he tenses, I step back.

He's not used to being touched.

"I know this scares you," I say.

"You have no idea."

"It scares me, too. Last night, when I went down on you, it was the hottest fucking thing I'd ever experienced."

He swallows hard. "I lost control, Ian. I was mindless."

"I know, and I liked it." I lean over and kiss his shoulder. "I'm not afraid of a hard fuck. I like it."

"When I saw you on your knees like that, I went a little nuts. Nothing's ever felt that good before."

"You just wait," I say, grabbing a slice of cucumber off the cutting board and popping it in my mouth. "The best is yet to come."

We finish our preparations and carry our food, two wine glasses, and the most expensive bottle of Cabernet Sauvignon I have up to the roof to eat in the greenhouse.

He follows me through the door that leads into the greenhouse. I flip the light switch, turning on a multitude of fairy lights strung overhead, all throughout the greenhouse.

The greenhouse is completely enclosed, attached to the stone exterior of the building and protected from weather. It's a lush, tropical escape filled with ferns, flowers, and potted trees that loom high overhead providing plenty of privacy.

While I set out our dinner on a round bistro table, Tyler tours the greenhouse.

"This is incredible," he says as he wanders around, taking it all in. He strolls past the small koi pond and fountain, and he pauses to look at the pillow and blanket lying on a futon sofa. "Is it climate controlled?"

"Yeah. I sleep up here sometimes, year-round. It's my escape when I feel cooped up."

It's too dark outside now to see the lake, but the stars are readily visible in the clear, cloudless sky. Plus, we have a perfect view of the Chicago city skyline as it juts out past Lake Shore Drive toward Navy Pier.

He joins me at the table. I open the wine and pour us both glasses.

"Is everything okay at work?" I ask him, midway through our meal. "Will there be any fallout from the shooting yesterday? Surely it was justified."

"It was. There's an investigation into the shooting, but that's standard procedure. It's nothing to worry about." Then he looks across the little table at me. "How about you? Are *you* okay?"

I nod. "Yeah, I'm okay. I just hated that Miguel was taking all the risk. I should have been up there, too, helping him."

"Miguel was doing his job. That's how it had to be."

"I still didn't like it. I'm not helpless, you know."

Tyler reaches out to squeeze my shoulder. "I know you're not."

* * *

After we finish eating, we carry our plates down to the kitchen. I clear off the plates and put them in the dishwasher. Tyler puts the leftover pasta in a storage container and sticks it in the fridge. It's all very domestic.

After we finish cleaning up, I pour us each another glass of wine.

This evening is a first for me, too. I'm used to hooking up at clubs, getting picked up and having quickies in the bathroom or in dark closets. I've had a lot of one-night stands, but I've always been careful. I've never had a guy at my house. I've never made anyone dinner before, and I've certainly never tried to woo someone. This feels different, and I like it.

I hand Tyler his glass. "Would you like to sit in the living room and relax? We could watch a movie."

He sets his glass on the kitchen counter and steps closer, his hands cupping my face. "I don't want to watch a movie."

The way he's looking at me sends a shiver down my spine, and my belly clenches in anticipation. "Then what do you want to do?"

"This." His thumb brushes the top of my cheek and his gaze lowers to my mouth. And then he kisses me.

He kisses *me!*

His lips nudge mine open, and then his tongue is inside my mouth, sliding against mine. He slides his hand down to grip my waist as he pulls me closer. His other hand slips behind my head, his fingers in my hair. My blood runs south, and my cock throbs.

His voice is rough and matter-of-fact. "If I do or say anything wrong, tell me. I'm flying by the seat of my pants here, and I don't want to fuck this up."

❧ 24

Tyler Jamison

Maybe it's the wine lowering my inhibitions. Or maybe it's the fact that two people who mean the world to me gave me permission to be happy. Apparently, my happiness hinges on having Ian Alexander in my arms, our mouths locked together. Our breath mingling. Our groans reverberating in our chests.

Suddenly, I'm desperate to know what it feels like to be with someone I want, not someone I *thought* I should want. Everything about Ian turns me on—the texture of his skin, the scratch of his beard against my palms and lips, the way he smells, the way he tastes, his rough, low groans.

I'm tired of fighting myself and denying what feels good. I'm tired of the guilt, the shame. I just want to embrace it.

I'm hard as a rock right now, my erection pressing against the front of my jeans. I lean into him, letting him feel my desire. I grind my erection against his.

Ian lets out a ragged moan and clutches my arms, his fingers digging into my biceps. "Tyler!" He reaches for the hem of his t-shirt and whips it off, dropping it to the floor.

I stare at his chest, unable to look away. He's leanly muscled, his torso tanned from spending time in the sun. His chest is smooth, and the sight of his pierced nipples makes my cock throb. My gaze locks on the line of hair running down from his naval, disappearing beneath the waistband of his jeans.

God, I want this. I want to taste him. I want him in my mouth. I want to make him come. I want to *fuck* him.

I whip my t-shirt off and toss it aside. I'm no gym rat, but I do work out. My shoulders and arms are bigger than his, my chest broader, and I outweigh him by at least twenty pounds. When I face him bare-chested, he stares at me with a hunger that makes my heart pound.

I slip my arms around his waist and draw him closer, until our chests are touching. I gently brush my nipples against his piercings, and he shivers.

"I got head the last time," I say. "It's your turn."

"No one's keeping score," he says, despite the glitter of excitement in his eyes.

I don't know where we're doing this, but it's not going to be in the kitchen. "Where to?"

He takes my hand and leads me down the hall, toward the parlor. "In here," he says, pointing to a room across the hall.

I steer him into a much larger room that's furnished with a couple of sofas, some upholstered chairs, a whole wall of bookcases filled with books, and a fireplace.

I walk him over to one of the sofas and reach for his belt buckle.

He grabs my hands. "Tyler, you don't have to do this."

"Hush," I say as I pull his belt free. "I want to." I can see that he's hard as a rock, his face flushed with arousal. He wants this as much as I do.

"It's not a competition," he says.

I meet his gaze. "I know that. I *want* to do this. Are you saying you don't want me to give you head?"

"Oh, hell no!" he says, laughing as he slides his warm hands up my chest. "I want anything and everything you're willing to give me. I'm just—I don't want to rush you. That didn't work out too well for us the last time."

"I want this, Ian. I want you in my mouth. I want to make you come, *hard*. Do you have a problem with that?"

Ian's eyes practically roll back in his head. "You're killing me."

I sit on the sofa and pull him to stand between my legs. "Don't get too excited. I've never done this before, and I may suck at it."

Ian laughs as he threads his fingers through my hair. "Somehow, I don't think that's likely. We're only *talking* about it, and I'm already on the edge."

I unsnap Ian's jeans and lower his zipper, careful not to catch his erection. *Damn.* He packs a lot in his briefs. When I tug his jeans halfway down his thighs, the warm scent of him wafts out at me and my belly clenches tightly.

As I trace the outline of his erection with my finger, a damp spot appears on the fabric of his briefs. He's excited, already leaking pre-cum. I smile, pleased that I'm affecting him like this. I want to turn him on. I want to make him hungry and desperate, like I was last night. Maybe I am keeping score, after all.

I pull his briefs down, freeing his erection. He's thick and long, crowned with a beautiful ruddy head, the tip glistening with pre-cum. My heart jackhammers in my chest as I stare at him. *God, I want to get this right.*

I wrap my fingers around him, near the base, my fist brushing up against his wiry hair. *Jesus.* The sight of his cock, with his sac nestled beneath it... he's gorgeous.

Ian brushes my hair back. His voice is little more than a husky whisper. "I'd like nothing more than to feel your lips wrapped around my cock, but I meant what I said earlier. You have nothing to prove."

"I'm not trying to prove anything. I want this. I want... *you.*" And then I clutch the back of his thigh with my free hand and draw him closer, guiding him toward my mouth. "Just don't expect much the first time, okay?"

I lick the length of his cock, from root to tip, teasing the rim before I swirl my tongue over the head, tasting salt and musk. He stares down at me, his gaze locked onto what I'm doing with his cock. His face is flushed, and his nostrils flare as he draws in a heavy breath.

It's true I've never done this, but I'm a man, and I know what feels good. I just do for him what I like done to me and hope for the best.

I want this to be good for him. I want to give him the best head he's ever had. My hand tightens on his thigh, my fingers digging hard into his muscles, holding him in place. My other hand strokes his cock from root to crown while I lick the head, teasing it with my tongue.

The heat and taste of him make my blood pound, and my own erection is confined and throbbing.

When I draw him into my mouth, my tongue stroking his length, Ian digs his fingers into my shoulders and arches his back, staring at me in awe. "Fuck!" he cries, his chest heaving.

I smile as I suck him in deep. I can feel the heated, throbbing pulse of his arousal against my tongue, his blood pumping madly. With a helpless groan, he starts moving, thrusting into my mouth. My head spins. It's like nothing I've ever imagined! The heat of him, the power. My own cock is hard as a rock, trapped in my boxer-briefs, the pressure and confinement killing me.

Ian grips the sides of my head, holding me where he wants me as he drives in and out of my mouth. My lips mold to the length of him, my tongue stroking him with each long slide in and out. The rough, desperate sounds coming from him drive my own arousal. He's just as turned on as I am, and that thrills me.

I was so afraid I wouldn't measure up to his previous partners, that I'd fumble my way through it, but if his harsh, panting breaths are any indication of his pleasure, I must be doing all right.

I glance up at him, lifting my gaze and locking with his. He's staring down at me, his lips tight, his jaw clenched hard. His eyes burn into mine.

With a groan, he clutches the back of my head and thrusts deep into my mouth. I work on relaxing my throat muscles and letting him in, breathing through my nose as his cock fills my airway.

He thrusts faster and faster, harder. He grits his teeth and practically growls. "Fuck, Tyler, I'm about to come."

I don't know if he's giving me a courtesy heads-up or warning me to disengage now if I don't want his cum in my mouth. But I do want it.

After a few more deep thrusts, he abruptly pulls out of my mouth, gasping. Before I can protest, he grabs a blanket off the back of the sofa and lays it on the sofa.

"Take off your clothes," he says as he kicks off his shoes. Then he steps out of his briefs and jeans, and strips off his socks. "Do it," he repeats when I just sit there, frozen. "We're not fucking, Tyler, so don't freak out on me. Just get naked."

I stand and do as he asked, kicking off my shoes and shucking off my jeans and boxer-briefs. He pushes me down onto the blanket, on my back. A moment later, he's stretched out beside me, one of his legs slipping between mine. "Relax, Tyler."

I let out a heavy breath and try to do as he says, but it's not easy.

A blowjob I can handle, but this—I don't know what he wants. I can feel my body tensing no matter how hard I try not to.

He clutches the back of my head with one hand and pulls me close for a deep kiss. His mouth is hot and demanding on mine. And then his cock brushes against mine, hot and wet from my mouth, and fire rages through me.

"I want us to come together," he says against my lips.

When he rubs his hot flesh against mine, the friction is enough to make my eyes roll back in my head. He grips both of our cocks, his grinding against mine, stroking us both.

The overload of sensations is just too much, and my head explodes. I clutch his hips and hold him to me, and we grind against each other, both of us straining for release. Now that we're free to thrust together, my length slides along his, our cocks a perfect match of heat and friction.

His lips slide down to the spot where my neck meets my shoulder, and he bites me lightly, then licks the spot. His mouth skims down my chest until he reaches a nipple, flicking it with the tip of his tongue.

Pleasure shoots through me, from my nipple straight to my cock. I cry out, shocked by how good it feels as he swirls the tip of his tongue over my nipple. My hips are bucking now, against his, desperate for more of that mind-blowing friction. "Ian!"

His mouth returns to mine, our tongues tangling, both of us seeking the same thing. Our cocks burn together, sliding and stroking against each other. My cock is throbbing, and my balls draw up tight. I'm desperate to come. He grips me tightly in his fist and jerks me off.

I press my forehead to his, my breath ripped from my chest. My lungs are burning. "Ian!"

"I've got you, baby," he murmurs against my temple, his lips gentle and coaxing. "Come for me."

My hips buck into his hold and then I see fucking stars as I come harder than I've ever come in my life. I feel a rush of heat, scalding hot, as my cock pulses in his fist. He tenses, too, right there with me, and we both strain together. I grip his cock and stroke him and soon he's arching his back, groaning loudly as he comes with me.

It takes us both a minute to catch our breaths. He settles down beside me, sliding his leg over mine, and I find myself gravitating toward his body heat. I lean my forehead against his, breathing in both his scent and the smell of sex in the air. My heart is pounding.

Finally, after milking my orgasm, Ian gently releases my cock. It was the best orgasm of my life. "Fuck." My voice is no more than a husky rasp.

Ian smiles as he turns to face me and throws an arm over my hips and cups my ass, squeezing lightly. "You can say that again."

I'm still trying to catch my breath. "Honestly, I've never experienced anything like it."

"That was just an appetizer. We haven't even had sex yet. The best is yet to come."

I laugh. "If that was an appetizer, I'm not sure I'd survive the main course."

He pats my hip. "Come upstairs with me. Let's shower and crawl into bed. Spend the night with me."

My throat tightens. I want to, but there's so much I don't know. I don't know what he expects of me. I don't know what I'm ready for, what I can handle.

"Hey, where'd you go?" he says, his voice teasing. He runs a hand over my chest, stroking my muscles before slipping around to the back of my neck. He catches my gaze, reading me easily. "We're just going to sleep, Tyler, that's all. We're not fucking, so relax."

I'm not ready to leave him. Not yet. Not after that. So I agree to stay. "All right."

He laughs. "You don't sound very enthusiastic."

"I want to stay. I'm just painfully aware of how ignorant I am… with all this."

He leans close and kisses me, a gentle melding of our mouths. "Everyone starts somewhere. Just a shower, then bed." He slides off the sofa and holds his hand out to me. "Come with me."

I take his hand and let him haul me to my feet. Thank God for the blanket, because we made a mess. Not just on the blanket, but our abdomens are sticky with semen. "I definitely need a shower."

After we gather our things, Ian takes my hand, linking our fingers, and tugs me toward the stairs. "Me too."

✺ 25

Ian Alexander

Carrying our discarded clothes, we head upstairs to my bedroom, both of us in a euphoric, post-orgasmic haze.

"Lights, twenty percent," I say, and the canned light fixtures in the ceiling come on, bathing the room in a faint glow of warm light.

"This is it," I tell Tyler as he surveys the room.

There's not much to look at—just a king-size bed with a gray upholstered headboard, and a couple of nightstands with lamps. The bed is covered with a gray comforter and a mound of coordinating pillows. Across from the bed is a 65-inch television with a kickass sound system that would give any movie theater a run for its money.

"This is where the magic happens," I say, winking as I nod at the bed.

He smiles, but I can tell he's a little on edge.

For the first time, I allow myself to get a good look at Tyler's body. He's a freaking work of art—broad-shouldered, his chest, arm, and shoulder muscles well-defined. His thighs are muscular as well, his legs long and lean. But it's his cock that draws my undivided attention. He's built perfectly, his shaft long and thick, still semi-hard even after coming just moments ago. He has good stamina.

I take his clothes from him and lay them over the back of a chair, along with mine. Then I nod toward the private bath. "Shower?"

He nods and follows me into the bathroom, his gaze surveying the spacious room. I head straight for the walk-in shower and turn on the water.

"Towels are in there," I tell him, pointing at a freestanding cupboard.

He grabs us each a towel, laying them on the bench right outside the shower. I take his hand and pull him into the shower with me, drawing him beneath the pulsating spray of hot water.

His gaze meets mine for a long moment, and then he glances away, pretending to be interested in the glass shelf that holds an array of body wash.

"Are you okay?" I ask him, suddenly afraid we might be moving too fast.

He turns back to me. "I'm fine."

"You don't seem fine."

He smiles. "I guess I'm still reeling from what just happened downstairs. Nothing has ever felt that good before." Tyler ducks his head beneath the water, pushing it back to wet it.

I can't stop staring at the sight of his naked body in my shower. Wanting an excuse to touch him, I squirt some body wash into my hands and work up a lather before laying them on his chest. "Have you ever thought about having intercourse with a man? About what it would be like?"

He eyes me warily as he nods. "Yes. Recently."

"Just recently?" I grin. "What did you think?"

He sighs. "I'll admit, the idea scares me."

"Why?"

He stands perfectly still, letting me wash his chest and shoulders. I slide my soapy hands down his muscular arms to his thick wrists, and finally to his hands.

He shrugs. "I don't know what to expect."

"I'm sure you have questions. We can talk about those tonight."

He nods. "I suppose most guys figure these things out in their teens."

"Not necessarily. You're not the only middle-aged, closeted gay who's just now figuring out which team he should be playing on."

Tyler laughs. "No one's ever called me middle-aged before."

"It's true. You are." I turn him and wash his back, admiring the lines of his musculature. My hands slide down to his waist, to his hips, but when he tenses, I go no farther. "You look pretty damn good for a middle-aged guy. I'll give you that."

Tyler turns back to face me and reaches for the body wash, but I hold it out of his reach. "Not so fast. I'm just getting to the good parts." And then I proceed to wash his abs, his hips, and thighs. Even flaccid, his cock hangs low and long. I remember full well the size of him when erect—not just his length, but his girth as well—and the knowledge blows my mind more than a little bit. I've never taken a cock his size before.

I guess I'm getting ahead of myself, though. I don't even know if that's something he wants. I hope he'll want to have anal sex, when he feels ready, but not all guys do. And then there's the question of whether he'd want to top or bottom. That's a discussion we still need to have.

I finish washing him, and then he returns the favor and washes me. I bite back a groan as his soapy hands skim over my body, from my shoulders to my ankles. He seems to enjoy the task, taking his sweet time as his fingers glide over my body, touching and stroking me.

By the time he's done, I'm hard again, and so is he. "You recover pretty quickly, too," I say, grinning at him. "For a middle-aged guy."

He grins, obviously relaxed enough to enjoy himself now. "I'm just making up for lost time."

After we both wash our hair, we shut off the water and towel dry. With our towels tied at our waists, we stand at the dual sinks. I toss him a brand-new toothbrush, which I pulled from a stash in a drawer, and we brush our teeth.

I watch his reflection in the bathroom mirror, his expression revealing a mix of curiosity, uncertainty, and hunger. His vulnerability makes my heart do a little flip. This may all be new for him, but it's new for me too. I've never been with someone who made me *care* this much before. It's always been fun for me, hot sex with hot guys, and sometimes I didn't even know their names. And that was fine. But with Tyler, it's different.

I find myself paying attention to the little things about him, like how he fingercombs his hair. I discover he's left-handed, like me, when we both brush our teeth.

He meets my gaze in the mirror. "If I'd known I was spending the night, I would have brought some things with me. Toiletries. A change of clean clothes."

"Next time," I say, trying to sound casual.

Tyler grins at the mention of a next time.

My heart beats faster at the idea of another sleepover. I guess I shouldn't jump the gun, though. He may decide this isn't want he wants after all.

Or, that *I'm* not the one he wants.

* * *

"Lights off," I say as we climb into bed.

As we slip beneath the sheet and comforter, my heart starts beating faster. I've never gone to bed with a man just to sleep, with absolutely no intention of having sex.

The moonlight shines through my bedroom windows, filtered by the canopy of trees outside, providing a decent amount of ambient light. I roll onto my side to face him. Tyler lies on his back, staring up at the high ceiling, his hands clasped over his abdomen. He glances at the bank of windows overlooking the street. "Do you want me to close the blinds?"

Oh, shit, here we go. My pulse picks up. I really don't want to get into this so soon. "If you don't mind, can we leave them open?"

He glances at the uncovered windows. "I just thought you'd want more privacy."

"No one can see in. There are too many trees."

"Okay." He shrugs. "That's fine."

I'd give anything to know what he's thinking right now... if he's regretting anything. If he has questions.

I lean closer and kiss his shoulder.

He shoots me a slightly frantic look. "Ian, I don't know the first thing about anal sex."

"You never had anal with a woman?"

He shakes his head. "No."

"But you've thought about it, with a man?"

"Yes."

I reach for his hand and link our fingers. "When you thought about it, were you giving or receiving?"

His fingers tighten on mine, but he doesn't say anything.

I rise up on my elbow and kiss his sternum. "Do you think you'd rather top or bottom? Do you want to fuck, or be fucked?"

Taking a deep breath, and not meeting my gaze, he says quite definitively, "Top."

"Thank you, baby Jesus!" Sighing, I roll onto my back.

He turns to face me. "What?"

"I want to *be* fucked. By you. Very badly."

A flush sweeps across his face, and he bites back a grin. "I think we can work something out."

ꞋꙞ 26

Tyler Jamison

Ian wears his emotions on his sleeve, holding nothing back. I can feel the energy, the anticipation radiating off him. He's a force of nature, beautiful, vibrant, courageous, and sexy as hell. He's also a lot younger than I am and way more adventurous. In a lot of ways, he's good for me. He's just what I need to get out of my own head.

His hair is still damp from the shower, the longer strands curling on top. I clutch the back of his head and draw him closer. When our lips meet, he moans softly, and the sound goes straight to my cock. We're both hard. I can feel his erection brushing against mine, hot and insistent.

This is all new for me. I've never felt this kind of heady anticipation, this level of constant arousal. I feel almost giddy just being with him.

I close the distance between us and kiss him with all the hunger trapped inside me. When I gently bite his bottom lip, he groans and slides his arm around my waist, clutching me tighter.

I loom over him, looking down into his eyes. Lying half on him, I align my erection to his, length to length, both of us hot and pulsing with need. His fingers dig into my biceps, and he pulls me closer. His mouth is just as eager, just as hungry as mine. He rubs himself against me, grinding his cock against mine, and the friction is mind-blowing.

When he reaches between us, gripping both our cocks, my brain implodes. "Ian!"

Why does this feel so fucking good? Why does his touch light me up like nothing else ever has? My mouth returns to his, and I drink in his harried breaths and muffled moans. His hand slides around to my ass, and he grips my ass and pulls me closer. His hips are rocking against mine now, and I can feel the tension ratcheting up between us. My blood is rushing south, my cock throbbing, and I feel light-headed.

"God," he growls, sounding frustrated. He moves his mouth to my shoulder and bites lightly before licking my skin. "I want you inside me so badly."

My heart stutters painfully. "Ian, I don't—"

"Relax. I said not tonight. But soon, I want you to fuck me."

"I don't want to hurt you, and I don't know how—"

"You won't hurt me."

"I don't see how I can possibly fuck you without hurting you." I pull back to fist my thick erection. "Ian, I've had women complain that I'm too big. All the lube in the world isn't going to change that."

He laughs, sounding part pained and part amused. "Trust me, Tyler, I know what I'm doing. I can bottom like a porn star."

Now it's my turn to laugh. I don't know how he does it. No matter the situation, he has the ability to make me smile.

He brushes my hand aside and grips my cock, spreading precum, both his and mine, down my shaft. "I can take this bad boy. I can take every inch of you, and I swear to you, it'll blow both our minds."

"You're already blowing my mind."

He starts stroking me then, his grip firm and determined. He rolls me to my back and leans up on his elbow while he jerks me off with his other hand. His gaze nails me with heat and promise, and he holds me under his spell as his hand works its torturous magic on my cock.

My breathing picks up and my hips start rocking. "Fuck, Ian."

He grins. "That's the point." And then he kisses me, his mouth hot and hungry.

I let out a ragged groan as his hand works me mercilessly, jacking me higher and higher until heat rushes down my spine. At the last minute, he replaces his hand with his mouth, swallowing me deeply until I hit the back of his throat. The tight heat is too much. I fist his hair, hard enough to make him groan, as a climax rips through me. "Fuck!"

I shoot my load into his mouth, my hips rising, bucking, and still he takes every inch of me, his nose buried against my groin.

* * *

I wake up in a strange place, startled out of a deep sleep, and it takes me a moment to realize where I am. *Ian's bedroom.*

Shit, I'm in bed with Ian.

What in the hell was I thinking last night? My family may have readily accepted my sexual orientation, but I'm pretty sure others in my life—namely my work colleagues—won't be so accepting. There are gay and lesbian police officers in my precinct, but they all probably face some type of discrimination, privately if not publicly.

As I lie on my back, Ian is tucked into my side, his head on my shoulder and his arm across my waist. I relax into his hold as my initial anxiety wears off.

Gently, so as not to wake him, I press my lips to his forehead and breathe in his scent. He moans softly, a yearning sound, and his hand tightens on my waist as he draws closer.

I'm shocked at how quickly Ian has gotten under my skin. I've only known him a short while, and already he's shattered my carefully-constructed life. It might have been fucked-up, but it was safe, orderly, and under control.

My world has been turned upside down, and it will never be

the same. I can't go back to being who I was before, not after experiencing this kind of desire. I don't want to go back.

But Ian's so young. He's vivacious and outgoing. He's the center of attention wherever he goes. And me? I'm always the outsider. I'm older, stuck in my ways, and I don't know if I can hold his interest for the long haul.

I don't know if I have what it takes to keep him.

* * *

My alarm goes off at six. I need to go home and change clothes before I head into the office. I'm sure there will be more questions today, more reports to read. More scrutiny into the Valdez case. I told Ian there was nothing to worry about, but there's likely to be repercussions of some sort. There always are.

At some point in the night, we shifted positions. He's now on his side, facing away from me, and I'm tucked up against his back, spooning him. My arm is around his waist, and I'm holding him close.

Jesus, this feels good.

I've never slept with someone before, not like this. Sure, I've fallen asleep with lovers before, but we weren't glued to each other. And as soon as I woke—usually in the middle of the night—I'd slip out of her apartment without a word.

This time is different. I'm in no hurry to leave. Having Ian nestled up against me like this makes my heart beat fast, and I find myself smiling like an idiot. But then reality intrudes, and I realize I might be jumping the gun here. This might be a life-altering experience for me, but for all I know, I could just be a diversion for him. The thought makes my chest ache. It's entirely possible that I've come out just to get my heart broken.

Gently, I release him and ease back. It's still early, and I don't want to wake him. I slip quietly out of bed. After a quick stop in the bathroom, I dress quietly in the dark, and then I head downstairs to retrieve the rest of my stuff.

Before I let myself out the front door, I leave him a quick text message.

I'm heading to the office. I didn't want to disturb you. – Tyler

As I start my car engine, I can't help wondering if I just made a dick move. Should I have woken him before I left? Should I have kissed him good-bye and said, *Thanks for the best night of my life?*

Should I have asked when I'd see him again? I wanted to, but I didn't want to come across as a desperate, needy son-of-a-bitch.

With my mind filled with what-ifs and should-haves, I head home to change. As I pull into the parking lot of my condo development, I'm struck by how odd it feels to be back here after only two nights away.

So much has happened in the past forty-eight hours. I'm not the same person. I came out to my family. I made out with a man—hell, I spent the night with him. But now, being back here, it feels like I'm right back where I started—isolated and alone— and it doesn't feel good. I guess there are too many bad memories associated with this place.

On my way in, I grab two days' worth of mail before I head

up to my unit and let myself in to a dark condo that doesn't feel like *home* anymore. For over two decades, this place has been my sanctuary. Now it feels cold and empty, like my life was for so long. How can meeting one person upend so much so quickly?

I grab a quick shower, dress, and carry a bag of trash out on my way back to the car. Then I head to the office. It's early, and folks are still coming in.

One of the admins seated behind the front desk flags me over. "Detective, I have a message for you." She hands me a slip of paper. "A call came in earlier this morning for you."

"Thanks."

As I head to my office, I unfold the slip of paper, not sure what to expect. A note from Ian, berating me for slinking off like a coward this morning? A note from Internal Review, wanting to ask questions about the shooting?

We need to talk. Come to my office at the courthouse at ten. – M. Alexander

M. Alexander? Shit. That's Ian's father, Martin Alexander. *Judge* Alexander. I laugh at the absurdity. Here I am, forty-four years old, with my first... what? What is Ian to me anyway? A crush? A hookup? What are we?

I can't imagine what Judge Alexander wants with me. His son is safe, and the killer is dead. It's not like he knows his son and I have been spending time together, or that we slept together last night.

As I head to my office, stopping only to grab a cup of coffee in the break room, my mind races through the possibilities. Why do

I have the sinking suspicion that Ian's father knows more than he should, and that I'm about to be called out on the carpet?

My neck heats at the thought of facing Ian's father. *Yes, Your Honor, I gave your son head.*

I check my e-mail, answer some questions from Internal Review and my captain. I field text messages from my sister and my mom this morning, asking how I'm doing. I eat a bagel, and it sits in my gut like a stone.

At nine-thirty, I walk over to the courthouse, wanting to get this over with as quickly as possible. I pass through the security check-point and head up in the elevator to the third floor, where the judges' private offices are located.

I don't know this judge personally, but I know of him. He has a reputation for being firm, but fair. I've never heard anything negative about him. I guess I'll soon be in a position to form my own opinion.

I find Judge Alexander's office door and step inside a small waiting room. His administrative assistant is seated at her desk, busy typing away on her computer keyboard.

"Tyler Jamison," I tell her. "Judge—"

"Yes, he's expecting you." She points at a closed mahogany door bearing the nameplate: *Judge Martin Alexander.* "Go right in, detective."

"Thanks." I knock once on the door, just as a courtesy.

I receive a booming reply. "Come in!"

I open the door and step inside the judge's inner office, having no idea what to expect.

"Shut the door, Jamison," he barks. He's on the phone. "Yes, that's fine. I have to go now. I'll call you later." He hangs up and points to a chair facing his desk. "Sit down, detective."

As I take a seat in front of a massive wooden desk, I quickly scan his office. Behind his desk is a solid wall of bookcases filled with thick legal tomes bound in leather, scores of them. There are several landscape oil paintings on the walls and some ornate brass lamps. It's a masculine room and a bit stilted for my taste.

I lean back in my chair and face him directly, hoping we can get this over with. "What can I do for you, Your Honor?" I say, hoping to get off on a good footing with the man. Hoping my worst suspicions aren't true.

I'd guess him to be in his late sixties, his short hair completely gray. His face is clean shaven, and his eyes are a cool blue. The tense expression on his lined face isn't promising, and I'm starting to think the worst.

Ian's father steeples his fingers and leans forward, his gaze direct. "I'll make this very simple, detective. Stay the fuck away from my son."

"I beg your pardon?" It takes a minute for my mind to stop reeling.

His gaze narrows on me. "You heard me, detective. Keep away from my son, or I'll have your badge so fast you won't know what hit you. You'll never work in law enforcement in this city again. In fact, if I have my way, you'll never work in law enforcement anywhere in this country. Is that clear?"

"Your Honor, no offense, sir, but I think you're overreacting."

"Am I?" He's glaring daggers at me now. "You have no business fraternizing with a vulnerable young man half your age, detective."

"With all due respect, sir, Ian is an adult. And he's not *half* my age. Not even close. He's old enough to decide who he spends time with. I don't think he needs your input."

"And I don't think he needs an opportunistic asshole—"

"I am not—"

"My son is a very wealthy young man, detective. Don't pretend you aren't aware of that fact."

"This is about money? Are you kidding me?"

"This is about you taking advantage of a vulnerable young man. Here you come, sweeping into his life like some big, strong protector. I know you hired a bodyguard to watch over Ian. Do you think his mother and I can't protect him?"

I shoot to my feet. "This is a ridiculous waste of time. I'm not the least bit interested in Ian's bank balance."

"Don't pretend you're ignorant of the fact that my son has a sizable trust fund. I will not stand by and let you take advantage of him!"

"I'm not taking advantage of him!"

"You have no idea what Ian has been through. You have no idea of the abuse he suffered before my wife and I adopted him."

"Ian is adopted?"

"Yes. He was five when we got him. His mother and I worked hard to give him a healthy, stable upbringing. It took us years to repair the damage that was done to him early in his life. You can't just waltz into Ian's life now and destroy everything we've helped him accomplish!"

Ian's father is clearly upset, his face flushed, his hands balled into fists. I keep reminding myself he's just trying to protect his son. The Alexanders don't know me. They don't know what kind of person I am. It takes all I have not to let this escalate. If anything, I need to de-escalate this—and quickly. This is Ian's *father*. I can't lose sight of that fact. "What makes you think I would do anything to jeopardize Ian's well-being?"

Martin Alexander jabs a finger in my direction. "Listen to me, detective. You don't know *anything* about my son. You don't know what he's been through. And I'm not going to let you undo all the good his mother and I have done for him. He's finally in a good place in his life, and I won't let you fuck that up."

Nothing I say seems to be getting through to Ian's father. "How did you even know about us in the first place?" *Jesus, we were only together one night.* "Did Ian tell you?"

He stares at me without answering, but I can see the truth in his eyes. He's hiding something.

"You have someone watching him, don't you?" I say. "Who? Private security? A private investigator?"

"That's none of your fucking business." The judge lifts a finger. "I know you spent the night at my son's house last night. This is your only warning, detective. You stay the fuck away from him. I won't tell you again."

"We're done here, Mr. Alexander. If you don't want to have a constructive conversation about Ian, then we have nothing more to say to each other." And then I turn and walk out.

On the way to my car, I realize there's a lot more to Ian Alexander than I'm aware of. Martin Alexander obviously cares about his son, and he's clearly worried.

It looks like Ian and I need to have a heart-to-heart.

27

Ian Alexander

When I wake up to an empty bed, my heart starts pounding. *He's gone.*

"Tyler?" Maybe he's in the bathroom.

But there's no answer.

I check my phone, which is on silent, only to find a short, impersonal text message from Tyler.

He didn't want to disturb me.

Translation: It wasn't worth my time to wake you up and say goodbye.

My chest tightens. *Of course, he's gone, you idiot. Why in the world would he stay?*

I exhale slowly and tell myself to calm the fuck down.

He had to go to work.

It's not a big deal.

It doesn't mean he's lost interest in you.

Stop the crazy train right now, before you derail completely.

My therapist's words play over and over in my mind, and I latch onto them desperately. "Ian, just because someone leaves, it doesn't mean they're leaving *you*. It just means they have somewhere they need to be. They'll come back."

I have abandonment issues. That's what happens when, at the ripe old age of five, you've been shuffled around from one home to another, never staying in one place long. Never getting attached and always getting handed off to someone else. Back and forth from my birth mother to foster homes, over and over, until the courts finally say *enough*. That's when I ended up with Martin and Ruth Alexander—my forever home. *My family.*

My throat closes up on me, making it difficult to swallow. Even to breathe. Tears sting my eyes as I fist the bedding and let out a frustrated growl.

Stop it!

"Think it through rationally, Ian," my therapist would say.

He had to go to work. He has responsibilities. It's not the end of the world. He's not leaving you. Get a grip.

He was just being considerate and didn't want to wake you. Maybe it's that simple, and you're making a mountain out of a fucking mole hill. It wouldn't be the first time.

Yeah, I have abandonment issues. Years of on-and-off therapy have helped a lot, but it's no magic bullet. My demons still come back to haunt me.

Desperate to get out of here, I climb out of bed, shower and get dressed, and then I grab my camera case—which doubles as a backpack—and hit the streets.

Photography is my therapy now. It helps me reframe my life, reframe the world I see. It helps me put my life into perspective when I see what others are going through. It helps remind me not to be a selfish bastard and be grateful for the things—and the people—I have in my life.

As I'm walking toward Millennium Park, I text my sister.

How's it going? How's the new bodyguard? – Ian

A few minutes later, I get a reply.

He sucks even more than the previous one, and my sugars are all over the place. Mom and Dad are hovering like crazy. And the voices are worse. Can I come live with you? – Layla

Shit. I was afraid this would happen. Miguel was right. Layla needs a medically-trained bodyguard. I'll talk to Mom and Dad about that. I just want my sister to be happy. I want her to live as close to a normal life as possible, without putting her at risk.

Mom and Dad would freak if you moved out. They're not ready for that. I'll think of something. – Ian

Half an hour later, I'm at Millennium Park, standing in front of the world-renowned metal sculpture lovingly referred to as 'The Bean.' The shiny, polished, stainless-steel sculpture reflects the Chicago cityscape behind me, along with an expansive skyline. Dark clouds are rolling in from the lake to the East, perfectly matching my mood.

My phone chimes with an incoming message.

I'm off to class now. Talk later. Luv u! – Layla

Be careful. Looks like a storm is rolling in. – Ian

You're such a worrywart! – Layla

I walk around the park for a while, taking pictures. But what interests me more is the *real* Chicago, not the tourists and not the famous landmarks. I'm more interested in the dark underbelly of the city, which is inhabited by the homeless, the mentally ill, drug abusers, and those simply down-on-their-luck. I might have ended up one of them if it weren't for the Alexanders.

I walk a few blocks more until my stomach threatens to abandon me if I don't feed it. I head to one of my favorite lunch spots. It's a small hole-in-the-wall Mexican restaurant run by a very close-knit family. As I approach the restaurant, I notice a familiar face. Jerry is sitting on the sidewalk right outside the door.

"Hey, Jerry," I say.

Jerry looks up, gazing at me with tired, weary eyes. He's a grizzled old guy, a military veteran from the first Gulf war. He suffers from PTSD, and he refuses to get help. I've offered to try to get him into a shelter, but he's not interested. The least I can do is put food in his belly.

I open the restaurant door. "Come on in, Jerry. I'll buy you lunch."

He hesitates for a moment, but then he heaves himself up to

his boot-clad feet and walks into the restaurant. I join him at the counter.

"Whatever my friend wants," I say to the kid behind the cash register.

Jerry glances at me, then turns to the kid. "Ten tacos and a large Coke."

When Jerry gets his food, he pats me on the back. "You're a damn fine young man, Ian." And then he leaves with his sack of tacos and large soft drink.

I watch him walk out the door, out onto the sidewalk, out into the elements. It's already started raining, and it's only going to get worse when those dark storm clouds reach this part of the city.

I order three tacos and a Coke. By the time I get my food and sit down to eat, the rain is coming down in sheets. My chest aches for Jerry and for others like him who are out there somewhere, with empty bellies and nowhere to go. As far as I'm concerned, food and shelter are basic human rights. While I've never been homeless, I have been hungry, and I know it's a miserable-as-fuck feeling.

As I finish my food, I check my phone. Besides my brief text convo with my sister, my phone remains silent. I've had no messages from Tyler. No checking in. No, "Hey, dude, how's it going? Thanks for last night. You give great head." Or, "Hey, dude, last night didn't totally suck for me. We should do it again sometime."

Nothing. Not a word.

I'm an idiot for thinking someone like him would ever be interested in someone like me.

He didn't abandon you!

Yeah, right. Then why haven't I heard from him?

Have you messaged him?

No. Good point. So I send him a quick text.

Hey. Hope ur day is going well. Sorry I missed u this morning. – Ian

When the rain lets up, I toss out my trash and hit the sidewalk to do some more walking and take some more photos. I come across half a dozen panhandlers and slip them each a twenty-dollar bill. That won't go far, but at least they'll be able to eat today.

Hell, I'd like to feed them all.

Twenty minutes pass without a reply from Tyler, and I have to tamp down my growing unease. I pop into a coffee shop for some caffeine. Once I'm done with that, I start walking the streets again, moving deeper and deeper into the rough parts of the city, taking photos of deteriorating buildings. I hand out money to a number of homeless individuals.

Layla and I both have an affinity for the down and out, the downtrodden, the lost and abandoned. Who knows what might have happened to either of us if we hadn't been adopted by a loving family? I could have ended up starving and homeless, easy prey, if it weren't for the Alexanders. We both feel a kindred spirit with these unlucky individuals.

When my phone chimes with an incoming message, my heart stutters. I'm almost afraid to look. I'm afraid I'll be disappointed if it's not Tyler.

It's going well. I didn't have the heart to wake you. I wanted to, but you looked so peaceful. – Tyler

I catch myself smiling at his message. I'm already so fucked up over this guy, and I haven't even known him that long.

A moment later, my phone rings, and it's my shipbuilder calling to confirm they're ready to replace the blood-stained boards on the deck of my boat. Fortunately, the repairs are manageable, and they're sending a maintenance crew to the marina today. It helps to be a VIP customer.

And then I get a follow-up text from Tyler.

Can you meet me for lunch around one? – Tyler

Sure. Where? – Ian

Your place. Order something in? – Tyler

Yes. Absolutely. See you then. Chinese? – Ian

Sounds good – Tyler

He wants to see me again. I feel stupidly giddy. Until I wonder why he wants to see me. Maybe it's not good after all.

✤ 28

Tyler Jamison

The incredible irony of this day is not lost on me. As I sit in my car outside the police station, I think back to the way I treated Shane when I first learned of his involvement with my sister. Beth was working at a medical school library when I found out that Howard Kline was going to be released early from prison.

Howard Kline, the monster who brazenly abducted my six-year-old sister from our mom's front yard in broad daylight, was being released early from prison on the basis of good behavior. I had no doubt he was a clear and present danger to my sister, even eighteen years later.

I remember those first few hours after we'd gotten the report of a missing child. My baby sister, an innocent little girl with her whole life ahead of her, had disappeared while riding her bike in the front yard. I'd never in my life known such abject terror. I was a rookie cop back then, not long on the force.

Fortunately, an observant neighbor remembered seeing a plumbing van parked on the street near my mom's house at the time of the abduction. We were able to track the van to a farm outside the city, where Howard Kline lived with his invalid mother.

We found Beth, bound and gagged, lying naked on a filthy mattress on the dirt floor of a pitch-black cellar. I was the first one down those cellar steps, descending into complete darkness with only a flashlight and a gun. I found her shivering from hypothermia and dehydration and immediately wrapped her in my jacket. It was a miracle Kline hadn't sexually assaulted her.

I hired Shane's company—McIntyre Security—to protect her, covertly, until something could be done to get Kline back behind bars where he belonged. I lost my head when I discovered that Shane had become involved with my sister. I accused him of every sort of unprofessional conduct imaginable, and I made his life hell.

My sister was twenty-four then, and Shane was in his early thirties. I railed at him for being too old for her, for taking advantage of her fragile emotional state. Since the day of her abduction, Beth has suffered from crippling anxiety. She wasn't equipped to deal with a man like Shane. I accused him of using her, of taking advantage of her.

But I was wrong.

I know that now.

He's proven himself over and over, and he's always been there for Beth.

And now the tables have turned, and I'm the letch who's being accused of taking advantage of someone younger. Someone vulnerable.

Someone who's apparently fragile.

* * *

I arrive at Ian's townhouse at exactly one o'clock, just as the delivery car from a Chinese take-out pulls away.

Ian's waiting for me at the door, holding two carry-out bags. "I wasn't sure what you like, so I ordered a few different things. We can share."

I step inside and close the door behind me, wondering who's watching us right now. After my talk with Martin Alexander, I have no doubt Ian's townhouse is being watched. I'm sure a report of my arrival will go promptly back to Ian's father.

I guess this means I've already violated his warning.

Can Judge Alexander get me fired? I honestly don't know. He does have a lot of clout in this city, though. If anyone can do it, he can.

Ian frowns. "What's wrong?"

I look at him—really look at him—and I see far more than a

pretty face. He's kind, caring, and full of empathy. And suddenly, I just want to protect him. I don't want him to be hurt or disappointed, and I'm afraid if he knew what his father was up to, that's exactly what he'd be. But I also don't want to lie to him. "Ian." I let out a heavy breath. "We need to talk."

His expression falls, and the light in his eyes dims. "Save your breath, Tyler. I don't need any explanations or excuses. Just go." And then he turns away and heads toward the kitchen.

What in the fuck just happened? I start after him. "Ian, wait!"

He raises a dismissive hand, not even bothering to look at me. "Just go, Tyler."

I follow him into the kitchen and watch him unpack the sacks of Chinese food. "What in the hell is going on?"

He turns to me, his reddened eyes filled with pain, but says nothing.

"Did your dad call you?" I say. "Is that what this is about? What did he say?"

Ian looks genuinely perplexed. "My dad? What are you talking about?"

"I saw your dad this morning. He called me to his office at the courthouse."

"Why?"

"To warn me to stay away from you."

Ian's voice rises a decibel. "Are you kidding me? What did he say?"

"He said I'd lose my job if I didn't keep my distance."

Ian's eyes widen, and it's clear he knew nothing about this.

"Wait a minute," he says, shaking his head. "How does he know we... it was just one night!"

"He has someone watching you. A private investigator, I imagine. He, or she, reported back to your dad that I spent the night here last night."

Ian shakes his head with a laugh. "I can't believe it. My parents sometimes go overboard trying to protect me and my sister. They mean well, they really do. They're not bad people. But sometimes they go a little over the top, especially my dad. I'm really sorry. I'll talk to him."

"Well, if that's not why you're upset, then what's bothering you?"

"I thought you came here to tell me you were done with me."

"What?" Now it's my turn to be surprised. "Why would you think that?"

"You didn't say goodbye this morning. You just left."

"And you thought that meant I was no longer interested in you?"

He shrugs. "I thought it was possible you'd changed your mind about me."

"You were asleep, Ian. I didn't want to wake you. I left you a text message." Martin Alexander's reference to Ian being vulnerable is starting to make more sense.

Ian shrugs off my explanation. "We should eat. The food will get cold."

"If you're hungry, Ian, go right ahead and eat. But we need to talk about this."

His eyes tear up.

"Hey." I close the distance between us, walk right up to him and lay my hands on his shoulders. "Talk to me, Ian. What's wrong?"

He looks away as a single tear rolls down his cheek. "Nothing."

"Ian."

Without meeting my gaze, he says, "I have issues."

"What kind of issues?"

"Abandonment issues." He draws in a shaky breath.

A sharp pain stabs me in the chest. "When I left this morning, did you think I abandoned you? Left you without a word? Without an explanation?"

He shrugs. "It might have crossed my mind."

I frown. "And here I thought I was doing you a favor by not waking you up. If I'd known how you would take it, I would have woken you." I bring my hands up to cup his face and make him look at me. "I would have told you how amazing you are and how much I want you." I lean in to kiss him gently. "I'm sorry, Ian. I'll never do that again."

Tears spill down his cheeks, and he wipes them away with a shaky hand. "I was just being stupid."

"No, it wasn't stupid." I brush fresh tears off his cheeks. "I'm sorry."

"And I'm sorry about what my dad said to you. I'll talk to him tonight and straighten things out."

"Are you sure that's a good idea? He was pretty clear that he wants me staying away from you."

"It's too late for that, if there really is a PI watching me. My dad will hear that you came by. Besides, don't worry. My parents are good people. They mean well. I'll tell my dad to back off. It'll be okay." Ian places his hands on my chest, then slides them up to my shoulders. "When do you have to be back to work?"

"I have a department meeting at three."

Ian leans in to kiss me. "I can think of a good way to spend the next hour."

"Can you?"

"Yes."

"Does it involve your mouth or mine?"

He grins. "Both."

"What about lunch?"

He eyes my mouth hungrily as he pulls me toward the staircase. "Lunch can wait."

* * *

An hour later, after cleaning up and dressing, we head back downstairs.

Ian walks me to the door. "Will I see you tonight?"

I nod. "I'll come by this evening, after work. Around seven?"

"That's perfect. It'll give me a chance to stop by my parents' house during dinner this evening and have a little chat with them."

"I don't want to cause problems with your family, Ian."

He reaches out to smooth my jacket. "Don't worry, you won't."

Once I'm outside, I stand on the front stoop and survey the

street in both directions. I mentally catalog the cars parked within view of Ian's townhouse: an Audi, two BMWs, a Lexus, a Mercedes, a Range Rover, two Escalades... and last but not least, a beaten-down piece of rusted junk. The townhouses in this Gold Coast neighborhood sell for a million dollars and up. I doubt the rusted-out economy car belongs to a resident.

I walk over to the vehicle and rap on the driver's window. There's a young man seated at the wheel pretending to read a magazine. *Sure.*

I flash my badge. "Chicago PD. Can I ask what you're doing here?"

He lays the magazine on the front passenger seat and stares up at me, completely unconcerned. "I'm not breaking any laws, officer. I'm allowed to sit here, at least until six pm." He points to a sign affixed to a nearby streetlamp: **RESIDENT ONLY PARKING FROM 6 PM – 7 AM.**

"I'm guessing you're a private eye," I say, scrutinizing the inside of his vehicle. The worn cloth seats are patched with electrical tape. There are half-a-dozen crumpled fast food bags on the floor, as well as twice that many empty energy drink cans. "It looks like private surveillance doesn't pay that well. Tell Judge Alexander that his son is a consenting adult, and that he needs to mind his own business."

As I walk back toward Ian's house, I hear the driver yell "Asshole!" out his open window.

ꙮ29

Ian Alexander

Ever since my parents adopted me, they made it a point to be home every evening for a family dinner at six o'clock. It isn't always feasible for a federal judge and a district attorney to pull off, but they succeeded more often than not. Sometimes only one of them made it home for dinner, but between the two of them, they made it work. And they still do it for Layla's sake. This evening is no different.

When I arrive at my parents' house, I park in the garage behind the house and walk in through the kitchen door.

"Ian!" A chorus of voices greets me as I walk into the kitchen.

Right now, the chef, two servers, Margaret, and the family butler are seated at the kitchen table, eating supper.

"Ian, you should have told us you were coming," Andre says, gently scolding me. He's the chef, originally from France.

My parents met Andre on a trip to Paris, and they managed to lure him back here to Chicago to be their private chef. He's been here twenty-two years now, is married to an American, and has four kids.

"Are my parents home?" I ask the question even though I already know the answer. I saw both their cars parked in the six-car garage behind the house. Layla's car—a cute, cherry red Fiat—is here too.

"They are," Charles says. The butler. He rises from his chair at the end of the kitchen table and pulls on his formal jacket.

"Don't get up, Charles," I tell him. "Sit down and enjoy your dinner."

"Very well," he says. "I'll have someone bring in a dinner plate for you."

"Thanks, but that won't be necessary. I'm just here for a quick visit."

My parents are wealthy, but they didn't get that way from working as a federal judge and a district attorney. No, the kind of money they have is old family money. My father's family, to be exact. My grandfather, Tobias Martin Alexander, founded a telecom company in the early twentieth century. His business made him a fortune, and I have a chunk of it in a trust fund, as does my sister. Both of us are independently wealthy, no strings attached.

We were each given our trust funds when we turned twenty-one.

I walk into the grand formal dining room, where my parents and Layla all sit together at one end of a long table. My parents must have just gotten home because they're still in their work attire. Layla's wearing a burgundy UChicago hoodie, her dark hair up in a messy ponytail, earbuds hung around her neck.

There's an impressive spread of roasted chicken with asparagus, baked potatoes, and salad on the table, along with a bottle of red wine for my parents and water for Layla.

"Ian, sweetheart!" my mother calls out when she spots me. She waves me over. "What a wonderful surprise! Come sit down." She pulls out the seat next to hers. "Are you hungry? I'll get you a plate."

"No, I'm not hungry, thanks."

"Why didn't you tell us you were coming?" Layla asks, a bit of a pout on her pretty face.

"Sorry. It was sort of a last-minute thing," I say.

"How's it going, son?" my father says as he refreshes his glass of wine. He's seated at the end of the table, Mom to his left and Layla to his right.

I sit next to my mom. "Good. I got a call from the shipbuilder today. They're replacing the blood-stained boards on the main deck."

Flinching, my mother pats my back. "I'm so sorry, honey. I just thank God you're all right."

"What brings you here this evening?" my dad says, as he cuts into his chicken.

I sit straighter and take a deep breath. I can think of only one way to derail his attempts to chase Tyler off, and that's to go public with my feelings for him. "I have an announcement to make."

There's a hint of a scowl on my father's face, probably because he knows what I'm about to say. "And what's that?" he says.

"I'm seeing someone."

My mom's eyes widen. "Really?"

"Oh my God, who is it?" Layla says. "Do I know him?"

"You don't know him, Layla, but I hope you'll meet him soon. His name is Tyler Jamison."

"That's wonderful, honey," Mom says. "What does he do? Where did you meet him?" She seems genuinely interested, which tells me she doesn't know what Dad's been up to.

"He's a police officer, a detective actually. I met him at the marina, the night Eric was killed."

"A homicide detective?" My mother frowns. "The name doesn't ring a bell." Then she glances at my dad. "Do you know him, Martin?"

My dad hesitates a moment before answering. Then, almost reluctantly, he nods. "I don't know him well, but yes, we met once."

"Well, I want to meet him," Layla says as she reaches for her water and takes a sip.

"I'm sure I can arrange it," I say, sitting back in my seat. "I really like this guy, Mom. This is different. He... means a lot to me."

"Why don't you bring him for dinner sometime soon?" Mom says. She turns to my dad. "Wouldn't that be nice, honey?"

"Of course," he says. He meets my gaze, giving nothing away.

I wait for him to say something more, but he doesn't. He just keeps methodically cutting up his chicken.

"So, how did you do on your psych exam, Layla?" I ask my sister.

She swallows her food before saying, "I got an A on my final, which means I'll have an A for the semester."

Well, that wasn't hard. That was all it took to get my dad off Tyler's back. Mission accomplished.

* * *

I stay a while longer as Layla catches us up on the status of her classes. She tells us all about the guy in her sociology class she likes. Mom tells me all about the ballroom dance lessons she's making my dad take with her. My dad listens in, responding where needed, but he doesn't say much himself.

When everyone is finished eating, my dad rises from the table. "Ian, come join me in my office."

"Sure, Dad."

When I stand, my mom reaches out and grabs my hand. "It's so good to see you, honey. I'm glad everything's going well."

I kiss her cheek and then excuse myself to follow my dad to his office.

"Take a seat, son," my father says, motioning toward a chair. He sits behind his desk and leans forward in his chair, his elbows propped on the desktop. In that moment, he looks very much like the judge he is. "Well played, son." He smiles at me, genuinely amused. "I guess Detective Jamison told you about our little talk this morning."

"His name is Tyler, and yes, he did. That was *so* not cool of you."

My dad makes a face, but it's only half-apologetic. "I'm just trying to protect you, Ian. Jamison is too old for you. I don't think it's a good idea for you to be seeing him."

"I meant what I said at the dinner table. I like him. I *really* like him. And I'm asking you, please, not to interfere. I'm not a kid. If I make a mistake, it's on me. But you have to let me live my life."

He frowns. "I don't want you getting hurt."

"Maybe I will, maybe I won't. But that's part of life."

He exhales as he runs his hand over his face. "Fine. I won't interfere. Just promise me you'll be careful. And I want to go on record as saying he's too old for you."

"You're eight years older than Mom," I remind him.

"Yeah, well, the age difference between you two is far greater, and I don't like it."

"Duly noted." I stand. "Promise me, Dad. No interfering."

Reluctantly, he nods. "All right, fine. Just don't come crying to me when he breaks your heart—and he will."

I head for the door, pausing at the last minute to turn back. "By the way, who do you have spying on me?"

My dad at least has the decency to blush. "I hired a private investigator to keep an eye on things. It's just a safety precaution, Ian. Don't worry about it."

I sigh. "Dad, please. I don't need you hiring people to watch out for me. That has to stop. Okay?"

He nods. "Fine."

* * *

When I get home, Tyler is parked in my driveway. I park my Porsche in the garage and meet him at his driver's side door.

He gets out of his car, walks to the rear of the vehicle, and pops the trunk. Then he pulls out an overnight bag. He's still wearing his suit, and the sight of him takes my breath away.

I can't help the grin on my face. "Are you staying the night?"

He nods. "Unless you have objections."

"No! Not at all." My face heats up in anticipation. I don't know if he's ready to take things to the next level, but I sure am.

"How'd it go with your dad?" he says as we walk up the front steps.

"Great. He promised to back off, and he agreed to get rid of the private eye. Not only that, my mom wants you to come to a family dinner."

Tyler laughs. "I'm impressed. This morning, your dad was threatening to get me fired, and now I'm invited to dinner."

"Honestly, he means well. The trick is to get my mom on board first. Then, my dad usually caves."

"I'll remember that. Get on your mom's good side."

"Have you eaten?" I ask him.

"Yeah, I got a bite to eat out of the office vending machines."

I unlock the front door and hold it for him as he steps inside and sets his duffle bag on the floor. I watch him remove his suit jacket first, then the holster and gun, hanging everything in the hall closet. His movements are precise and efficient, and I find that sexy as hell.

After Tyler shuts the closet door, he turns to me, grasping my shoulders and walking me backward until I'm against the wall. His mouth collides with mine, his lips controlling a very fierce and hungry kiss. My pulse instantly skyrockets.

"I've been thinking about this all day," he says against my lips. He leans into me, his chest pressed against mine, our hips aligned. "About you. About us. About *this*."

When he grinds his erection against me, my cock immediately hardens.

"You said you want me to fuck you," he says, his breath coming hard. "Do you still feel that way?"

I clutch his shoulders, desperate for what he's offering. "God, yes." The thought of him inside me—*fuck*! I can't even imagine. My knees go weak at the thought.

He picks up his duffle bag, grabs my hand, and pulls me toward the stairs. "Then come show me how it's done."

〜 30

Tyler Jamison

I've thought about this long and hard, and I finally decided I'm doing it. I may be scared shitless, but I'm tired of being stuck where I've been. I'm tired of being afraid to take chances. Since I met Ian, and especially since I came out to my family, I've realized the only thing holding me back from having what I want are my own fears.

I'm done with that.

I'm tired of being alone and afraid to feel something.

Ian makes me feel things I've never allowed myself to feel before. He makes me want things—a future with someone. He makes me think it's possible.

"Lights twenty percent," I say once we're in Ian's room. The overhead lights flicker on, bathing us in soft light. I dump my overnight bag on a chair and rummage around inside, retrieving the supplies I bought on the way over here. I drop a box of condoms and lube on the bed.

Ian glances down at the supplies, a huge grin on his face. "That'll do." He picks up the lube which, according to the package, is specifically intended for anal sex. "Good choice. I approve."

"I Googled it." I palm my erection through my trousers. "You'd better be sure, because this is going in your ass." I'm not trying to brag, but I want him to know what he's signing up for.

He flushes as he whips off his shirt and tosses it aside. "I'm not complaining, mind you, but what's gotten into you? I like it when you're bossy."

"Good. Get used to it. I've been told on numerous occasions, and by good authority, that I'm a controlling bastard. I've waited a long time for this." I lay my hand on the center of his chest, my palm flush on his smooth skin. Those nipple piercings beckon me. Heat surges through me, and my belly tightens. My cock throbs. "If you're game—if you're willing to trust me—then let's do it."

Ian looks me in the eye as he unbuttons my shirt, from the neck down. "I'll need to shower first," he says, very matter-of-factly. "There's some preparation that goes into this, you know, for me anyway. You can't just stick it in me like you would a pussy."

He shoves my shirt off me, and then he frees my undershirt

from my waistband and pulls it up and over my head. His gaze goes to my bare chest, his eyes burning and his chest rising. He lays his warm hands on me, stroking my pecs, then my shoulders and deltoids. When his gaze lands on one of my nipples, he licks his bottom lip.

He leans forward and swipes his tongue across the flat disc. Pleasure shoots through me. Then he slides his palms down the front of my trousers, squeezing my erection. The pressure is incredible. When I groan, he smiles.

"Make yourself at home," he says. "Relax. There's a bottle of whiskey on my dresser over there and some glasses. I won't be long."

After Ian disappears into the bathroom, I wander over to his dresser to find a half-full bottle of Glenfiddich. At least the kid has good taste in liquor. I pour myself a shot and knock it back, reveling in the firestorm. I try not to think about what he's doing in there. I'm already nervous as hell.

I pour a second shot and take the glass with me when I sit in an armchair by the window. It's dark out now, and the streetlights flicker through the dense canopy of leaves outside.

I'm nervous. Mostly because I'm afraid I'll do something wrong, like commit some sort of gay sex faux pas.

I lose track of time as I sit and stew over this. It all comes back to one thing: I'm afraid of hurting him. He says I won't, and I have to trust him because he knows what he's doing. But still, he's the one taking all the risk here.

"Hey! Stop overthinking."

I glance across the room at Ian, who's standing half-naked in the bathroom doorway, with only a towel wrapped around his lean waist. From here, I can see light glinting off one of his piercings, and all I can think about is how much I want to lick them. I stand, holding my empty glass in my hand.

"How many of those have you had?" he says, grinning at me as he crosses the room to join me.

"Two."

"You've had enough." He grabs the bottle and pours himself a shot. Then he raises his glass to me. "To Tyler, who's about to pop his man-cherry."

"To us," I counter, nodding as he downs his shot.

After setting down his glass, he reaches for my belt buckle. "We need to get you naked."

I grab his hands. "Ian, wait. Before we go any further, there's something I need to say." I look him in the eye, and he watches me just as intently. "I suppose we should have talked about this before now. It's a little late to spring this on you, but it's important. I want you to know... I want you more than anything, but I won't share you."

His eyes widen.

"I need to make that clear. I've seen you at the clubs. I've seen how the guys flock around you. I'm okay with you dancing with your friends, and I'm okay with harmless flirting, but if we're going to be *together*, it has to be exclusive. I'm just not wired for anything else. Can you live with that?"

He nods, his throat working as he swallows. "Jesus, you scared me. I thought you were going to say something crazy. Yeah, I can live with that." He cups my face and steps closer as he finishes unbuckling my belt. "I'll let you in on a little secret."

Ian lowers his voice as he tugs my slacks and boxers off. "I've never wanted anyone the way I want you. I'll gladly agree to anything you say if it means we're together." And then he kisses me, his lips gently clinging to mine, nudging mine apart as he licks his way inside.

After I pull the towel free from his waist and toss it to the floor, we're both naked. Ian's already hard, his impressive erection straining upward. I wrap my fingers around him and squeeze, hard enough to get his undivided attention. He sucks in a breath.

"Tell me if I do something wrong," I say.

"Stop worrying. It's not rocket science. You've had sex before."

"Yeah, but not like this. Fine. I'll stop worrying."

I've had two shots of whiskey, but I'm far from drunk. I almost wish I was drunk, because my nerves are shot to hell.

I walk Ian back toward the bed, until he falls onto the mattress. I follow him down, looming over him on my hands and knees, caging him in. He gazes up at me with eager anticipation as he skims my sides with his hands. Looking down at him, I feel a heady sense of power. This beautiful man is about to be mine.

My heart hammers in my chest, partly from nerves and partly from desire. There's no doubt my body has hopped on board the arousal train. My cock strains against gravity, hot and throbbing. Already the tip is glistening as pre-cum leaks out.

I brush Ian's hair back from his face and gaze into a mesmerizing pair of green eyes. His chest rises and falls with quick, heavy breaths.

I run my thumb over his lush bottom lip, wanting to taste it. "You're so beautiful."

His lips turn up. "I bet you say that to all the cute guys."

I scoff. "Hardly. You're the first."

He slips his arms around my neck, his hands warm against my nape. "I'm glad I'm your first."

I lean down and kiss him, and he opens up to me, our tongues colliding, stroking. The kiss goes from hesitant to hungry in a matter of seconds.

I kiss my way down his throat, past his collarbone, to his sternum before crossing over to one nipple. When I flick my tongue over a piercing, he arches his back with a hoarse cry.

"Are they sensitive?" I say.

He nods. "God, yes. Do it again." His hands are in my hair now, gripping and tugging, and he brings my mouth back to his nipple.

I lick one nipple, teasing the piercing with the tip of my tongue. He bucks upward with a groan.

I kiss my way across his chest, tasting his skin along the way, and I then I lick his other nipple, toying gently with the barbell before kissing it.

"Fuck," he groans.

His nipples have tightened into little points, and I imagine that makes them even more sensitive. I lick one again, then blow warm breath on it; he cries out and arches his back off the mattress.

My lips move lower, skimming down his torso, past the slight ridges of his abs and the indent of his belly button, which is also pierced. I tongue the curved barbell, and then I kiss my way to his hip bones, first one and then the other. As my mouth moves lower, closer to his straining erection, his hips shoot up off the mattress.

"Fuck, Tyler!" he gasps. "Are you going to fuck me or torture me to death?"

"Patience, Ian. I assume men enjoy foreplay too, right?"

"Yeah, but damn! You're killing me."

I wrap my fingers around his thick erection and lick the tip before sucking the head into my mouth. I want our first time to be good for him. I want him to remember this night and want more. Using my hand and my tongue, I ratchet up his pleasure until his cock is throbbing. He grips my biceps hard, his fingers digging into my muscles.

When I feel the blood pulsing in his cock, I release him, slowly backing off. I don't want him to come just yet.

He growls in frustration. "You are such a cock tease!"

I smile, moving up to kiss him again. "You haven't seen anything yet."

"Oh my God, I've created a monster."

I grab a condom packet and tear it open, setting it aside.

"XL?" Ian says, eyeing the packet with a smirk on his face.

"You'd better believe it."

He wraps his hand around my cock. "Damn."

"How do you want to do this?" I ask him.

He bucks his hips. "Let me turn over. Doggy style will be easier for you to see what you're doing."

I stand at the foot of the bed, and he rolls onto his hands and knees. While he positions himself at the edge of the mattress, I quickly sheath myself and reach for the lube. *Jesus, this is really happening.*

"I don't want to hurt you," I say, running my hands over his smooth, taut ass cheeks.

"Stop overthinking and just fuck me. I told you, I bottom—"

"Like a porn star. I know." I slap his ass once, the sound startlingly loud. There's a pink mark on his fair complexion.

"Ow! What was that for?"

"I don't want you to get complacent." I run my hands over his round ass, learning the feel of his skin, the shape of him. When I squeeze his buttocks, he moans.

I admit to watching a few gay porn videos this past week, when I lay in bed unable to sleep. I don't know how realistic they were, but at least it was something to go on. I'll have to trust Ian to correct me if I make a mistake.

I apply lube, which is in a handy squirt bottle, directly to the condom. Then I dribble some between his ass cheeks. He moans low in his throat, and I can't tell if that's good or bad. "Are you okay?"

He presses his face into the sheet, groaning. "Yes! Just hurry up. You're killing me."

I apply lube to my middle finger, and when I run the slippery tip of my finger around the rim of his puckered hole, he groans.

"Finally!"

When I press my finger in, just a bit, he relaxes, loosening his muscles, and my finger slides in easily. I stroke him, spreading the lube. I curl my finger toward his belly and search for his prostate. I want to make this damn good for him. I know when I find it, because he moans loudly as he clutches the sheet. I keep stroking him inside, slow and steadily, until he drops his head to the mattress and his thighs start to shake.

"Are you sure you've never done this?" he says, fisting his cock.

I sink my finger deeper, then slide it out and back in, lubing him up and brushing against his prostate each time. I don't know if what I read was bullshit or not, but I did some research. I didn't want to go into this completely blind.

I slide a second finger inside him and stroke, the lube making it easier.

He cries out, the sound garbled as he presses his face into the bedding. "Shit! I thought you didn't know what you were doing!"

"I told you, I Googled it."

"Fuck, Tyler!"

As I stroke him, I monitor his breathing and the sounds he's making, judging his level of arousal. His muscles tense.

"Okay, stop!" he gasps. "You're going to make me come, and I don't want to come yet. Not until you do."

I remove my fingers and grasp my cock instead, which is rock hard and throbbing with need. Positioning the head at his opening, I lean into him, letting my weight do most of the work. I watch, mesmerized, as the head of my cock presses against his opening. He sighs, breathing out, and suddenly his body opens for me, and the head of my cock sinks into him. He fists the bedding, and I hear him panting. And then I hear a long, agonized groan.

"Ian?"

"I'm fine!" He gasps, and then makes a plaintive sound. "Damn, you're big."

I laugh. "I warned you."

"Shut up." Without warning, he pushes back against me, groaning loudly as my cock sinks farther into him. "Oh, God, fuck!"

My brain is short circuiting. He's so damn tight, my cock feels like it's being squeezed in a vice. I've never felt anything this fucking good. I rock forward a bit, then back, and he moans, his fists flexing on the bedding. He keeps pushing back against me, impaling himself on my cock, and I think it's his way of signaling that he's fine, and that I should stop worrying and start fucking.

I clutch his hips, my fingers digging into his flesh, and slide deeper. Forward and back I move, trying to lube him up well. Each time, I sink a bit deeper, and his moans get a little hoarser. I have to trust that he'll let me know if something's wrong.

I work myself in, a bit at a time, my cock hard and throbbing, until finally my groin is pressed up against his ass. I hold my position for a moment, gritting my teeth at the exquisite tightness. My breath shallows and my heart pounds. Already my balls are drawn up tight, and I'm so close. My nerves are on fire, every inch of my spine electrified.

When I start to move, I reach around and stroke his cock again in rhythm with my own thrusting. I want him with me. Slowly, I rock in and out of him. The pleasure is mind-blowing, and I have to grit my teeth against coming too soon. He's a lot younger than me, so I have a reputation to worry about. If I blow my load within the first two minutes, I'll never hear the end of it.

As my fist pumps his cock, his breathing quickens. With a loud cry, he comes on the comforter, his cock bucking and pulsing in my hand. His entire body shudders as I milk him, gently coaxing each spasm.

His legs are shaking, and he collapses on the mattress, face down. I follow him down, my cock still deeply embedded, my body covering his. I wrap one arm around his shoulders, holding him close. "Is this okay? I'm not crushing you?"

"I'm fine," he says. He clutches my wrist tightly and leans over to kiss the back of my hand. Then he bucks his ass against me. "Fuck me, Tyler."

That's all the green light I need to resume thrusting. I pull back to the tip and then sink inside him. His body is relaxed and open, accepting my thrusts.

"Harder," he murmurs.

I start moving, harder, faster.

"God, yes, like that," he cries. "More!"

My hips slam against his backside as I power into him, my cock sliding easily. His muffled moans and hoarse cries only encourage me. I let loose and tunnel into his ass, my loins slapping against his ass cheeks.

I can barely catch my breath as my lungs and heart work over-time. Ian bucks up into me, meeting me thrust for thrust. His hand has a death grip on my wrist, holding me to him. I lean down, angling my head to reach his mouth, and we kiss hotly, our mouths devouring each other's.

"Oh, fuck yes!" he cries against my lips. "Shit! Yes!"

When I come, it's like nothing I've ever felt before. My cock explodes, jettisoning liquid heat into the condom. I'm on a whole new plane. I see stars, literally, and for a minute I'm afraid I might actually pass out on him. I slow my strokes, my body shuddering from an overload of sensation. I savor every second, every pulsing beat, as I milk my climax.

When I finally slide out of him, I collapse beside him on the mattress. I can barely catch my breath. "Ian, are you okay?"

He rolls to face me, his arms going around my waist. "I'm dead." And then he tucks his head into the crook of my shoulder, nestling against me. His lips skim over my heated skin as he trails tiny kisses across my shoulder to my throat.

I lie quietly for a moment, giving my heart rate a chance to come down to a more normal level. My lungs billow as I try to catch my breath. I wrap my free arm across his shoulders and hold him to me. "That was amazing." I know it sounds trite, but it's the truth. I had no idea it would be like that. Nothing I've ever felt in my life has come anywhere near it.

"No shit," Ian says, laughing softly against my skin. He's just as winded as I am. "Jesus, where've you been all my life?"

At his quiet words, my heart twists painfully. My throat tightens and I feel tears pricking the backs of my eyes. I think of all the years I suffered through loneliness, sadness, and confusion. I think about all the guilt and self-loathing.

I pull him closer and press my lips to his forehead. "I'm here now."

With a groan, Ian rolls to his back and turns to look at me. "I've never been fucked so well in my life."

I laugh. "You're just saying that."

"No, I'm not. I mean it." He sits up, making a face. "I jizzed all over the comforter. I'll grab a clean one, and then we can cuddle. I need you to hold me after that."

I shove him playfully, and he gets up to grab another blanket while I dispose of the condom. We quickly change the bedding. I know he was just kidding about needing me to hold him, but I suspect both of us are a bit shaken. Or maybe it's just me being overly emotional after popping my man-cherry. *Is that even a word?*

Since we're already up, we head to the bathroom to get ready for bed. Then we both climb under the covers.

"I hope that was okay," I say.

He nudges me with his elbow, and then he slides his arm across my waist and presses close to me. "Did you not hear me say I've never been fucked so well?"

"I figured you were just being nice."

"I was being totally serious." He brushes his thumb across my nipple. "Have you ever thought about getting piercings?"

I laugh. "No."

"You'd look hot."

"Yours are pretty hot." I roll him onto his back and loom over him. "Lights off."

The room darkens, and I can barely make out his features. There's just a bit of moonlight filtering through the trees into the room.

I lower my mouth to his, and he sighs into a kiss.

I grab both of his wrists and pin them to the pillow above his head. Then I gaze down at him, searching his expression. His chest rises and falls steadily, his breath coming fast. He struggles half-heartedly against my hold before settling down. Then I kiss him, and he melts into me with another satisfied sigh.

I roll him to his side and spoon behind him, wrapping my arm around his waist and drawing him close. *He's mine.*

There are a million and one things I want to say to him, but I can't. It's too soon. And I'm probably feeling a bit over-emotional after having the best sex of my life. At least I can be honest with him and tell him that much. "Now I know what I've been missing. That was the best sex I've ever had."

His lips curve upward. "Me, too."

"No, I mean it."

"So do I, Tyler." He brings my hand to his mouth and kisses the back of it.

31

Ian Alexander

I wake the next morning with a start, expecting Tyler to be gone like he was yesterday morning. But he's not gone. In fact, he's still sound asleep. He's lying on his belly, one arm tucked beneath his pillow. His hair is disheveled, and he looks sexy as hell. Everything about him is sexy. I don't know how I got so lucky.

He's here in my bed. He wants me. And I was his *first*.

Tyler doesn't give himself easily. And right now, he's all mine.

Last night was fucking amazing. He was so determined to do things right. I loved his strength and his power, and that little taste of domineering personality. I have a feeling I'm going to be seeing more and more of that as he grows comfortable being with me. I certainly hope so.

I keep thinking about what he said last night. *I won't share you.*

I'm okay with that. I'm okay if he wants to get all possessive and snarl at guys who get up in my personal space. I picture the two of us at the clubs, me dancing with my friends, and Tyler watching from the bar, glaring at any guy who gets too close. I shiver just thinking about it.

Damn. I'm definitely okay with that.

Lying on my side, I watch him sleep. My cock hardens as I replay last night in my head. *He* was amazing. I want that again. Now! All day, and every day. But I know I'm getting ahead of myself. Just because last night was amazing doesn't mean he wants more. It doesn't mean we're on the same page.

I'm his first. Now that he's taken the first step down this path, he might want to move on, see what else is out there, explore and experiment. Isn't that what I've been doing my whole adult life? I've never before wanted to settle down.

I check the time. It's seven already on a Friday, and I'm surprised he's not up getting ready for work. I wonder if I should wake him.

The sheet has slipped off his shoulder, and I have a front row view of his muscular arm and shoulder. I want so badly to reach out and touch him.

"Hey," Tyler says, his voice husky from sleep.

My gaze shoots to his. He's watching me with a very satisfied and amused expression.

"Hey yourself." I reach out and run my fingers through his tousled hair. "Don't you have to go to work?"

He shakes his head. "Nope. I took the day off."

My belly clenches at the realization he doesn't have to rush off to work. We're naked, in my bed, and we have the whole day ahead of us. "Do you have plans today?"

He grins. "None at all." And then he rolls onto his back and stretches, groaning loudly. "What about you? Do you have plans today?"

I'm hard just watching him, and based on the action I see beneath the bedding, it appears he woke up with a hard-on. My heart rate picks up in anticipation. "Maybe we could shower and then go out for breakfast. I was planning to go to the marina today to check on the repairs to my boat. Would you like to come?"

He turns to me with a grin on his handsome face. "I'd love to. What else?"

"It's Friday. I usually meet the guys at a club around ten." I practically hold my breath as I wait for his reaction. Going out with friends, cutting loose, and dancing are a big part of my life. It's something I look forward to.

He shrugs. "Okay. As long as you don't expect me to dance. That's just not my thing. But you can. I like watching you."

"Really? You wouldn't mind?" I find the idea of bringing Tyler with me to a club very appealing. I love the thought of him *watching* me dance. "Since Diablo's is closed, the guys have been hanging out at Sapphires."

When he sits up, the sheet falls to his waist. My gaze roams down his torso, past his broad shoulders and muscular arms, past his abs, to the happy trail that leads below the sheet.

"Honestly, I don't mind," he says. "Relationships are all about give and take, right? You want to dance, so dance. As long as you're okay with me just watching."

Is that what we have? A relationship? My heart stutters before kicking into overdrive. I sit up beside him and turn to face him, cupping his cheeks and pulling him close for a kiss. "I'm more than okay with that."

* * *

We decide to take my Porsche to the marina, since I have a member's permit to park there and Tyler doesn't. The weather's nice this morning, so I put the top down. I grab my Ray-Bans from the glovebox and hand Tyler a spare pair.

I peer into the rearview mirror at my own reflection, then tilt the mirror so he can see himself. "Damn, we look boss."

Tyler grins at me as I start the engine and back the car out of the carriage house.

It's a short drive to the marina. I take the access road down to the private club and park. There's a members-only clubhouse at the end of the boardwalk with a café that serves up an awesome breakfast.

We walk along the pier to the restaurant, passing a bait and tackle shop and a Jet ski rental business. When we reach the clubhouse, Tyler opens the door for me. *Quite the gentleman.* I get goosebumps when he ushers me inside, his hand grazing my lower back in a fleeting gesture. No guy has ever done that for me before.

Breakfast is in full swing, but there are a few tables available. We don't have to wait long. A young woman escorts us to a table for four. Tyler pulls out a chair for me, and I sit. Then he takes the seat catty-corner from me instead of opposite me.

Our server comes to the table and pours us each a cup of coffee.

"The food here is great," I tell Tyler. "Try the breakfast special. It's got a bit of everything."

Tyler lays down his menu. "Sounds good to me." Then he takes a sip of his black coffee.

I pour a generous amount of French vanilla creamer into mine, along with three packets of sugar.

He watches me stir my coffee, scowling when I take a sip. "Is that supposed to be coffee or a milkshake?"

Laughing at his expression, I lay my arm across his shoulders. "It's delicious. That's what it is."

An older couple sitting near us looks our way and stares unabashedly. Noticing them, Tyler shifts uncomfortably away from me, and I drop my arm.

I shouldn't let it get to me. He's obviously not ready for displays of public affection. He might never be ready for that. This is all new to him, and it's going to be an adjustment for both of us. Still, I'd be lying if I said that didn't sting. I pick up my menu and pretend to be engrossed in it.

Our server comes to take our orders.

"I'll have the breakfast special," Tyler says.

My heart is thudding hard and I avoid looking at him. Instead, I glance up at our server. "I'll have the same. And some orange juice, please."

She collects the menus and leaves to fill our orders. I can feel Tyler's gaze on me. I look anywhere but at him.

After a long moment of dead silence, Tyler lets out a heavy sigh. "Ian, I'm—"

"No, don't," I say, lifting a hand to cut him off. My throat is so tight it hurts, and I can already feel the tears threatening to spill. "I'm sorry I touched you. I won't do it again."

I glance over at the elderly couple, and it appears we now have their undivided attention. *Wonderful!* It's our first meal out together, and people are staring.

Tyler sets his coffee down. "Ian." His voice is low enough that only I can hear him. "I'm sorry. I—you took me by surprise. I didn't mean to pull away. It was an automatic reflex."

My chest tightens, and I feel a searing pain where my heart should be located. Right now, it's up in my throat as I realize how much this—he—is affecting me. I've never had a relationship that lasted more than a night. It's always been that way for me, and it was intentional. I never wanted to get close to anyone before. Looking down at the table, fidgeting with my spoon, I say, "This is new to me, too."

He takes a sip of his coffee and eyes me over the rim of his cup. "What is?"

"No one's ever spent the night before, and you've done it twice now."

I glance over at our curious audience to find them still watching us. I stare right back at them, and the man has the decency to look away. But the woman elbows her husband and continues watching us.

Our server returns with our food. She refills our coffee cups and asks if we need anything else.

"No, thank you," Tyler says, looking to me for confirmation. "This looks good."

I keep my eyes on my plate as I concentrate on eating. I can tell Tyler's watching me, but I'm trying to ignore him. I don't want to call any more attention to us. He's uncomfortable enough as it is.

After we finish our meal, our server returns to our table. "Will this be one check or two?" she says.

My head snaps up. "Two."

"One check, please," Tyler says in a firm voice, as if I hadn't spoken.

The girl looks from me to Tyler, obviously needing clarification.

Tyler smiles and says, "Just one check."

"Yes, sir." She pulls a single check from her apron pocket and hands it to him.

My heart does a somersault as I watch Tyler pull his wallet from his back pocket and hand her a credit card.

While she's processing the payment, I look at him, trying to ignore the old lady who's still openly staring. "You didn't have to do that. I can pay for my own food."

The corner of his mouth turns up. "I know you can."

When the transaction is completed, we head out of the restaurant. As we pass by the table of the couple who'd been staring, I can't resist leaning close to the woman and saying, "Next time, do everyone a favor and take a picture. It will last longer."

Tyler stifles a laugh as he herds me out the door.

Once we're safely outside, I growl out my frustration. "God, what a nosey old bitch!"

"Does that happen a lot?"

"What? The staring? Yes. Sometimes it's a lot worse. Sometimes they're openly hostile."

We walk along the pier toward the dock that leads out to my boat. We have to pass by Eric's boat first. The police tape is still in place. Next is my boat. The police tape has been removed, and there's no obvious sign that my boat was the site of a shooting.

I step aboard and climb up to the main deck, Tyler right behind me. He joins me on the main deck, standing beside me as I study the new boards. The repair work is flawless.

Tyler steps closer, his arm brushing against mine. "They did a great job."

I nod. "No more blood stains."

He slips an arm around my waist. "Ian, I'm sorry."

My heart thuds in my chest. I don't think he's talking about my boat, or even about Eric. He's referring to what happened at breakfast. "Don't worry about it, Tyler. It's fine." I pull away and head toward the galley steps. "I want to check below real quick. I'll just be a minute." And then I head down the steps, needing a moment to myself.

I do a quick visual sweep of the galley, making sure everything looks right. You never know what might happen when there are strangers on your boat.

Tyler follows me down and looks around, studying the galley, with its custom cherry cabinetry, stainless-steel appliances, and the built-in seating for four beside a large window. "Nice."

I realize he's never been below deck before. "Thanks."

I continue down the narrow corridor that leads to the front of the ship. I know I'm reading too much into what happened at the restaurant—I'm overreacting—but I can't seem to help it.

The close walls of the ship are pressing in on me, tighter and tighter, and I'm having trouble breathing. I shouldn't have come down here. I'd be better off up top, out in the open.

"Ian."

I slip inside the stateroom and close the door behind me. My emotions are spiraling out of control. I sit at the foot of the bed and lean forward, my arms propped on my thighs. I work on controlling my breathing, slow and steady.

The doorknob turns, and Tyler walks into the stateroom. He quickly scans the room—the king-size bed, a small round table and two chairs in front of a panoramic window that spans the whole front of the boat.

I flinch when he crouches in front of me. He lays his hands on my thighs, gripping me firmly. His touch grounds me.

"Ian, what's going on? Talk to me." His low voice steadies me.

I move to stand, to push him away, but his hands tighten on

my legs, and he's not so easy to dislodge.

"Look at me."

Reluctantly, I meet his concerned gaze.

"Talk to me, please," he says. "Tell me what you're thinking."

"It's nothing. I shouldn't have touched you in the restaurant. I'm sorry I made you feel uncomfortable." I shrug. "I won't do it again."

Tyler frowns. "None of that was your fault, Ian. I was caught off-guard, and I didn't react well. And those people staring at us— I'm definitely not used to that."

"It's okay."

"This is all new to me, Ian. I'm not used to that type of public scrutiny. It's going to take some getting used to." He stands and pulls me to my feet and into his arms. "But one thing I am sure of... I like it when you touch me. In private and in public."

When I feel tears threatening to spill, I attempt to pull away, to put some space between us, but he holds me fast.

"Be patient with me, Ian. I'm trying to figure it all out."

I don't even realize my cheeks are wet until he brushes my tears away.

His hand slides behind my head, and he draws me in for a kiss, at first gentle, just a touching of lips. But soon, he increases the pressure, and his lips coax mine open. When his fingers tighten on the back of my head, I groan.

"Do you like that?" he murmurs against my mouth.

My response is breathy. "Yes."

"We both have a lot to learn about each other," he says. "And it's going to take time. But I've learned one thing already." His voice gentles. "You feel rejection easily, don't you?"

As fresh tears sting my eyes, I try in earnest to push him away, but he doesn't budge.

"Shh." He wipes my tears. "I'm not going to let you run," he says.

The tighter he holds onto me, the harder my cock gets.

"Let's make a deal," Tyler says. "You be patient with me, and I'll try not to fuck up. Okay?"

When I laugh, he smiles.

"Is that a yes?"

I nod. "Yes."

"Good." Then he leans in and kisses me. His arms go around me, holding me close. I feel surrounded by him, cosseted, and it comforts me. It's also a hell of a turn-on.

"Now, it's a beautiful day, and we're here on your beautiful boat. Are you going to take me out on the lake, or what? We have time to kill before we go out tonight."

I smile. "You're still willing to go clubbing tonight?"

"If it's something you want to do, then yes, I'm willing."

"But it's a public place. Are you sure you're ready for that?"

"I've been to Diablo's a few times with you already."

"Yeah, but that was different. That was before."

"Before what?" He releases one of my hands and presses his palm to the front of my jeans, caging my erection. "Before I fucked you?"

My face heats. "Yes." *Please do it again.*

"It's fine. I don't mind going. There's nothing to worry about, Ian, as long as your friends don't cross the line. Remember, I don't share. You might want to tell them that."

32

Tyler Jamison

Ian is in his element as he pilots his yacht through the marina and out onto the lake. I don't have any boating experience, but he did let me help prep the boat to cast off.

Once we're out of the marina and out in open water, I sit beside him in the cockpit and watch him operate the controls. "I'm impressed that you can operate this boat alone."

"It's only forty feet," he says, as if that's no big deal.

"*Only?* What if you got injured or sick out on the water? What then?"

"I'd radio the Coast Guard for assistance."

"What if you'd broken your leg and couldn't get to a radio?"

He pats his back pocket, where his phone resides. "I'd text them. My phone's always on me."

I laugh. "Smart-ass." He's got an answer for everything. "I still think it's pretty risky to come out by yourself."

He leans into me, bumping his shoulder against mine. "Then it's a good thing you're here, isn't it? If I get sick or break my leg, *you* can call the Coast Guard."

I watch as Ian lifts his face into the wind, smiling up at the sunshine. He clearly loves it out here. He's happy now, carefree—nothing like the insecure man I kissed earlier below deck.

Frankly, his insecurities baffle me. He's incredibly handsome and charismatic. He's smart. He's adored by his friends. He's close to his family. So, where does the insecurity come from, and why is he so susceptible to feeling rejected?

His father's cryptic words come back to me. *You don't know anything about my son. You don't know what he's been through. And I'm not going to let you undo all the good his mother and I have done for him. He's finally in a good place in his life, and I won't let you fuck that up.*

I gently clasp the back of his neck. "Ian, tell me about your life before you were adopted."

He turns to me, his brow furrowing. "How do you know I was adopted?"

"Your father told me. He said I had no idea what you'd been through. What did he mean?"

"My dad has a big mouth." Ian frowns down at the console in

front of him, inspecting the myriad dials. He increases the speed, and the boat skims high over the waves.

"Ian, please. Answer my question. I need to understand."

"I really don't want to talk about this."

"I think we should."

He shakes his head. "There's not much to tell, Tyler. I was born to a single mother who had a drug habit she couldn't kick. Child Protective Services took me from her. I was in and out of foster care for a few years. She'd try to get clean and promise I could come home again. I'd get placed back with her, but every time she'd mess up and start using again, and I'd be back in the system. Finally, the powers that be had enough of the revolving door that was my life, and I was put into care permanently—with the Alexanders. Once my birth mother's rights were terminated by the state, they adopted me. The rest is history."

I can hear the pain in his voice as he recites his history. "I'm so sorry."

He shrugs off my touch. "Don't be. The Alexanders were the best thing that ever happened to me. Besides, other kids have had it worse."

"Ian, don't minimize what you went through." I reach for his hand, linking our fingers together. "Where's your mom now?"

"I have no idea."

Ian's insecurities make a lot more sense now. He grew up with so much uncertainty, his mother coming and going from his life. I admire the Alexanders for giving him a stable home and for trying to help him overcome his early childhood. Ian lived his formative years knowing nothing but disappointment. I'm not surprised he struggles with rejection and feeling abandoned.

Ian turns the boat in a wide arc, changing direction as we head northward. We cruise the shoreline, past Kenilworth. Ian's attention is focused solely on the controls. Honestly, I think he's gone somewhere else in his head.

I rub gentle circles on his back. "Do you want to talk about it?"

He runs his fingers through his hair and blows out an agitated breath. "She traded her body for heroin."

"Jesus, Ian." *He was just a little kid.* "I'm sorry."

Ian swallows hard, shaking his head as if trying to clear the memories from his head. "Before the men came over, she'd lock me in an upstairs bedroom. I realized later she was probably trying to protect me."

He stops talking as tears track down his cheeks into his beard. I don't say anything. I just wait to see if he'll say more.

"Sometimes, she'd pass out after shooting up, and I'd be locked up there for hours. Sometimes it felt like days. There weren't any lights in the room, and the window was boarded up. So at night, it was pitch-black in there. I used to sit in the closet and shake until I fell asleep."

"Is that why you leave the blinds open on your bedroom windows? So your room isn't dark?"

Staring straight ahead at the water, he nods. "She'd leave me boxes of dry cereal and bottles of water, but sometimes I couldn't get the water bottles open. Or I'd run out of cereal and have nothing to eat. I had to go to the bathroom in a training potty."

I watch, horrified as he shuts down right before my eyes. His expression grows flat, emotionless. The more he tells me, the less emotion he displays. I feel him distancing himself, and it scares me. Wanting to pull him back to me, I lean close and kiss his temple. "I'm so sorry, baby."

He shakes himself. "Somebody reported her to Child Protective Services. When they came to the apartment to do a welfare check, they found her passed out on the sofa downstairs, naked and covered in semen. They found me upstairs, locked in a dark room with nothing to eat or drink. They took me away that day, and that's when the revolving door started. She'd do rehab and sober up, and they'd let me go back, until the next time. This went on, over and over, until the state stepped in and terminated her rights. That's when my parents took me in, and within a year, they adopted me."

Ian wipes away the tears streaming down his cheeks. Then he stops the boat and drops anchor. As the boat rocks gently on the waves, he climbs down from the cockpit and heads to the bar on the main deck.

I follow him, at a complete loss as to how to help him. How to comfort him. I feel like a total shit for reopening all those painful memories.

He opens the fridge behind the bar and pulls out a bottle of water. He viciously unscrews the cap and guzzles half the bottle.

"Ian, I'm sorry, but I have to ask. Did any of those men ever hurt you? Did they touch you?"

He shakes his head. "No. I think that's why she locked me upstairs, so they wouldn't know I was there. I remember her telling me I had to be quiet like a mouse. She'd play loud music downstairs, and I think it was so no one could hear me crying."

He's shaking now. I take the bottle from him, set it on the bar, and wrap him securely in my arms. "I'm so sorry." I know the words are wholly inadequate, but I don't know what else to say. All I can think is, *Thank God those men never knew he was upstairs.*

I place my hand on the back of his head and force it down onto my shoulder. I turn toward him, my mouth close to his ear, and whisper to him, "It's okay, baby. No one can hurt you again. I won't let them." And then I think about Roy Valdez, and my stomach drops like a stone. Someone almost did hurt him, worse than anything imaginable.

My words are little comfort, and far too late. The damage was done to him years ago. I understand him so much better now, and instead of thinking he's insecure, I think it's a miracle that he's as strong and healthy as he is.

He's still shaking, and I'm sure it will take a while for those painful memories to fade once more into the background.

I kiss him. "I think you're incredibly brave and strong. Your mom was in a very bad situation, but it sounds like she did the best she could to protect you. She loved you, Ian. Even if she couldn't take care of you properly, she loved you."

He gazes at me with reddened eyes. "She didn't love me enough."

Now's not the time to talk to him about the insidious nature of drug addiction. Instead, I hold him firmly in my arms, and together we sway with the rocking motion of the boat.

"Addiction is complicated, Ian. It doesn't mean she didn't love you enough. I'm betting she loved you so much she knew she had to let you go."

When he starts sobbing, all I can do is hold him. I'm not letting go.

ꙅ 33

Tyler Jamison

An hour later, we raise the anchor and head back to the marina. Ian is quiet, lost somewhere deep inside his thoughts, but that's okay. I stay at his side, watching his cues, ready to help when he needs me.

Ian teaches me how to help him dock the boat. After he steers the boat into its slip, I hop out and secure the lines. Then I reconnect shore power. Finally, we can disembark.

We head back to Ian's place to grab a bite to eat before we head out clubbing. We end up grilling burgers on the roof. Ian's dark mood has lifted, and he's clearly in his happy place up here under the open sky. His need for open spaces and fresh air makes a lot more sense to me now. It's the antidote to having been locked up during his most vulnerable years.

When the sun begins to set, we clean up dinner and get ready to go out. I get a huge kick out of watching Ian decide what to wear. He's going to end up wearing jeans and a t-shirt, but my God, it takes him half an hour to decide *which* pair of jeans he should wear. I've never seen so many pairs of ripped jeans in one closet.

And then there's a decision to be made about which t-shirt to wear. His clothes rack looks like a gay pride flag, with all the hues of the rainbow, organized by color.

"What do you think?" he says to me as he surveys his options.

I'm standing in the closet doorway, leaning against the door-jamb, and enjoying the hell out of myself. Ian's wearing a pair of bright blue boxer-briefs that lovingly hug his perky apple butt cheeks. I'm torn between staring at his chest or his ass.

"I think you look amazing no matter what you wear," I tell him. It's true. I'm not just trying to flatter him. He would look good in a paper bag. I'm sure he considers me grossly underdressed in my jeans and gray Henley t-shirt.

Ian pulls a bright aqua t-shirt off the rack and holds it up to his chest. "How about this?"

"Perfect! Now put it on and let's go."

He rolls his eyes at me as he slips the shirt over his head. "You have no imagination whatsoever, Tyler."

Personally, clubbing is the last thing I want to do tonight. I'd rather we stay in and watch a movie, or just sit and talk, but Ian wants to see his friends, and I want him to be happy. So, we're going out.

We arrive at Sapphires at half past nine. According to the text messages that have been flying back and forth all evening between Ian and his buddies, many of his friends are already here.

I'm the designated driver tonight, which means Ian can drink, within reason of course. I'm not about to let him get drunk. I find a parking spot a block over from the club, and we walk. As always, there's a line of people wanting in, mostly men, but there are a couple of women in the line, too. As we walk past the entrance, the bouncer waves Ian forward. I imagine Ian could jump the line like he could at Diablo's, but he doesn't.

I know Ian is wealthy. How else could he afford his townhouse, a Porsche 911, and that yacht without having a paying job? I don't know the balance of his bank account, and frankly I don't want to know. I live on a detective's salary, and I do just fine. I live in a modest condo in a decent part of Lincoln Park, my BMW is paid off, and I don't need a lot.

I can understand why Ian's father thinks I'm out for his son's money. I can't really blame Martin for wanting to protect his son. The man doesn't know me from Adam. But hopefully, in time, if Ian and I are still seeing each other, Martin will come around.

Ian looks amazing tonight. His t-shirt lovingly hugs his lean torso and yes, the color does make his green eyes pop. I'm trying to prepare myself mentally for what it will be like inside the club. I've seen how much attention he attracts.

The bouncer, Nico, greets Ian warmly and motions him inside. I don't get the same degree of welcome, but when Ian grabs my hand and says, "He's with me," Nico nods reluctantly and lets me in.

Inside the club, just as it was in Diablo's, it's dark and the music is loud. The floor is literally shaking, as are my eardrums. The lights are predominantly blue—hence the club's name, Sapphires. A sprawling bar is the focal point of the room, with small, elevated dance floors scattered throughout the space. Men wearing iridescent G-strings—and nothing else—dance for money. Customers are lined up three-deep hoping to slip bills into those flimsy excuses for costumes.

I skim the premises, taking it all in, from the bar to the main dance floor to the raised stages. There's a VIP loft upstairs where patrons are lounging on sapphire blue velvet sofas.

I've been here before, at least a couple of times, in a professional capacity, but never off-duty. As I watch Ian, his face lit with excitement as he scans the crowd in search of his friends, I have a feeling we'll be doing this quite often. He's practically radiating energy.

When he turns to me, I plaster a smile on my face, but not quite fast enough.

Ian frowns. "We can leave if you want to." His smile fades and he starts to reach for my hand, but he stops himself.

Nightclubs, big crowds, loud music... it's just not my thing. And a dance floor... *God no.* I'd rather be doing just about *anything* else. But then I see the hopeful expression on Ian's face, and

I don't want to be the guy who rains on his parade. I reach for his hand and link our fingers. "No, it's fine. We can stay. I want you to have fun."

A moment later, two of Ian's friends descend upon us. I recognize them both from Diablo's.

"Ian, my God," one of them says, pulling Ian close for a quick hug. Then he holds Ian at arm's length and gives him a thorough once-over. "You look hot!" And then the guy turns his gaze to me.

"This is Chris," Ian tells me, introducing his friend. "And this is Trey."

Chris, blond-haired and blue-eyed, is wearing a pair of skin-tight bright orange skinny jeans and a billowy white pirate shirt, open at the chest, revealing two nipple piercings that sparkle beneath the bright blue strobe lights.

Trey, on the other hand, dark and brooding, is more subdued in black jeans and a black, sleeveless t-shirt that showcases his muscled, tattooed arms.

Trey watches me warily, while Chris gives me blatant fuck-me eyes.

Ian grins. "Guys, this is Tyler."

Chris grabs my hand and squeezes it. "Hello, gorgeous. Are you here on official police business?"

I shake my head. "Not tonight."

"Too bad," Chris says, "because I've broken a half-dozen laws already. You should arrest me."

Ian grabs Chris by the arm and pulls him away from me. "He's mine. No flirting!" Ian links his arm with Chris's. "Let's get drinks and then we'll hit the dance floor."

I follow Ian and his friends to the bar, where there's standing room only. They order shots with suggestive names, like *Rim Job* and *Blow Job*.

"And what about you, sugar?" the bartender says to me as he flashes a dazzling pair of dimples. "What can I get you?"

"I'll have a club soda."

The bartender looks incredulous. "Honey, surely you can do better than that."

Ian throws his arm over my shoulders. "He's my designated driver."

"Ooooh!" the guy says, giving Ian a high-five. "Lucky you, sweetie."

A *Rim Job* turns out to be scotch and Bailey's Irish Cream. Chris and Trey order the same, and after that round, they all order *Blow Jobs*. Maybe it's my age, but I feel like I'm out with a bunch of college kids who are looking to get hammered.

Their third round is *Sex on the Beach*. The alcohol is definitely having the desired effect. They're laughing at the most ridiculous things.

"Come on, let's dance," Chris says, grabbing Ian's hand and pulling him from the bar.

Ian turns back to me, a grin on his face. "You don't mind?"

I wave him on. "Go. Have fun. Don't mind me."

Ian pulls free from his friend and comes right up to me. By now, I've managed to grab a vacant barstool, and I'm sitting with my back to the bar.

Ian steps between my knees and clutches my thighs. He leans in close. "I want to kiss you right now, because you're so sweet," he says, barely loud enough to be heard over the music. "But I know you don't like PDA, so I won't."

I return his grin, tempted to call his bluff and kiss him instead. Part of me wants to stake my claim on him, right now, right here. I've noticed men eyeing him since we arrived, and I can't say I blame them. "I'll take a raincheck."

"Deal!"

And then Chris grabs Ian and pulls him away from me. The three of them head to the dance floor to dance to a Cher remix.

As I watch Ian dance, I'm amazed by his lack of inhibition. He throws himself into the dancing, his movements sharp and precise. On the dance floor, at least, he exudes confidence.

He's come so far from the abused toddler he once was. I wonder if his mother is still alive. I wonder if she grieves for the son she lost, or if she had any other children. When I asked Ian if his mother was still alive, he said he didn't know. I don't think he wants to know. He could have easily tracked her down if he did.

The Cher remix quickly morphs into a Beyoncé remix. Ian's at the center of attention, again. Several other guys have joined their little party. Ian's laughing, clearly enjoying himself, but every once in a while, his gaze returns to me, latching onto me as if I'm his security blanket. As if he's making sure I'm still here. That I haven't left him.

Damn. It's hard to imagine this outgoing, confident guy as unsure and insecure.

He locks gazes with me, and I can see the heat in his eyes.

When he crooks his finger at me, inviting me to join him on the dance floor, I shake my head and laugh. "Not going to happen, pal."

Ian breaks away from his entourage and rejoins me at the bar. "Come on," he says, grabbing my hand and pulling. "Just one dance? Please?"

I shake my head. "Nope. Sorry. I have two left feet."

He reaches for my glass and takes a swig, then makes a disgusted face. "Oh God, that's nasty!"

"It's club soda," I say, laughing at his pained expression.

He flags down a bartender. "Can I get a water, please? Just plain water." And while he's waiting for his water, he leans close enough to whisper in my ear. "I might be a little bit drunk."

As he wavers a bit, I reach out to steady him, my hands on his waist. "You think? You've had three shots."

He traces my brow with his index finger. "Then it's a good thing I have my own designated driver."

"Yes, it is." I bite back a grin. I love Ian's playful side. Maybe it's true that opposites attract. I'm pretty reserved, and he's anything but. I actually admire how fearless he can sometimes be.

The bartender hands him a bottle of spring water, and Ian chugs half of it before setting the bottle down next to my glass. He leans close and whispers in my ear, his warm breath sending a shiver down my spine. "I'm going back out on the dance floor. Try not to miss me, detective."

My hands slide down to his hips. "No promises, but I'll try."

His gaze burns into mine, and I know he's fighting the urge to kiss me.

I catch his gaze. "Ian?"

He sways a little drunkenly. "Yeah?"

"When we get home, I'm going to fuck you."

His eyes widen in slow motion, heat building, and I can't resist smiling at him. But then Chris is there, pulling Ian back toward the dance floor. Reluctantly, I release him and watch him go.

As I sit here sipping my club soda, watching Ian on the dance floor, I realize I'm sinking deeper and deeper into an infatuation with him. I have no idea where this is going. This is all new territory for me.

A few minutes later, a new face appears on the dance floor, out of nowhere. It's someone I recognize all too well, after having spent quite a bit of time sitting across an interrogation table from him. Brad Turner.

I stiffen as I observe the dynamic shifting around Ian. As Turner moves in closer, he pushes Ian's friends away. The expression on Ian's face transforms the instant he sees Turner. *He's afraid.*

Ian shakes his head as Turner slips behind him and wraps his arms around his waist. Turner presses his mouth to Ian's ear and says something that makes Ian flinch.

I'm already on my feet and halfway to the dance floor when Ian breaks free from Brad Turner and makes a beeline for the restrooms. Chris is hot on Ian's heels.

Turner stalks after Ian, disappearing down the hallway that leads to the restrooms.

Hell no!

34

Ian Alexander

Brad's threat reverberates in my head as I stalk down the hallway to the bathroom. "I'm going to fuck you until you scream my name and beg for more."

I think of Eric, and it breaks my heart. Brad might not have killed Eric, but he did fuck him, and the thought makes me sick. Eric deserved better.

Chris follows me into the restroom. "Are you okay? What did he say to you?"

A moment later, the restroom door opens. Strong hands latch onto my shoulders, turning me to face a seething Brad Turner.

Grimacing, he slams me against the cement wall, pinning my shoulders against the cold, hard surface.

"Get off me!" I yell as I plant my palms against his shoulders and push as hard as I can. He doesn't even budge.

"Let go of him!" Chris shrieks, tugging futilely on Brad's arm.

Brad slides one hand to my neck, his long fingers wrapping around my throat and cutting off my air. He leans in close, his face just inches from mine, his breath hot. "You've been a very bad boy, Ian. I saw the cop staring at you. He watches you like he *owns* you. You let him fuck you, didn't you?"

My head is spinning, partly from an alcohol buzz and partly from lack of air. My cheeks are burning, and blood pounds in my ears. I grab his wrist and try to dislodge his grip on my throat, but I'm too weak to be effective. I see bursts of light behind my eyes, and my lungs are on fire. I try desperately to suck in air, but I get nothing.

When the bathroom door slams into the wall, Brad turns to look. A moment later, he's wrenched off me so abruptly I sink to the floor, coughing and wheezing as I try to catch my breath.

I watch, horrified, as Tyler slams Brad against the wall. Brad's head hits the wall with an audible crack.

Tyler fists Brad's shirt and holds him in place. Teeth gritted, he growls, "Keep your fucking hands off Ian!"

Brad swings his fist, aiming for Tyler's face, but Tyler dodges the blow. Then Tyler hauls off and slams a fist into Brad's face.

There's a horrible crunching sound as blood sprays from Brad's nose. "Let go of me, you motherfucker!" he shouts.

Brad shoves Tyler hard, and Tyler stumbles back a few steps before righting himself. Brad charges Tyler, his fist connecting with Tyler's jaw. Tyler staggers back, wiping blood from his chin. And then he's on Brad again, driving his fist into Brad's belly, over and over, knocking the breath out of him. Brad folds over, wheezing as he sucks in air.

I'm still trying to catch my breath as Chris pulls me aside, out of the way of flying fists. I notice someone has propped the bathroom door open, and there's a crowd gathered in the doorway, spilling out into the hall. Numerous phone cameras are out, filming.

Two club security guards shove their way into the bathroom. They grab Tyler by the arms and drag him away from Brad, who's still hunched over, his arms clutching his waist. He's spitting blood and struggling for air.

"You'll pay for this, asshole!" Brad gasps. He straightens partway, still holding his abdomen. "I'll have your badge for assault!"

Brad pulls his phone out of his back pocket and starts filming. He points the camera at his own battered and bloody face, and then he points it at Tyler, who's disheveled, his lip split. He's struggling as the security guards restrain him.

His voice shakes as he narrates the video. "Here we have one of Chicago's finest, assaulting a citizen in the public restroom of a gay dance club. *Tyler Jamison.* Here you go, Chicago. This is what your hard-earned tax dollars are paying for."

Furious, Tyler jabs his finger at Brad. "You're under arrest, asshole, for assault and battery!"

"Tyler, no! You can't!" My voice is so hoarse, I'm not even sure he heard me. But I can't let him do this. If he arrests Brad, everyone at his precinct will find out about us. And I refuse to be the reason he gets outed.

"Go ahead, I dare you!" Brad spits out at Tyler. Then Brad turns his phone camera on me, where I'm kneeling on the floor next to Chris. "And here's Ian Alexander, the little cunt who started it all."

Tyler breaks free of the security guards and rushes Brad, ramming his shoulder hard into Brad's abdomen, knocking him back into the wall. Tyler manages to punch Brad twice more before the security guards can pull him back.

And all the while, numerous cameras in the open doorway are pointed right at us, filming everything.

A third security guard pushes his way through the crowd and into the bathroom. He takes one look at the scene, grabs Brad's arm, and hauls him out the door.

Tyler pulls free of the two guards who'd been restraining him and crouches down in front of me. "Are you okay?" He searches my face and neck, gently examining my throat. "Are you hurt?"

"I'm okay." My voice is shredded. "Get me out of here, please."

Tyler helps me to my feet and puts his arm around my waist, supporting my weight. The guards clear the clogged doorway, and Tyler walks me out into the hall. The onlookers lining the hallway stare at us as we head toward the exit.

This is all my fault. I was so fucking stupid for letting this happen. I should have done something different, anything, other than let Brad Turner get leverage against Tyler.

My throat feels raw, and I'm still struggling to catch my breath. I hardly pay any attention to how we make it outside. We walk to the next block, where Tyler's BMW is parked. He opens the front passenger door and helps me inside. I sit there, numb, as he buckles my seatbelt.

My gaze follows Tyler as he jogs around the front of the car to the driver's seat and slips in.

"Are you sure you're all right?" he says, turning in his seat to face me. He scans me from head to toe.

"I'm fine." I stare out the rain-streaked windshield at the darkened street. "It's raining," I say, stating the obvious. I hadn't even noticed. Tears sting my eyes as my throat tightens. "I'm so sorry."

Tyler cups the back of my head, and his touch feels so good I just want to close my eyes and lean into it. But I can't. I fucked up big time.

"You have nothing to be sorry for, Ian. None of that was your fault. Turner fucking assaulted you."

"He got video, Tyler! Of *you*! Of the security guards trying to restrain you. What if he presses charges against you? We have absolutely no proof that he assaulted me in the bathroom. It's just my word against his. And there's plenty of video evidence of you assaulting him."

Tyler's expression hardens. "I'll deal with that when the time comes." Frowning, he brushes my hair back from my forehead. "Right now, let's just get you home."

I lean my head back as hot tears burn my cheeks. "I'm a shit lousy boyfriend."

Tyler laughs. "Is that what we are? Boyfriends?"

My heart stops when I realize what I said. *Fuck!* Can this night get any worse? "Shit, I'm sorry. I shouldn't have said that."

"You need to stop apologizing." Tyler squeezes my hand and studies me like he's memorizing every detail. He wipes his bloody lip on the hem of his shirt before leaning in close and pressing his forehead to my temple. "Is that what we are? Boyfriends? Because this is all new to me, and I don't know the rules."

"Fuck the rules," I say. I haven't known Tyler that long, but I know he makes me feel things I've never felt before—things I've only dreamed of. I know enough to know I'm keeping him.

Tyler starts the engine and pulls out onto the street. Then he reaches for my hand and presses my palm to his thigh, covering my hand with his, linking our fingers. My heart soars.

"So, boyfriends then?" he repeats, as if he needs clarification. "It's official?"

I sigh into a smile. "Yeah, boyfriends. I'm definitely keeping you."

That might not have been the most romantic declaration in the history of declarations, but it got the job done.

35

Ian Alexander

Tyler is quiet on the drive back to my townhouse—too quiet—and that sends my anxiety through the roof. He said what happened tonight wasn't my fault, but now that he's had time to think about it, reality is probably setting in. It is my fault. And now his career is in jeopardy. He could lose everything because of me.

The rain kicks up, along with the wind, and he releases my hand to put both of his on the wheel. As the weather worsens, rain lashing the car, he white-knuckles the steering wheel, his gaze never leaving the road.

He must be furious, and I don't blame him. I feel like absolute shit. I'm the one who got us into this. I'm the one who Brad fixated on.

As soon as Tyler pulls into my driveway and parks, I'm out of the car and racing through the downpour up the steps to my front door. I fumble to get the door unlocked, and then I rush inside, leaving the door ajar in case he decides to come in. I wouldn't be surprised, or blame him, if he simply up and leaves.

Buzzing with nervous energy, I head for the kitchen to grab something cold to drink—I just need something to do. Just as I pop open a bottle of beer, I hear the front door close quietly.

My heart starts hammering because I don't know what to expect. A lecture? Censure? Blame?

I hear the hall closet door open. A moment later it closes, and Tyler walks into the kitchen sans jacket and holster. He must have hung them up. *He's still here.*

Tyler stands in front of me, his fingers latching on to the waistband of my jeans. He pulls me close. "It's okay, Ian. You don't have to run. I'm still here. I'm not going anywhere."

My eyes burn, and I blink away tears. "I wouldn't blame you."

He smiles, but it's a sad one. "Nope. I'm still here." He starts to lean in for a kiss, but he stops himself. "I need to wash up." He grabs a paper towel from the rack and wets it at the sink before wiping the mostly dried blood off his face.

I set down my beer and take the paper towel from him. "I'll do it." I wipe the dried blood from his bottom lip and tenderly dab the corner of his mouth. When he winces, I flinch. "Shit! I'm sorry."

"Ian." His voice is low and even, comforting. I'm starting to recognize that tone—it's the one he uses when he's talking me off a ledge.

"Don't talk," I tell him. "You'll start bleeding again."

Tyler stills my hand and takes the paper towel from me, wadding it up and tossing it into the wastebasket. He cups my face and gently brushes my throat with his thumbs. "Forget about me. How's your throat? Does it hurt?"

"It feels bruised." I clasp his wrists, just wanting the physical connection. "I'm really sorry about tonight."

He frowns. "I told you, there's nothing to apologize for. It wasn't your fault. If anyone should apologize, it's me, for losing my temper. But God, Ian, when I saw his hands on you, I snapped. He may not have killed Eric and the others, but he abused them all. I saw the photographic evidence. He *hurt* them, and then he took pictures. The thought of him even *touching* you made me see red." He steps closer and gently presses his forehead to mine. "I'd kiss you, but I'm a mess right now."

I laugh. "You look wonderful." It's true. The blood is gone from his face and beard, but his lip is slightly swollen.

His hands skim up the sides of my throat, then he frames my face, his thumbs gently brushing my lips. His gaze is locked on mine, and there's so much emotion in his eyes, unspoken and raw.

Tyler pulls me into his arms, our chests melding. He cups the back of my head, and we draw near each other. His touch makes me moan. I've had guys grope me and feel me up, but this is nothing like that. This is tenderness, caring.

"Let's go upstairs," he says.

I nod.

Tyler takes my hand and leads me up the staircase and down the hall to the master suite. He follows me into the bathroom, where we both undress quietly. He peers into the bathroom mirror to examine his lower lip. "It's fine."

We turn on the water and step into the shower, each of us taking turns standing beneath the hot spray. I can't take my eyes off him. The water sluices off his broad shoulders, trailing down his arms over rock-hard biceps, down his torso and onto his muscular thighs.

I lather up my hands and run them over every inch of his magnificent body. He does the same for me. And then we quickly wash our hair and rinse off.

"I want you," Tyler says, pulling me close beneath the soothing spray of hot water.

I run my fingers through his wet hair, making the dark strands spike. Then I lean forward to gently kiss the unblemished corner of his mouth. "You have me. I'm all yours."

He palms my ass, squeezing lightly before slipping a finger between my butt cheeks to tease me. "I mean, I want inside you."

My cock swells as heat and desire surge through me. *He still wants me.* "Dry off and make yourself comfortable. I'll finish up in here."

* * *

Tyler's eyes follow me as I walk into the bedroom in nothing but a towel around my waist. He's wearing a pair of gray flannel pants that hang low on his cut waist. The sight of him takes my breath away. Muscular chest and arms, ridged abs. There's a thin trail of dark hair heading down from his naval, disappearing beneath his waistband. He crooks a finger at me, beckoning me closer.

I walk across the room to join him by the dresser and gaze down at his erection, which strains the fabric of his bottoms. I drop to my knees and gently work the waistband of his pants down past his cock, then yank them to the floor. He steps out of them, watching me intently.

His cock is gorgeous, long and thick as it strains upward. I reach out and grasp him firmly, his throbbing heat heavy in my palm. I rub my face against him, reveling in his scent. Then I lick the tip, getting a hit of salt and musk on my tongue. I circle the head of his cock with my tongue, teasing and stroking beneath the sensitive rim.

He grips my head tightly. "Fuck!"

I bring him into my mouth, taking him deep. With my free hand, I reach around to grasp one of his ass cheeks, my finger slipping between them to tease his tight hole. His ass clenches tightly as I work his cock with my hand and mouth, sucking and stroking every inch of him, driving his arousal higher. His cock is throbbing, and I know he's close.

When I bring him to the very back of my throat, he groans loudly, his fingers tightening on my skull. "Ian!" I'm not sure if he's praising me or cursing me.

The truth is, I love getting on my knees for him. I love giving him head. Hands down, he's the sexiest guy I've ever been with. I look up at him and our gazes meet. The heat in his expression scorches me to the bone, and that only drives my need to please him even higher.

"That's enough! You're going to make me come." Without warning, he withdraws from my mouth and pulls me to my feet, steering me toward the bed. "When I come, it'll be inside you. Get on the bed."

Just as I kneel on the bed, he pulls the towel off me and tosses it aside. Then he walks to the nightstand and retrieves a condom and lube.

"Lights twenty percent," he says, and the recessed ceiling lights dim, leaving us bathed in a soft glow.

Tyler tosses the condom and lube onto the bed. "Lie on your back." After I do as he says, he crawls onto the mattress and kneels between my thighs. He positions me higher up on the bed until my head is resting on a pillow. Looming over me, he grips my jaw and makes me look him in the eye. "I keep thinking it could have been *your* body discovered that night at the marina, and it makes me a little crazy."

I reach up to stroke his cheek and then brush back his damp hair. "Valdez is dead."

"I know. But you were next on his list. After Eric died, Valdez started fixating on you."

"I remember when I first heard your voice at the marina, when you arrived on the scene. My whole body responded. Even in the midst of such carnage, and such heartbreak, my body responded to your voice. And when I saw you—when I saw it was *you*—I couldn't look away."

Tyler lies down half on top of me. Our erections are nestled together, both of us hot and straining. He grasps my cock and strokes me as he leans down and kisses me gently.

He lifts to meet my gaze. "When I saw Turner with his hands on you tonight, his fingers around your throat, I lost it. All I could think about was how close I might have come to losing you."

I lift my face and kiss the underside of his jawline, and then I trail kisses down his throat to his clavicle. He looms over me, dark and intense, and my body lights up for him as he grinds his cock against mine. The pleasure is mind-blowing.

His fingers are in my hair, alternately stroking and tugging the strands, and I groan.

Tyler drops his forehead to mine. "I want you like this," he says. "Missionary. I want to see your beautiful face when you come."

He moves back onto his haunches and grasps the condom packet, tearing it open and sheathing his erection. Kneeling between my thighs, he opens my legs wide. He drips lube between my butt cheeks, and I can feel the silky fluid slide down to my opening. Tyler's finger is there, catching the slippery wetness and teasing me open.

I arch my back, hissing with pleasure as his long finger sinks inside me. He strokes me, grazing my prostate, again and again, and my cock swells even more. My body sings with pleasure. He's diabolically relentlessly, driving my arousal higher and higher. I gasp. "Where the fuck did you learn that?"

He laughs. "Gay porn can be very instructive."

"Damn!" As he continues to work my prostate, my erection strains wildly and my balls draw up tighter. Fuck, he's going to make me come like this. I grab his wrist. "Wait. I want to come with you."

He withdraws his finger and reaches for the lube once more, this time slicking up his sheathed erection. Then he's there, the head of his cock pressing against my opening. He rocks against me, easing himself in as I exhale a long, slow breath and will my body to relax for him. My muscles go soft, and I let him push in.

He holds my gaze as he sinks slowly inside me, rocking in and out in gentle waves, sliding deeper each time.

I grit my teeth, because the mind-numbing pressure feels so good. Finally, he's all the way in, his body pressing against my ass. He reaches down to tease one of my nipple piercings, and pleasure zings down my spine to my balls. With a gasp, I arch my back.

Tyler pulls out slowly and slides back in, the head of his cock grazing my prostate.

"Fuuuck, Tyler!"

He starts moving then, his cock sliding in and out of me. My balls are nestled against his loins. He reaches between us and wraps his fingers around my straining cock and strokes me in tandem with his thrusts. His fingers are lubed, and his hand moves smoothly on me. He strokes me steadily, and the pleasure builds perfectly—so perfectly it steals my breath, and I'm left shaking.

He leans down and kisses me, his lips coaxing mine, teasing me.

This isn't fucking. This is making love. The realization blows my mind. I've never had this before. All of my sexual encounters have been hookups with guys who just wanted to get their rocks off—just like I did. But this is completely different. This is about *us*. This is about making a connection. This is about *giving* pleasure, not taking.

Tyler nudges my lips open and slides his tongue in to find mine. He strokes my cock faster, his grip tight and demanding. My heart slams against my ribs, my pulse out of control. My hands frantically skim his body, his chest, his arms and shoulders. Both of us are breathing hard.

His grip on me is so fucking perfect, as if he knows what I need. He strokes me from root to tip until my cock is throbbing, and I'm so close. He thrusts faster, long and deep, and we climb together.

"Come with me, baby!" He grinds out the words, his voice hoarse.

Baby. He called me baby.

As if on command, I buck into his grasp and shoot my load. He milks me through my orgasm, and we both watch as creamy ribbons of jizz coat my abs and chest.

He grits his teeth and bucks into me with a cry as his own orgasm follows right after mine.

I am so fucked, and I mean that metaphorically as well as literally. Tyler has ruined me for anyone else. Hell, he hardly knows what he's doing yet, and he's already blown my mind.

36

Tyler Jamison

After pulling out, I collapse beside Ian and draw him close. I'm still learning what the hell I'm doing, and I'm sure I'll get plenty wrong. I can only go with my gut instincts, and they tell me to hold Ian close, love him, give him every pleasure I possibly can, and then give him more. And most of all, make him feel secure.

He's given me something precious—something I've craved my entire life and have never been able to find—passion and a connection with another human being. I'm talking about a *partner*. Somebody to hold. Somebody to love. And for some reason, I've found that with another man. I'm not going to question it, because he's given me more in just a matter of weeks than I've experienced in decades.

I head to the bathroom to dispose of the condom and grab a warm, wet cloth, which I bring back to the bed to clean Ian up. When I'm done, I lean down and kiss him gently. "I'll be right back."

"Lights off," I say, and the room goes dark, except for the moonlight filtering through the tree branches. After disposing of the wet washcloth, I slide beneath the covers with him and he turns to me, his arm going across my waist and his cheek against my chest.

He draws lazy patterns on my chest with his finger. "Tall, dark, and handsome... where have you been all my life?" he teases.

I know he meant it as a joke, but I suspect there's an underlying grain of truth in his words. I tighten my hold on him. "I was looking for you in all the wrong places."

He laughs. "Well, better late than never."

I roll onto my side to face him, my hand stroking his back. With a groan, he presses his face into the crook of my neck.

Now that I've had a taste of what it's like to be with someone—to connect with someone and feel real, mind-numbing pleasure—I don't know how I can ever go back to my old life.

My stomach drops at the thought of Ian growing tired of me. We're so different. I'm not outgoing. I'm not comfortable in crowds, not like he is. It scares me to think I might not be able to meet all of his needs. I don't ever see myself dancing in a nightclub.

I lie awake for a long time, long after Ian has fallen asleep. He rolls over in his sleep, and I roll with him, spooning him from behind. I revel in the feel of his ass nestled against me. My cock starts to harden, and I imagine what it would be like to enter him like this, lying on our sides... spooning. Next time, I want him like this. I could stroke him off so easily while I fuck him.

I'm wide awake, my mind racing as thoughts careen inside my brain. I imagine introducing him to my family. My sister would love him. So would my mom. Ian's one of those people everyone loves. He's charming, handsome, caring. *He's everything.*

As my eye lids begin to grow heavy, I press my nose into his hair and revel in his scent. It's my new addiction.

Finally, I am content, dozing off with a man in my arms.

* * *

On Saturday morning, I wake with a hard-on that just won't quit. I'm guessing it's because my morning wood is inches from Ian's ass. For half-a-second, I contemplate waking him with my cock sliding into his ass—but no, that's definitely something we should discuss ahead of time.

Our bed—Ian's bed—is warm and comfortable, and I don't want to get up. He stirs in my arms, making sleepy, satisfied sounds that make me even harder.

He shifts to his back and looks at me as he stretches lazily. "Good morning, handsome."

My dick throbs. "Good morning."

He rolls toward me once more, yawning as he wraps his arm around my waist. "What time is it?"

"Six."

He groans. "Go back to sleep, Tyler. It's the weekend." Then he presses his lips to my chest.

Normally, even on weekends, I'd be up early. I've never been one to sleep in. But now that I have a warm body to snuggle up with, I'm not in such a hurry to get up. "Ian?"

"Hmm?"

"Tomorrow is my nephew's first birthday, and my sister is hosting a party for him in the afternoon. Would you like to come with me?"

Ian raises his head. "Seriously? You're inviting me to a family event?"

"Yes."

"I'd love to go! Are you kidding? Meet your family? Oh my God! Have you gotten his birthday gift yet?"

"I thought I'd do that today."

"We have to go shopping. What does he like?"

"Ian, he's a baby. I have no idea what he likes. And probably, neither does he."

Ian rolls his eyes. "Leave it to me. I'm great with kids."

I laugh. "Fine. You're in charge of picking out Luke's birthday present."

Ian kisses my shoulder and he rolls over onto his side, pulling me with him so that I'm spooning him. I close my eyes, enjoying the feel of him in my arms as I drift back to sleep.

A couple of hours later, my stomach is growling loud enough to wake the dead. It certainly wakes me. Not wanting to disturb Ian, I climb out of bed and take a quick shower, then dress in the clothes I brought in my overnight bag.

I head downstairs to the kitchen and raid the refrigerator, finding everything I need to cook a nice breakfast for Mr. Sleepyhead.

Half an hour later, Ian comes ambling down the stairs in nothing but a pair of shorts. His hair is sticking up in tufts, and his eyes are only half-open. "Do I smell bacon?"

"Yes." I point to the kitchen table. "Have a seat. Breakfast will be right up."

Ian sits, and a few moments later I bring him a plate with eggs, bacon, and toast. I pour him a cup of coffee, and he drowns it in flavored cream and sugar.

As we eat together, he checks his phone for messages. He responds to a text from his mother and two from his sister. "My mom wants you to come for dinner sometime. She's anxious to meet you."

I sip my coffee. "I'd love to meet your family, but how do you think your dad will react?"

Ian brushes off my concern. "He won't do anything to upset my mom or rock the boat. Trust me, it'll be fine."

As we finish up breakfast, I say, "We need to go grocery shopping. The fridge is pretty bare, and this is the last of the coffee."

Ian blushes. "I've been a little too busy lately to remember to do such mundane things as buy groceries. My mind has been otherwise occupied."

I grin. "Really?"

"Yeah. You see, there's this new guy I've been seeing. He's got me all twisted up in knots."

When Ian casually reaches up to tease one of his nipple piercings, my cock twitches in my pants, and my whole body heats up. *Fuck.* My pulse is racing now.

I rise from my seat and pull Ian out of his. Slowly, I walk him backward until he's flush with the wall. My gaze keeps dipping down to those damn piercings, the silver barbells nestled in those dusky pink flat discs. I don't know what it is about them that sends my body into overdrive, but I can't look at them—or even think about them—without getting hard.

I gently brush one of his nipples with the pad of my thumb and he shudders with a groan. My voice drops to a rough octave. "If someone's going to mess with your piercings, Ian, I think it should be me."

He swallows hard. He opens his mouth to speak, but only a shaky, hot breath escapes.

I lean close, my lips grazing his ear as I whisper, "When I look at those piercings, all I can think about is fucking you. It's like waving a red flag in front of a bull."

Ian moans as another shudder ripples through him. He clutches my arms, his fingers digging into my biceps, and his lips part as he blows out a long breath. "Tyler."

I dip my head and tongue one of the piercings, the metal warmed by Ian's body.

With a loud cry, Ian arches his back and tightens his hold on me. "Oh, fuck!"

I slip a hand down his front to cup his cock through his shorts. He's hard as a rock. I can feel his erection throbbing, swelling even more.

Watching him growing more and more aroused only increases my own arousal. It's thrilling to feel this with him. To want him this badly, all the time, and know that he wants me just as much.

I kiss his trembling lips, and then I take his hand and lead him upstairs. We're both aching for it now. And I know just how to take care of him.

$\backsim$ 37

Ian Alexander

Sunday afternoon, Tyler drives us to his sister's apartment building for his nephew's birthday party. I've never been anyone's plus one before. I'm excited.

We park in a reserved spot in the underground parking garage and take a private elevator up to the top floor. The doors whoosh open, and we step out into a formal foyer. An impressive chandelier hanging high overhead is decorated with baby-blue streamers.

I'm holding Luke's gift bag. We went shopping at a toy store yesterday, and when I saw this, I just had to get it. I hope Luke loves it as much as I do.

Tyler looks a bit panicked. I reach for his hand. "Don't be nervous."

He squeezes my hand. "I'm not nervous."

I step in front of him, face-to-face, and grasp the back of his neck. "Relax. It'll be fine. We're just two guys going to a birthday party, right? No big deal."

He grins as he takes a deep breath. "Right. Just two guys. No big deal."

"By the way, you look hot as hell."

Tyler debated for over an hour this morning on what to wear. He ended up going with blue jeans, a white button-down, and sneakers. Classic, casual, yet well put together.

I'm wearing ripped jeans, a form-fitting dark gray graphic tee, and boots. We look good, if I do say so myself.

"Okay, let's do this," I tell him, tugging on his hand as I lead him toward the doorway. "Come introduce me to your family and friends."

He nods. "Right."

I have no idea how he's going to introduce me. Will he call me his boyfriend? Or just his friend? We did have the boyfriend conversation, sort of, but that was in private. This is our first real, public test. I have to keep reminding myself not to get my hopes up.

Just before we step through the foyer door, I release his hand to give him a little breathing room. To ease the pressure. But to my surprise, he grabs my hand and links our fingers together.

Okay, I guess we're going all in.

Tyler leads me through the open doorway into the penthouse. There are at least two dozen people here—sitting, standing, milling about, talking, laughing, drinking.

All conversation comes to a dead stop, and everyone turns to face us. The sudden quiet is deafening.

A little boy about five years old, with spikey brown hair, runs up to us. He's holding a well-loved, stuffed dinosaur in his arms. "Hi, Uncle Tyler!"

"Hello, Aiden," Tyler says as he squeezes my hand.

The kid looks at me with big, curious brown eyes, then back at Tyler. "You brought a friend to the party."

I bite my lip to keep from laughing. There's a crowd of people staring at us, waiting with bated breath to hear Tyler's answer. My heart is pounding, because I'm dying to hear it, too.

Tyler's gaze sweeps the room, then he looks down at the kid. "This is Ian. He's my boyfriend."

The kid looks at me, then he eyes the gift bag I'm holding. "Is that for Luke? He's my cousin."

I can't help grinning. This kid didn't miss a beat. There's been no yelling, no screaming, no pitch-forks thrown our way. No one fainted. I squeeze Tyler's hand. "Yes, this is for Luke."

Aiden holds out his hand. "I'll put it on the table for you, if you want me to. That's where the other presents are."

"That would be fantastic," I say as I hand over the gift bag.

"This is Aiden McIntyre," Tyler tells me, finally remembering his manners. "His father, Jake, is my sister's husband's brother."

"God, I hope there's not going to be a test." And then to the boy, I say, "It's nice to meet you, Aiden."

When the kid races off with Luke's birthday present, the conversations pick up throughout the room and the excitement has passed. Tyler Jamison has just publicly come out of the closet to a room full of people, and no one seemed to mind.

"See how easy that was?" I say.

But he's still tense, clearly prepared for the worst.

A gorgeous blonde girl with an obvious baby bump comes forward, her arms out to Tyler. There are tears in her blue-green eyes—the same color as Tyler's. She has to be his sister, Beth.

Tyler envelops the girl in his arms, hugging her carefully so as not to crush her belly. And then an older woman with long silver-blonde hair appears at their side. She looks just like the sister, only much older, probably in her sixties, although it's hard to tell. She looks young to be Tyler's mother. She has tears streaming down her pale, softly lined cheeks. My breath catches as I watch the three of them hug.

These two women are the people he loves most in the world. This is his *family*. And I desperately want to be a part of that.

"Mom, this is Ian," Tyler says, releasing his mom and motioning for me to step forward. To me, he says, "My mother, Ingrid, and my sister, Beth."

Ingrid opens her arms to me and hugs me with all she's got. I wrap my arms around her too, and we hold each other. She's shaking.

When she pulls back, she smiles at me through her tears. "I'm so glad to finally meet you, Ian. Welcome."

* * *

After meeting Tyler's family, I shake hands with a steady stream of people who come up to greet us. The first one is Tyler's brother-in-law, Shane. After that, I lose track of who's who. But I do remember that most of them are named McIntyre.

After all the introductions, Tyler and I gravitate to the bar, where most of the guys are hanging out.

"See, you had nothing to worry about," I whisper to Tyler, as a silver-haired fox standing behind the bar makes me a Cosmo.

Tyler leans close, his shoulder pressing against mine. To the gentleman behind the bar, he says, "This is Ian." And to me, he says, "Ian, this is Daniel Cooper."

Mr. Cooper gives me the once-over, his sharp blue eyes missing nothing. For an older guy, he's extremely well-built—and hot.

"I'm Sam," says a red-head about my age. Sam offers me his hand, and as we shake, he winks at me. "Welcome. Glad to meet you."

This one's gay, no doubt about it. And if the slightly possessive look the older guy is giving him is any indication, the silver-haired fox is too. This must be the couple Tyler's sister and her husband live with.

The caterers announce that the food is ready, and folks meander over to the spread on the dining room table. And then, with plates of hot finger foods, the ladies congregate in the seating area, on two sofas and two stuffed armchairs. Besides Aiden and the little birthday boy, there are two infant girls being passed around.

Tyler's sister joins us at the bar, her adorable baby boy perched on her hip. Then Shane joins us, slipping his arm around Beth's waist.

The baby raises his arms to his daddy, squealing. "Da-da!"

Shane reaches for the baby. "So, Tyler."

Tyler eyes Shane. "Yes?"

"I'm only going to say this once," Shane says, raising a brow as he pins Tyler with a mock glare.

Beth laughs.

Tyler actually looks guilty. "All right, Shane, let's hear it. Get it off your chest."

Shane points a finger at Tyler. "I don't *ever* want to hear you griping about the age difference between me and my wife, is that absolutely clear?"

Tyler laughs. "Crystal."

"Good," Shane says. "Because you two have us beat, hands down. I don't want to hear another word about it."

Tyler extends his hand to his brother-in-law, and they shake. "Got it."

Then the red-haired guy—Sam—slips in beside me and puts his arm over my shoulders. "I dig older men, too," he says with a grin as he tips his head toward his partner behind the bar.

Tyler points from me to Sam and back to me. "You two are not allowed to be friends."

"You know, we should double-date sometime," Sam says to me with a wink.

❧ 38

Tyler Jamison

I swallow past the knot in my throat as I observe my lover sitting on the great room floor, cross-legged, with the birthday boy perched on his lap, and Aiden seated beside him, leaning close and watching in fascination as Ian shows Luke how to operate his new toy camera. It's just a simple little toy, one designed for toddlers, with a couple of flashy buttons that make noise, but Luke is absolutely captivated by his birthday gift.

Even with all the money at his disposal, Ian picked a simple, inexpensive gift for Luke, and he couldn't have chosen better. The kid loves it, and Ian's passion for photography shines through as he pretends to demonstrate to Luke how to take pictures.

My mom is seated on a sofa, holding one of Jake and Annie's twin baby girls. Jake's mother is seated beside her, holding the other twin. The babies look identical to me, and I have no idea which one is which. Besides the parents, I think Aiden is the only one who can tell his sisters apart.

I'm standing at the dining room table with my sister, while she puts the finishing touches on an elegant, three-tiered birthday cake.

Ian lifts his gaze and searches the room until he spots me. He gives me a smile before he goes back to entertaining the kids.

Beth inserts a single blue candle, shaped like the number one, into the cake's pristine white icing. Then she glances over at Ian. "I really like him, Tyler," she says, giving me a heart-felt smile.

"So do I." I laugh.

Beth puts her arm around me and leans her head against my shoulder. "I'm so happy for you both."

This whole afternoon has been surreal. Every person here has patted me on the back, shaken my hand, or hugged me. And everyone has welcomed Ian with open arms. I know the world won't always be so accepting of our relationship, but it feels good to start here in a safe place.

Everyone comes to gather around the table to sing *Happy Birthday* to my nephew. It's hard to believe he's a year old already. He had a rough start in the beginning, born prematurely and under dire circumstances. Beth had a difficult time of it, too. I think of her new baby, due to arrive this fall, and I hope she has an easier delivery this time around.

"You still don't know what you're having?" I ask my sister, as we're eating birthday cake.

She lays her hand on her bump and grins. "Nope. We want to be surprised."

"Does Shane still think it's a girl?"

She smiles. "Yes. He's convinced we're having a girl."

"Any names picked out?"

"Maybe."

"Look what I have," Ian says as he joins us. He's cradling one of the twins in his arms.

"Where did you get her?" I say.

"From your mom. This one is Everly. Isn't she adorable?" Ian glances at Beth. "You have two boys in your family and two girls. I guess your new baby will be the tie breaker." Ian bounces little Everly in his arms as she coos at him. "Aiden told me he's hoping you have a boy, so the boys outnumber the girls."

"I wish him luck," I say. "That's going to be a moving target. With a family this big, there are bound to be a lot more babies on the horizon."

* * *

Ian and I say our good-byes amidst lots of hugs and good wishes.

"Your mom and sister are great," Ian says, as we step out of the elevator into the parking garage.

"Yeah, they are. Everyone was great."

I open the front passenger door for Ian, but before getting into the car, he steps in front of me, just inches away.

He reaches for my hands. "You were wonderful, too." He leans in to kiss me. "Thanks for letting me be your plus one."

A car speeds past us in the hushed garage, headlights flashing in our faces, and someone shouts, "Go to hell, faggots!"

I freeze, my heart suddenly pounding.

"Shit," Ian says, stepping away. He ducks into the car. "Fuck them. Let's go."

I slide into the driver's seat and start the engine, letting it run for a minute while I process what just happened. It was the first time I'd heard a slur directed at me—at *us*—but I know it won't be the last time.

Ian reaches for my hand, giving it a comforting squeeze. "I'm sorry."

"It's all right," I say as I buckle my seat belt. "I knew it would happen sometime."

I'm a bit preoccupied on the short drive back to Ian's townhouse. I keep hearing that hate-filled jeer in my head, on a repeating loop, and my blood boils. I'm not naïve enough to think a gay man can go through life without hearing slurs like that, but until I heard it firsthand, directed at me, it was a bit academic. Now it's personal.

I am a gay man, and some people will hate me for it.

Ian's quiet too, his eyes fixed on the road. When I pull into his driveway, I realize he hasn't said a word since we left my sister's apartment building. I shut off the engine, and we both sit in the car, tensions high, staring straight ahead. I'm not even sure what to say. I guess it's just something I'll have to get used to.

Ian lets out an audible sigh as he reaches for his door handle. "Thanks again for inviting me." And then he opens the door and steps out, quickly closing it behind him.

I watch him jog up the steps to his front door. *He's running again.* "And there he goes."

It's a pattern. Whenever he feels afraid that I'll find a reason to not want to be with him, he panics. And then he runs. I guess he thinks it's better to run than be rejected.

I sigh. "That's my high-maintenance boyfriend." I can't help smiling, not because he's high-maintenance, but because he's *mine.*

He's halfway down the hallway when I catch up to him, grabbing his arm to slow him down. "What's the rush?"

He pulls away from me and keeps going.

Just like on previous occasions, he's quick to assume the worst.

"Ian, wait." I follow him into the kitchen. "Talk to me. What's going through your head right now?"

"Nothing." He jerks open the refrigerator door and peers inside.

"Ian—"

"I'm fine," he says, his voice cracking. "You don't have to say anything. I get it." He grabs a bottle of beer from the fridge, pops the cap, and heads up the stairs.

For a moment, I'm stunned. I think I'm still reeling from being called a faggot by a complete stranger who knows absolutely nothing about me. And now Ian's having a melt-down because he expects the worst. He's already assuming I'm going to bail on him because I can't handle a homophobic jibe. Well, I'm sure as hell not going to let that happen.

I grab a bottle of beer from the fridge and follow him upstairs. When I can't find him on the second floor, in any of the bedrooms, I walk up another flight to the roof. And that's where I find him, in the greenhouse, seated on a wooden bench facing the lake.

The sun is setting, and the city lights are starting to flicker on. Up here, surrounded by potted trees and assorted foliage, it feels like we're in a spacious treehouse, above and apart from the rest of the city, in our own secluded hideaway.

I join him on the bench, and we both stare out at the water, at the cruise ships slowly making their way out from Navy Pier for evening excursions. Smaller boats zip past them.

"That'll take some getting used to," I say, and then I take a sip of my beer.

"What will?" He sounds hesitant, as if he's curious about my remark but not entirely sure he wants to have this conversation.

"Hearing slurs thrown at us. People are such idiots."

He laughs. "Yeah. They are."

"So, you think I'd bail on you just because some asshole called me a *faggot?*"

He shrugs. "You're not used to hearing that."

"No, I'm not. But do you really think I'd walk away from *you* just because some jackass called us a name?"

He turns to me, his eyes flashing angrily. "It's not just the name-calling, Tyler. Wait until they find out at your work. What if Brad files charges against you for assault? What then? You could lose your job because of *me*! You could lose the respect of your peers because of *me*! Have you really thought this through?"

There's so much fear brimming in his eyes, in his words, in his tone of voice. His eyes are red, his expression guarded. He's really afraid I'll bail on him.

I reach out to brush his hair back from his forehead. "Yeah, I've thought about all that, a thousand times over. And I'll think about it a thousand times more. But you know what? I'll also think about how happy I am when I'm with you. How even the *thought* of being with you makes me happy. And the thought of being *without* you guts me."

I press my lips to his temple, savoring the heat of his skin, breathing in his scent. My gut tightens with longing and desire.

I cup the back of his head and skim my lips down the side of his face to his jawline, and then below, to his throat.

Ian's rigid posture softens, and he arches his neck to give me better access.

I turn him to face me and stare into a pair of hopeful green eyes. I realize it's going to take a lot of work to convince him I won't abandon him every time we hit a road bump. It might take years. Decades. Maybe the rest of our lives. I sigh. "I'm not going anywhere, Ian."

He squeezes his eyes shut, and his expression twists in pain. I massage the back of his head and his neck, and he groans.

Darkness is falling fast, and the sky fills with the flickering light of distant stars. Up here, we have a front row view of the universe.

I put my arm around him and draw him close. "Since I met you, I've never been happier. You're the last thing on my mind at night before I fall asleep, and you're the first thing on my mind in the morning. When I'm at work, part of my brain is wondering what you're doing, and I count the hours until I can see you again. I realize we haven't known each other long, and maybe this is too soon—"

"It's not." Ian turns to face me, his eyes filled with a mixture of hope and skepticism. He searches my gaze, as if measuring the truth of my words.

Yeah, this may not always be easy, but he's so worth it. He's turned my life upside down and given me what I've always craved—a connection. A partner. A soulmate. "I want you, Ian. In my life and in my bed. I want *all* of you, including your hopes and dreams, even your fears and insecurities. I've spent a lifetime without you, and now that I've found you, I don't ever want to lose you."

He exhales a shaky breath. "I know I can be difficult sometimes. I'm just so afraid you won't think I'm worth the effort."

I trace the shape of his ear with the tip of my index finger. "You are worth *everything*."

He shivers, his eyes searching mine desperately.

"Have you ever made love up here on the roof?" I ask him.

His eyes snap wide open as he considers my question. "No. I've never brought anyone up here."

"You brought me up here once."

He grins. "Well, maybe you're special."

I turn on the bench, sitting astride it to face him, and then I coax him to shift so he's facing me. As I lean in to kiss him, I grab the hem of his t-shirt and lift it up over his head. It's warm and humid up here in the climate-controlled greenhouse. It feels good. I run my hands up his arms, skimming over his muscles to his broad shoulders.

His fingers go to the buttons of my shirt, as mine go to his belt buckle. We undress each other slowly, under the purview of the night sky and a multitude of stars. We're bathed in moonlight, and the foliage surrounding us provides ample privacy from curious eyes.

We stand to kick off our shoes and pull off our socks, and then it dawns on me. "Fuck! We need a condom and lube."

Ian laughs. "Nightstand drawer. I'll go get them."

I reach out and grip his cock firmly. "I'll go. You stay and think about how I'm going to take you up here, because there's no bed."

He laughs. "We don't need a bed."

I race downstairs to Ian's bedroom and grab a condom and lube. I also grab a hand towel, in case we need it for clean-up.

When I return to the roof, I find him standing at the glass wall looking out toward the lake. My breath catches in my chest as I stare at him, the contours of his body illuminated by moonlight. He reminds me of a Grecian statue, pure male perfection—tall, lean, cut muscles. His legs go on forever, and his cock juts out from his loins—thick and long—begging for attention. He takes my breath away.

I can't take my eyes off him. "So, how do we do this?"

"We can do it standing up," he says. "Or..." He grins as he points at the futon. "You can lie on the futon and let me ride you like a cowboy."

The mental image alone puts a smile on my face. "Definitely that last one."

"Cowboy it is. Yeehaw!"

39

Tyler Jamison

On Monday morning, after showering and dressing for work, I stand at the side of the bed and watch Ian sleep. He looks so peaceful I hate to wake him, but I know it would be a mistake if I didn't.

Leaning down, I place a gentle kiss on his temple. "I'm heading to work now," I whisper.

He wakes with a start, and it takes him a second to orient himself. When he does, he rolls to his back and gives me a lazy smile. "Have a great day," he mumbles sleepily.

The sheet has slipped down to his waist, and I have a front row view of his piercings. My gaze skims down his torso to his happy trail, and I smile. This beautiful man is *mine*.

I press a kiss to his lips. "Thanks. You too."

I smile as he rolls onto his belly and closes his eyes with a contented sigh. "Sweet dreams, baby," I whisper, forcing myself to walk away.

It feels weird going our separate ways today after having spent an entire three-day weekend together. It's back to business as usual. I'm heading to work, and he's planning to meet Miguel for lunch today. And later in the afternoon, he's going to see his sister. He wants to personally evaluate her new bodyguard.

My day turns out to be pretty quiet, and I'm afraid it's the calm before the storm. We still haven't heard a peep from Brad Turner, and my gut tells me he's biding his time. But I have no idea if or when he's going to strike. I guess I'll deal with that when the time comes.

I'm holed up in my office for most of the day, catching up on e-mails, reading forensics reports, DNA test results, the usual stuff. Captain Walker assigns me to a new case: a stabbing death in Rogers Park. Fortunately, there were two eyewitnesses, so it should be an easy case to resolve.

By mid-morning, I can't resist sending Ian a text.

How's it going? – Tyler

I receive a reply just a minute later.

Good. Getting ready to meet Miguel. – Ian

At lunch time, I drive out to Roger's Park to interview the two witnesses to the stabbing death. Turns out it was a drug deal that went south. The dealer was stabbed and killed by a paranoid customer hyped up on heroin. The customer thought the dealer was an undercover cop, and the transaction didn't end well.

The killer is a forty-seven-year-old man with a history of mental illness who lives in the neighborhood. It's a quick, easy arrest. After bringing him in for booking, I head to my office to type up my report.

By late afternoon, my mind keeps drifting to Ian. After spending an entire weekend together, it feels odd to be apart.

After leaving the office, I'm feeling out of sorts. Ian's still at his parents' house, so I decide to do something productive with my time instead of wondering when he'll be home.

I head to my condo, which I've been neglecting lately. I need to collect the mail, empty the trash, and clean out some food in the fridge that has probably gone past its use-by date. I also need to do laundry and pick up some more clothes to take to Ian's house.

When I walk through my front door, into a dark and quiet condo, I'm once again struck by how *unfamiliar* it feels. I've spent so much time at Ian's lately, that my own place no longer feels the same.

I walk through the condo, through the darkened living room and kitchen, flipping on lights as I go. I walk down the hallway to my bedroom and step inside. I flip on a light and open the blinds in an attempt to dispel the gloom.

I stand at the foot of my bed, with its navy-blue comforter and matching pillow cases, and I'm struck by a wave of crushing anxiety. *Jesus, I don't want to be here.* Not anymore.

I want to be with Ian.

The place I've called *home* for so long is suddenly a dreary, lonely place. As I stare at my bed, one thing becomes crystal clear. I don't want to sleep here again. At least not alone. My chest feels hollowed out.

My phone chimes with an incoming message, and I grab it, looking at the screen. It's from Ian.

Had a good day with Miguel. My sister's new bodyguard is a prick. — Ian

I smile. I can almost hear his voice. Another message comes in on the tail of the first one.

I'm starving! How about pizza for dinner? What time will you be home? — Ian

He asked me when I was going to be *home*.

This condo *isn't* my home anymore. My home is wherever Ian is.

I send him a quick reply.

I'll be home in 40 minutes. Go ahead and order. — Tyler

I grab all the clothes from my closet and pile them on the bed. I fill a duffle bag with socks, underwear, and t-shirts. I bag up my toiletries, fill a cardboard box with my books and financial records, and grab my laptop bag and my tablet. That's it. That's all I need. Ian has a workout room at his place. I can use his equipment.

I manage to carry everything out to my car in just two trips. Then I empty the fridge of anything perishable and take the trash out to the dumpster.

I'm in my car and heading back across town to Ian's house twenty-five minutes later. Despite rush-hour traffic, I make good time, pulling into Ian's driveway just as the pizza delivery guy is backing out.

Ian waits at the door for me, holding an extra-large pizza box. "Perfect timing," he says as I step inside.

I take the box from him, carry it into the kitchen, and set it on the island counter. Then I turn to him and pull him into my arms.

He opens his mouth. "What's—"

"I missed you like hell today." And then I kiss the fuck out of him, like he's oxygen, and I'm suffocating. I realize I *need* him, like I need air to breathe.

He kisses me back, just as hungrily. And then, smiling, he breaks our kiss. "Tyler—"

I gaze hard into his eyes. "I went to my condo after work and packed up everything important and brought it with me. It's in the trunk of my car. This is my home now, Ian. *You're* my home. Please let me stay. Don't send me back to my empty condo because my life is here with you."

Tears fill his eyes, and his arms go around my waist. "It's been on my mind all day," he says. "Wanting to ask you to move in with me."

"Ask me."

Laughing shakily, he cradles my face in his hands. "Would you like to move in with me?"

"Yes."

"That was easy. I was afraid you'd say no. I thought you'd say it's too soon, that we don't know each other well enough."

I cup his head and draw him close to place a tender, reverent kiss on his perfect lips. "It's not too soon, Ian. I've been waiting for you for *years*."

* * *

We're sitting on the sofa in the living room, with the pizza box on the coffee table in front of us and two beer bottles. We're watching an episode of *Grey's Anatomy* on the massive TV screen hanging on the wall in front of us. Apparently, this is one of Ian's favorite shows as he's got a crush on a gay intern.

Ian grabs another slice of pizza and scoots back onto the sofa beside me.

After we finish eating and clean up the trash, we put a movie on. *Deadpool*. Ian about had a coronary when I told him I hadn't seen it.

My attention is split between the movie and the man seated beside me. We're sitting close enough that our arms brush, and our thighs touch. I can feel the heat of his body through our clothing. When Ian lays his hand on my thigh, I feel the connection all the way to my bones.

This is what I missed out on for so many years. I think of all the times I sat on sofas with women and watched movies just like this—I never once felt this sense of connection. My heart never pounded in anticipation that one touch might lead to another, and then to another. I simply never cared.

To be honest, I've given up trying to understand it. It just is. My body, my heart, my brain, they're all wired for *this*. I'm done questioning it.

I draw Ian closer, and he leans into me, his head ending up on my shoulder. He's stroking my thigh, and the friction and heat of his palm on my leg is giving me ideas. I can think of a better use for his hand.

I don't think either one of us is really paying any attention to the movie at this point, and it's getting late. All I can think about is going upstairs to bed. I just want to be naked in bed with this guy.

I press my lips to his ear and whisper, "I want to take you to bed."

He reaches for the remote and turns the TV off. "I thought you'd never ask."

* * *

Ian nestles against my side, his head on my shoulder, his arm across my waist. I stroke his arm, my fingertip following the path of a vein that travels down his forearm to the back of his hand. His hand slides up to my chest, and he draws lazy circles on my pecs.

I don't think I'll ever take this for granted. As much as I love sex with Ian, it's the quiet moments like these that tie me to him.

He traces a circle around one of my nipples, sending a shiver down my spine. "Has there been any word from Brad?"

His tone is nonchalant, but I know he's worried. And for good reason. A Chicago police officer beating up a man in a gay nightclub is sure to bring a lot of unwanted attention on the department.

"No, nothing yet." I lean over and kiss his forehead. "Don't worry about it, Ian. Turner assaulted you in the restroom at Sapphires. Chris and I both witnessed him choking you."

"But it's his word against ours," Ian says. "The security guards who pulled you off him—they only saw you beating Brad. They didn't see what came before. And the people recording in the hallway came only after you started hitting Brad."

I roll Ian to his back and lean over him, gazing down into his face. "Don't worry. I'll deal with what comes."

"But if you get in trouble because of me—"

"Brad Turner *assaulted* you, Ian. I did what I had to do, to protect you. I'd do it again in a heartbeat." I kiss him, our lips clinging.

"My protector," Ian says, smiling into our kiss.

Our kiss starts off slow and gentle and quickly morphs into something hungry. When we're both hard and throbbing, I roll Ian to his side and press up behind him. I run my hand down his side, to his waist, and over his hip. Then my hand slides down to cup his ass.

Ian shivers when I slip my finger between his ass cheeks, exploring. Groaning, he presses his face into his pillow. "You're such a tease."

He reaches over to open the nightstand drawer and retrieves

lube and a condom, passing both to me. He laughs. "What else have you Googled?"

I press my erection against his ass. "I want to take you like this. Spooning."

He reaches back to grab my ass and press me closer to him. "Have at it."

"Ian?"

"Hmm?"

My heart pounds at the idea of asking him this, but it's only right that I do. "I've been wondering... do you want me to bottom sometime for you?"

He's quiet for a moment—a long moment. "Ian? Did I say something wrong?"

"No, you didn't. It's just—you would do that for me?"

"Yes."

"No hesitation? Just an unequivocal yes?"

"Yes. If that's what you wanted."

"The truth is... I love it when you fuck me. I love feeling your strength. I love how you take care of me. I love feeling like I'm *yours*. So, no. Topping isn't something I feel the need to do. I will, if you want me to, if you want to try bottoming. Do you?"

"The thought makes me nervous as hell. If we're both okay with what we're doing, then I see no need to change anything."

"Good."

I slick my finger with lube and run it around the rim of his hole, teasing him open with slow, languid strokes.

Ian moans into his pillow. "You sure are a fast learner."

"I have a lot of catching up to do."

When I eventually ease into him, sliding through a tight ring of muscle, I gasp at the sensation. I kiss the back of his neck as I reach around to stroke his erection, which is straining madly for attention.

I stroke him relentlessly, from root to tip, teasing the head and building his pleasure and the friction until he comes undone, shooting his load into my palm.

"Tyler, *fuck!*" he cries.

I stroke his cock gently, milking his orgasm. Then I allow myself to finish, and the exquisite pleasure of his tight channel makes my eyes roll back in my head.

We're both breathing hard, both of us hot and sweaty. I tell him not to move when I go clean up in the bathroom and dispose of the condom.

When I return to bed, he's already half-asleep. I pull him close. *Yes, Ian's my home now.*

Epilogue

Tyler Jamison

I never dreamed I would get so much enjoyment out of watching my boyfriend decide what to wear on a date.

Ian pulls an aqua-blue Henley off its hanger and holds it up to his naked chest. "What about this one? The color makes my eyes pop."

I push away from the doorjamb and walk into a dressing room that's bigger than the living room in my condo. It's got a multitude of clothing rods and drawers and shelves, all of his clothes and accessories organized neatly by color. It looks like we're standing in a department store.

I shake my head. *Rich people.*

All of my clothes are in this closet, too, hanging on a rod Ian cleared off for me. I don't have a lot of clothes, so I only need one. He cleared out half the drawers in the dresser for me. And my shoes are lined up on the floor beneath my suits and jeans.

Ian frowns at his reflection in a full-size mirror, his shoulders falling. "You don't like it?"

I snap my attention back to Ian and his wardrobe dilemma. "I love it. It's perfect."

I've never seen him so nervous. In the two months we've been together, I've learned that Ian is full of contradictions. He can be self-assured and brazen one moment, but when his insecurities surface, his confidence takes a nose-dive. He's high maintenance, but I don't care. I know what my life was like before Ian, and I don't ever want to go back to that. I'll fight his insecurities tooth and nail before I ever give up on him. On *us*.

I pull him into my arms and gaze into his beautiful green eyes. "Ian?"

"Yeah?"

"You look amazing no matter what you wear."

He scowls. "You're just saying that."

"No, I mean it. Now, please, finish getting dressed." I glance at the digital clock on the wall. "It's seven-thirty. If we don't leave in fifteen minutes, we'll miss our reservation."

"All right! Sheesh. Have a little patience."

I was serious when I said he'd look amazing in whatever he chose. Although he is a bit of a clothes horse, he's usually never this worked up about it. But tonight is a big night for him. For both of us. It's our first *official* date. We have reservations for two at Tavern on Rush.

"You're nervous," I say.

He shrugs, not bothering to contradict me.

"It's just a date, Ian. Relax."

He turns to face me. "It's not just a date. We're going out on the town, to a really nice restaurant, in public. I want tonight to be perfect."

"It will be."

He rolls overly dramatic eyes at me just before he pulls the shirt over his head. The shirt molds itself to his torso, accentuating his musculature. The only problem is I can see hints of his nipple piercings through the soft cotton fabric.

"I'm going to have to sit through dinner tonight trying *not* to stare at your piercings," I say. When I brush my thumb over one, he shivers. "Maybe you should wear a hoodie instead, something bulky that hides them."

"Not a chance." Ian grins as he pulls me close, wrapping his arms around my shoulders.

"We could cancel our reservation," I say, grinning because I know how this will go.

"Cancel? God, no! I've been waiting all week for this, Tyler. We are not cancelling!" Ian smacks a kiss on my lips then storms out of the closet and into the bathroom to finish getting ready.

I've been ready for almost an hour, dressed in black trousers and a white button-up, sans tie. I hardly own anything other than black and white, so it wasn't a hard decision for me.

I find Ian in the bathroom spritzing on some cologne. After

brushing his teeth, he fingercombs his hair, which is still a bit damp from a shower. "How do I look?" he says.

"Amazing." I walk up behind him and wrap my arms around his waist to pull him against me. I'm sure he can feel my erection pressing into his ass. "Watching you primp and preen gives me a hard-on."

He grins as he meets my gaze in the bathroom mirror.

I run my hands over his broad shoulders, unable to resist teasing him. "Are you sure you don't want to just stay home and fuck?"

He frowns at my reflection. "You really don't want to go out tonight?" He looks crushed.

Crap. Now I feel like an ass for putting a damper on his excitement. He's been talking about this date all week. "Of course, I want to go. I was just teasing you."

Actually, I *would* rather stay in tonight, but that's not an option. We need to be gone from the townhouse for two hours this evening. I have a surprise for Ian, and he can't be here when it arrives. Besides, I can't disappoint him. Every day I spend with this guy, the deeper I fall under his spell.

I run my fingers through Ian's hair. "Let's go."

* * *

It's a nice night, and the restaurant is only a few blocks away, so we decide to walk. Ian has a light jacket on over his Henley, and I'm wearing my typical black leather jacket to conceal my holster.

We walk side-by-side along the pavement, crossing from Ian's quiet residential neighborhood to Rush Street, which is a huge tourist attraction. Occasionally, Ian's hand brushes mine, and I have a feeling he's aching to hold hands. But he doesn't press the issue. He knows I'm not exactly comfortable with public displays of affection, especially not after the jeer thrown at us in the parking garage of Shane's building.

Despite the lack of PDA, Ian looks happy, his smile radiant. Still, I feel like I'm letting him down.

When we reach the restaurant, I open the door for Ian. He grins as he steps inside. There's a short line at the host's podium. The waiting area is packed with guests.

"We have a reservation," Ian says to the two young women standing behind the podium. "Jamison, party of two."

While one of the women checks the guestbook, the other grabs two menus and tucks them into the crook of her arm. She's a cute blonde, her long hair hanging in a complicated braid. Her blue eyes sparkle as she gazes at Ian a little longer than necessary.

Forget it, honey. You're barking up the wrong tree.

Ian seems completely oblivious to her charms as he glances back at me. His enthusiasm is a bit infectious, and I can't resist brushing my hand against his lower back as I escort him into the dining room.

We follow the hostess to a corner table for two. As she lays our menus on the table, I pull out a chair for Ian, and he sits.

A young man stops at our table and fills our water glasses.

"So, what looks good?" I say to Ian.

He opens his menu with a flourish and scans the pages. I'm

sure he's been here a hundred times before and knows exactly what he wants. "Crab cakes for an appetizer. A prime burger—medium rare—fries, and grilled veggies. And a Cosmo."

I shake my head. "Where are you going to put all that?"

"Are you kidding? That's nothing. If I have room, I'm getting dessert, too. They serve a wicked 7-layer chocolate cake. We'll just have to burn some calories when we get home." He winks at me.

Home. That never gets old.

Our server comes to take our order. I order a steak with a baked potato and coffee.

While Ian chats about his day, I surreptitiously check my phone for a text message.

We're at the townhouse now. Setting up. – Miguel

This surprise is something I think Ian will really appreciate, and something I know we'll both enjoy.

Our server brings our meals, and as we dig into our food, we chat about everything—Ian's boat, his sister's new bodyguard, his family, mine. It doesn't matter to me what we talk about. I just like to hear Ian talk.

Out of habit, I make a visual sweep of the room. My gaze lands on a nearby table where two women are enjoying a bottle of red wine after their meals. They look to be in their early thirties. I've caught their curious gazes on us more than a few times this evening. I'm not sure if they're checking us out or trying to figure out the nature of our relationship.

"Ignore them," Ian says, when he notices where my attention has gone.

I realize he's been monitoring them too.

"You guys look like you're having a good evening."

We both turn to look at the pretty brunette now standing beside our table, one of the women who've been watching us this evening. She has a big smile on her face, her brown eyes glittering a little too brightly. They must have polished off that entire bottle of wine, and maybe more.

"I'm Ashley," she says, swaying slightly as she braces herself on the back of Ian's chair. She glances back at her table. "Stacey and I were wondering if you guys would be interested in a private party this evening. Our hotel isn't far."

"Thanks for the offer," I say, "but we'll pass."

The brunette frowns as she transfers her gaze to Ian, as if hoping he'll give her a different response. When he doesn't, she says, "Your loss," and heads back to her table.

Ian pops a fry into his mouth and chews to hide his amusement.

I realize this is the first time I've been hit on by a woman and it didn't faze me in the least. Because it doesn't matter anymore that I'm not interested in her, or any other woman. I've got what I want right here in front of me.

I stretch my arm across the table, toward Ian, my hand resting palm up on the table. "Give me your hand," I tell him when he hesitates.

Slowly, glancing around to see if anyone is watching, he lays his hand in mine. I squeeze his hand, holding it securely in mine.

"You don't have to do this," he says, eyeing our joined hands.

"I know. I want to."

The smile he gives me is worth any degree of discomfort on my part. I want this evening to be special for him, and I'll do whatever it takes to make that happen.

Our server approaches our table, and when Ian tries to pull his hand away, I tighten my grip.

"Can I get either of you gentlemen anything else?" she says.

"Yes," I say. "He'll have a slice of your 7-layer chocolate cake, and I'll have another coffee."

Not long after, our server brings Ian's dessert and my coffee refill. As I watch Ian enjoying his dessert, I know there's a stupid smile on my face.

I'm still holding his hand, and he's grinning between bites.

Tonight is about as perfect as it gets. And it's only going to get better.

* * *

Ian Alexander

Something's gotten into Tyler tonight. He's been holding my hand for fifteen minutes and refuses to let go. The two women who were ogling us earlier up and left after Tyler made his grand gesture. I know he's self-conscious when it comes to PDA, and that makes our hand-holding even sweeter.

After a long and leisurely meal, our server brings us the check, which Tyler snatches up.

"I'll get it this time," I say, holding my hand out.

Tyler shakes his head as he reaches into his back pocket for his wallet. "Thanks, but dinner's on me."

"I can at least pay half." This restaurant is many things, but inexpensive isn't one of them.

He shakes his head. "Nope."

After Tyler pays the bill, we head outside. The sun is just setting to the west, over the lake. The sky is a stunning orangey-pink-red this evening.

"Let's walk back," Tyler says.

As we step onto the sidewalk, Tyler takes my hand again, holding it securely in his. Holding my hand in the restaurant was a magnificent gesture, and I appreciated it greatly, but *this?* This is epic because the sidewalk is bustling with pedestrians, and traffic is heavy. People can *see* us.

A passing car honks, and Tyler flinches, but to his credit he doesn't let go.

"You don't have to hold my hand," I tell him. "It's the thought that counts."

He just smiles at me and tightens his grip. As we walk home, my chest tightens with each step. Tyler's really pushing his comfort zone tonight, just for me. This night couldn't possibly be any more perfect.

"Thank you for tonight," I tell him when we reach the townhouse. "Everything was perfect."

It's nearly ten o'clock, and the sun has dipped below the horizon. There's only the faintest orange ribbon of glow hanging on the horizon, and that will be gone in a matter of minutes. Thanks to a clear night sky, a multitude of stars are visible tonight.

As we climb the steps to my door, Tyler still has my hand squarely in his. He pulls out *his* house key—the one I had made for him after we decided he was moving in—and opens the front door.

Once we're inside, he hangs up his jacket and holster in the hall closet. Then he turns to me, pulling me into his arms. "I have a surprise for you, up on the roof." He takes my hand and leads me to the stairs.

We climb the stairs to the roof and step out into the greenhouse. Tyler flips on the strands of fairy lights, and I gasp when I see the transformation. The old futon has been replaced with a king-size bed in a black, wrought iron bedframe. The bed is made up with pristine light gray sheets, a matching blanket, and pillows. In the center of the bed is a tray containing two empty champagne flutes, scattered rose petals, and little chocolates wrapped in gold foil.

Next to the bed is a nightstand holding a bottle of champagne in a bucket of ice.

I stare, dumbfounded. It's beautiful. It's a secret oasis tucked in amongst all the greenery. The profusion of plants blocks anyone from looking down through the glass. No one can see the bed. No one can see us together. We can sleep up here—we can *be together* up here—and no one would ever know.

I turn to Tyler, my vision blurred by tears. "You did this for me?"

He nods. "I thought you'd enjoy sleeping under the stars."

I shake my head in disbelief. "How did you manage all this?"

"Miguel and a couple of his buddies from McIntyre Security took care of it this evening while we were at dinner. I gave him instructions and a key. He took care of delivering the bed and setting it up so I could surprise you. He did it all. The champagne, the rose petals, the chocolates."

My teary gaze sweeps the cozy sleeping nest. *Fresh air, no solid walls closing in on me.* He brought the outside in.

He knows me. Tyler knows me.

Overwhelmed, I shove my hands into my hair, gripping the strands hard. He knows my greatest weaknesses, my greatest fears, and instead of thinking less of me for them, he does *this*.

"Hey, easy." Tyler gently pries my hands from my hair. "It's okay, Ian. Just breathe."

My face is hot, my eyes burning as I face him. "I don't know what to say."

He pulls me into his arms. "You don't have to say anything. Come check it out."

Tyler moves the tray to a side table, and we both kick off our shoes and crawl onto the bed. It's spacious and comfortable and perfect. We lie on our backs and gaze up through the greenery at the stars overhead.

Tyler reaches for my hand and links our fingers together. "Let's sleep up here tonight."

Nodding, I roll to my side to face him. He rolls toward me.

"I..." The words stick in my throat. There's so much I want to say, but I'm afraid it's too soon.

He brushes my hair back. "What is it, Ian? You can tell me anything."

I take a deep breath. "When my birth mom locked me upstairs in a dark room, I used to pretend that someone was coming to rescue me. Sometimes I fantasized it was Superman, or Batman, or GI Joe. Sometimes, it was a policeman or fireman who came to set me free. But that never happened. In the end, it was Child Protective Services that came for me."

I lean close and kiss him tenderly. "I think it's fitting that you, Tyler, a real-life police officer, are the one who truly rescued me." I swallow against a painful knot in my throat. "Even if it's too soon to say this, I need you to know. I love you, Tyler."

Tyler's eyes glisten with tears. "It's not too soon. I love you, too." He leans close to kiss me. "And I think you got it backwards. You're the one who rescued me."

That's it for now…

I hope you'll come back for more of Tyler and Ian's journey.

Books by April Wilson

McIntyre Security Bodyguard Series:

Vulnerable

Fearless

Shane – a novella

Broken

Shattered

Imperfect

Ruined

Hostage

Redeemed

Marry Me – a novella

Snowbound – a novella

Regret

With This Ring – a novella

(with more coming...)

A Tyler Jamison Novel:

Somebody to Love

(with more coming...)

Coming Next!

I hope you'll stay tuned for the next installment of Tyler and Ian's journey. They have a lot more story coming, new challenges, and many new joys.

You might also be interested to know that Ian's sister, Layla, has her own book coming.

If you're a fan of my McIntyre Security bodyguard series, stay tuned for more books on the way, including books for Sophie McIntyre and Dominic Zaretti, Hannah McIntyre and Killian Deveraux, Liam McIntyre, Cameron and Chloe, Ingrid Jamison and Joe Rucker, and many more! There are too many books in my head and not enough hours in the day!

For updates of future releases, follow me on Facebook or subscribe to my newsletter at www.aprilwilsonauthor.com.

I'm active daily on Facebook, and I love to interact with my readers. Come talk to me on Facebook by leaving me a message or a comment. Please share my book posts with your friends. I also have a phenomenal reader group on Facebook (April Wilson Fan Group) where I post daily with new book updates and share weekly teasers for new books. I also love to run giveaway contests. Come join me!

You can also follow me on Instagram, Amazon, BookBub, and Goodreads!

Visit my website: www.aprilwilsonauthor.com

Please Leave a Review on Amazon

I hope you'll take a moment to leave a review for me on Amazon. Please, please, please? It doesn't have to be long... just a brief comment saying whether you liked the book or not. Reviews are vitally important to authors! I'd be incredibly grateful to you if you'd leave one for me.

Goodreads and BookBub are also great places to leave reviews.

Acknowledgements

As always, I owe a huge debt of gratitude to the generous people who help me bring my books to life.

Thank you to my sister and best friend, Lori, for being there with me every step of the way. Her tireless support and encouragement are priceless.

Thank you to my personal assistant, Julie Collier. I never realized how much I needed a PA until she started making my life easier.

Thank you to Sue Vaughn Boudreaux for her extraordinary editorial support. She has single-handedly prevented me from making so many disastrous blunders.

Thank you to my dear friend Rebecca Morean for her friendship, mentoring, and support. You mean the world to me.

A special thank you to Christina Hart, my editor. She's simply a dream come true. Thank you, Christina! And thank you for loving Tyler and Ian's story.

Thank you to my amazing team of beta readers who share their invaluable feedback with me.

Finally, I want to thank all of my readers around the world and especially the amazingly kind and wonderful members of my reader group on Facebook. I am so incredibly blessed to have you in my life. Your love and support and enthusiasm mean the world to me. You've become dear friends to me, and I am grateful for you all. Thank you from the very bottom of my heart for every review, like, share, and comment. I wouldn't be able to do the thing that I love to do most—share my characters and their stories—without your support. I thank my lucky stars for you every single day!

With much love to you all... April